Colleen Hoover is the #1 *New York Times* bestselling author of the Hopeless series, the Maybe Someday series, *Ugly Love, Confess, It Ends with Us, All Your Perfects*, and many more. She lives in Texas with her husband and their three boys.

To find out more, visit: www.ColleenHoover.com

Verity

COLLEEN HOOVER

SPHERE

SPHERE

First published in 2018 by Colleen Hoover
This edition published in 2022 by Sphere

9 10 8

A CIP catalogue record for this book
is available from the British Library.

Cover design by Murphy Rae Fennell.

ISBN 978-1-4087-2660-0

Papers used by Sphere are from well-managed forests
and other responsible sources.

MIX
Paper from
responsible sources
FSC® C104740

Sphere
An imprint of
Little, Brown Book Group
Carmelite House
50 Victoria Embankment
London EC4Y 0DZ

An Hachette UK Company
www.hachette.co.uk

www.littlebrown.co.uk

This book is dedicated to the only person this book could possibly be dedicated to.

Tarryn Fisher,
thank you for accepting the darkness in people as much as you accept their light.

1

I hear the crack of his skull before the spattering of blood reaches me.

I gasp and take a quick step back onto the sidewalk. One of my heels doesn't clear the curb, so I grip the pole of a *No Parking* sign to steady myself.

The man was in front of me a matter of seconds ago. We were standing in a crowd of people waiting for the crosswalk light to illuminate when he stepped into the street prematurely, resulting in a run-in with a truck. I lunged forward in an attempt to stop him—grasping at nothing as he went down. I closed my eyes before his head went under the tire, but I heard it pop like the cork of a champagne bottle.

He was in the wrong, looking casually down at his phone, probably a side effect of crossing the same street without incident many times before. *Death by routine.*

People gasp, but no one screams. The passenger of the offending vehicle jumps out of the truck and is immediately on his knees near the man's body. I back away from the scene as several people rush forward to help. I don't have to look at the man under the tire to know he didn't survive that. I only have to look down at my once-white shirt—at the blood now splattered across it—to know that a hearse would serve him better than an ambulance.

I spin around to move away from the accident—to find a place to take a breath—but the crosswalk sign now says *walk* and the thick crowd takes heed, making it impossible for me to swim upstream in this Manhattan river. Some don't even look up from their cell phones as they pass right by the accident. I stop trying to move, and wait for the crowd to thin. I glance back toward the accident, careful not to look directly at the man. The driver of the truck is now at the rear of the vehicle, wide-eyed, on a cell phone. Three, maybe four, people are assisting them. A few are led by their morbid curiosities, filming the gruesome scene with their phones.

If I were still living in Virginia, this would play out in a completely different manner. Everyone around would stop. Panic would ensue, people would be screaming, a news crew would be on scene in a matter of minutes. But here in Manhattan, a pedestrian struck by a vehicle happens so often, it's not much more than an inconvenience. A delay in traffic for some, *a ruined wardrobe for others*. This probably happens so often, it won't even end up in print.

As much as the indifference in some of the people here disturbs me, it's exactly why I moved to this city ten years ago. People like me belong in overpopulated cities. The state of my life is irrelevant in a place this size. There are far more people here with stories much more pitiful than mine.

Here, I'm invisible. Unimportant. Manhattan is too crowded to give a shit about me, and I love her for it.

"Are you hurt?"

I look up at a man as he touches my arm and scans my shirt. Deep concern is embedded in his expression as he looks me up and down, assessing me for injuries. I can tell by his reaction that he isn't one of the more hardened New Yorkers. He might live here now, but wherever he's from, it's a place that didn't completely beat the empathy out of him.

"Are you hurt?" the stranger repeats, looking me in the eye this time.

"No. It's not my blood. I was standing near him when..." I stop speaking. *I just saw a man die.* I was so close to him, his blood is on me.

I moved to this city to be invisible, but I am certainly not impenetrable. It's something I've been working on— attempting to become as hardened as the concrete beneath my feet. It hasn't been working out so well. I can feel everything I just witnessed settling in my stomach.

I cover my mouth with my hand, but pull it away quickly when I feel something sticky on my lips. *More blood.* I look down at my shirt. So much blood, none of it mine. I pinch at my shirt and pull it away from my chest, but it sticks to my skin in spots where the blood splatters are beginning to dry.

I think I need water. I'm starting to feel light-headed, and I want to rub my forehead, pinch my nose, but I'm scared to touch myself. I look up at the man still gripping my arm.

"Is it on my face?" I ask him.

He presses his lips together and then darts his eyes away, scanning the street around us. He gestures toward a coffee shop a few doors down.

"They'll have a bathroom," he says, pressing his hand against the small of my back as he leads me in that direction.

I look across the street at the Pantem Press building I was headed to before the accident. I was so close. Fifteen— maybe twenty—feet away from a meeting I desperately need to be in.

I wonder how close the man who just died was from *his* destination?

The stranger holds the door open for me when we reach the coffee shop. A woman carrying a coffee in each hand attempts to squeeze past me through the doorway until she sees my shirt. She scurries backward to get away from me, allowing us both to enter the building. I move toward the women's restroom, but the door is locked. The man pushes open the door to the men's restroom and motions for me to follow him.

He doesn't lock the door behind us as he walks to the sink and turns on the water. I look in the mirror, relieved to see it isn't as bad as I'd feared. There are a few spatters of blood on my cheeks that are beginning to darken and dry, and a spray above my eyebrows. But luckily, the shirt took the brunt of it.

The man hands me wet paper towels, and I wipe at my face while he wets another handful. I can smell the blood now. The tanginess in the air sends my mind whirling back to when I was ten. The smell of blood was strong enough to remember it all these years later.

I attempt to hold my breath at the onset of more nausea. I don't want to puke. But I want this shirt off me. *Now.*

I unbutton it with trembling fingers, then pull it off and place it under the faucet. I let the water do its job while I take the other wet napkins from the stranger and begin wiping the blood off my chest.

He heads for the door, but instead of giving me privacy while I stand here in my least attractive bra, he locks us inside the bathroom so no one will walk in on me while I'm shirtless. It's disturbingly chivalrous and leaves me feeling uneasy. I'm tense as I watch him through the reflection in the mirror.

Someone knocks.

"Be right out," he says.

I relax a little, comforted by the thought that someone outside this door would hear me scream if I needed to.

I focus on the blood until I'm certain I've washed it all off my neck and chest. I inspect my hair next, turning left to right in the mirror, but find only an inch of dark roots above fading caramel.

"Here," the man says, fingering the last button on his crisp white shirt. "Put this on."

He's already removed his suit jacket, which is now hanging from the doorknob. He frees himself of his button-up shirt, revealing a white undershirt beneath it. He's muscular, taller than me. His shirt will swallow me. I can't wear this into my meeting, but I have no other option. I take the shirt when he hands it to me. I grab a few more dry paper towels and pat at my skin, then pull it on and begin buttoning it. It looks ridiculous, but at least it wasn't *my* skull that exploded on someone else's shirt. *Silver lining.*

I take my wet shirt out of the sink and accept there's no saving it. I toss it in the trashcan, and then I grip the sink and stare at my reflection. Two tired, empty eyes stare back at me. The horror of what they've just witnessed have darkened the hazel to a murky brown. I rub my cheeks with the heels of my hands to inspire color, to no avail. I look like death.

I lean against the wall, turning away from the mirror. The man is wadding up his tie. He shoves it in the pocket of his suit and assesses me for a moment. "I can't tell if you're calm or in a state of shock."

I'm not in shock, but I don't know that I'm calm, either. "I'm not sure," I admit. "Are you okay?"

"I'm fine," he says. "I've seen worse, unfortunately."

I tilt my head as I attempt to dissect the layers of his cryptic reply. He breaks eye contact, and it only makes me stare even harder, wondering what he's seen that tops a man's head being crushed beneath a truck. Maybe he *is* a native New Yorker. Or maybe he works in a hospital. He has an air of competence that often accompanies people who are in charge of other people.

"Are you a doctor?"

He shakes his head. "I'm in real estate. Used to be, anyway." He steps forward and reaches for my shoulder, brushing something away from my shirt. *His* shirt. When he drops his arm, he regards my face for a moment before taking a step back.

His eyes match the tie he just shoved in his pocket. *Chartreuse.* He's handsome, but there's something about him that makes me think he wishes he weren't. Almost as if his looks might be an inconvenience to him. A part of him he doesn't want anyone to notice. He wants to be invisible in this city. *Just like me.*

Most people come to New York to be discovered. The rest of us come here to hide.

"What's your name?" he asks.

"Lowen."

There's a pause in him after I say my name, but it only lasts a couple seconds.

"Jeremy," he says. He moves to the sink and runs the water again, and begins washing his hands. I continue to stare at him, unable to mute my curiosity. What did he mean when he said he's seen worse than the accident we just witnessed? He said he used to be in real estate, but even the worst day on the job as a realtor wouldn't fill someone with the kind of gloom that's filling this man.

"What happened to you?" I ask.

He looks at me in the mirror. "What do you mean?"

"You said you've seen worse. What have you seen?"

He turns off the water and dries his hands, then faces me. "You actually want to know?"

I nod.

He tosses the paper towel into the trashcan and then shoves his hands in his pockets. His demeanor takes an even more sullen dive. He's looking me in the eye, but there's a disconnect between him and this moment. "I pulled my eight-year-old daughter's body out of a lake five months ago."

I suck in a rush of air and bring my hand to the base of my throat. *It wasn't gloom at all in his expression. It was despair.* "I'm so sorry," I whisper. And I am. Sorry about his daughter. Sorry for being curious.

"What about you?" he asks. He leans against the counter like this is a conversation he's ready for. A conversation he's been waiting for. Someone to come along and make his tragedies seem less tragic. It's what you do when you've experienced the worst of the worst. You seek out people like you...people worse off than you... and you use them to make yourself feel better about the terrible things that have happened to you.

I swallow before I speak, because my tragedies are nothing compared to his. I think of the most recent one, embarrassed to speak it out loud because it seems so insignificant compared to his. "My mother died last week."

He doesn't react to my tragedy like I reacted to his. He doesn't react at all, and I wonder if it's because he was hoping mine was worse. It isn't. *He wins.*

"How did she die?"

"Cancer. I've been caring for her in my apartment for the past year." He's the first person I've said that to out loud. I can feel my pulse throbbing in my wrist, so I clasp my other hand around it. "Today is the first time I've stepped outside in weeks."

We stare at each other for a moment longer. I want to say something else, but I've never been involved in such a heavy conversation with a complete stranger before. I kind of want it to end, because where does the conversation even go from here?

It doesn't. It just stops.

He faces the mirror again and looks at himself, pushing a strand of loose dark hair back in place. "I have a meeting I need to get to. You sure you'll be okay?" He's looking at my reflection in the mirror now.

"Yes. I'm alright."

"*Alright*?" He turns, repeating the word like a question, as if being *alright* isn't as reassuring to him as if I'd said I would be *okay*.

"I'll be alright," I repeat. "Thank you for the help."

I want him to smile, but it doesn't fit the moment. I'm curious what his smile would look like. Instead, he shrugs a little and says, "Alright, then." He moves to unlock the door. He holds it open for me, but I don't exit right away. Instead, I continue to watch him, not quite ready to face the world outside. I appreciate his kindness and want to say more, to thank him in some way, maybe over coffee or by returning his shirt to him. I find myself drawn to his altruism—a rarity these days. But it's the flash of wedding ring on his left hand that propels me forward, out of the bathroom and coffee shop, onto the streets now buzzing with an even larger crowd.

An ambulance has arrived and is blocking traffic in both directions. I walk back toward the scene, wondering if I should give a statement. I wait near a cop who is jotting down other eyewitness accounts. They aren't any different from mine, but I give them my statement and contact information. I'm not sure how much help my statement is since I didn't actually see him get hit. I was merely close enough to hear it. Close enough to be painted like a Jackson Pollock canvas.

I look behind me and watch as Jeremy exits the coffee shop with a fresh coffee in his hand. He crosses the street, focused on wherever it is he's going. His mind is somewhere else now, far away from me, probably on his wife and what he'll say to her when he goes home missing a shirt.

I pull my phone out of my purse and look at the time. I still have fifteen minutes before my meeting with Corey and the editor from Pantem Press. My hands are shaking even worse now that the stranger is no longer here to distract me from my thoughts. Coffee may help. Morphine would *definitely* help, but hospice removed it all from my apartment last week when they came to retrieve their equipment after my mother passed. It's a shame I was too shaken to remember to hide it. I could really use some right about now.

2

When Corey texted me last night to let me know about the meeting today, it was the first time I'd heard from him in months. I was sitting at my computer desk, staring down at an ant as it crawled across my big toe.

The ant was alone, fluttering left and right, up and down, searching for food or friends. He seemed confused by his solitude. Or maybe he was excited for his newfound freedom. I couldn't help but wonder why he was alone. Ants usually travel with an army.

The fact that I was curious about the ant's current situation was a clear sign I needed to leave my apartment. I was worried that, after being cooped up caring for my mother for so long, once I stepped out into the hallway I would be just as confused as that ant. Left, right, inside, outside, *where are my friends, where is the food?*

The ant crawled off my toe and onto the hardwood floor. He disappeared beneath the wall when Corey's texts came through.

I was hoping when I drew a line in the sand months ago, he'd understand: since we no longer have sex, the most appropriate method of contact between a literary agent and his author is email.

His text read: *Meet me tomorrow morning at nine at the Pantem Press building, floor 14. I think we might have an offer.*

He didn't even ask about my mom in the text. I wasn't surprised. His lack of interest in anything other than his job and himself are the reasons we're no longer together. His lack of concern made me feel unjustly irritated. He doesn't owe me anything, but he could have at least acted like he cared.

I didn't text him back at all last night. Instead, I set down my phone and stared at the crack at the base of my wall—the one the ant had disappeared into. I wondered if he would find other ants in the wall, or if he was a loner. Maybe he was like me and had an aversion to other ants.

It's hard to say why I have such a deeply crippling aversion to other humans, but if I had to wager a bet, I'd say it's a direct result of my own mother being terrified of me.

Terrified may be a strong word. But she certainly didn't trust me as a child. She kept me fairly secluded from people outside of school because she was afraid of what I might be capable of during my many sleepwalking episodes. That paranoia bled into my adulthood, and by then, I was set in my ways. A loner. Very few friends and not much of a social life. Which is why this is the first morning I've left my apartment since weeks before she passed away.

I figured my first trip outside of my apartment would be somewhere I missed, like Central Park or a bookstore.

I certainly didn't think I'd find myself here, standing in line in the lobby of a publishing house, desperately praying whatever this offer is will catch me up on my rent and I won't be evicted. But here I am, one meeting away from either being homeless or receiving a job offer that will give me the means to look for a new apartment.

I look down and smooth out the white shirt Jeremy lent me in the bathroom across the street. I'm hoping I don't look too ridiculous. Maybe there's a chance I can pull it off, as if wearing men's shirts twice my size is some cool new fashion statement.

"Nice shirt," someone behind me says.

I turn at the sound of Jeremy's voice, shocked to see him.

Is he following me?

It's my turn in line, so I hand the security guard my driver's license and then look at Jeremy, taking in the new shirt he's wearing. "Do you keep spare shirts in your back pocket?" It hasn't been that long since he gave me the one off his back.

"My hotel is a block away. Walked back to change."

His hotel. That's promising. If he's staying in a hotel, maybe he doesn't work here. And if he doesn't work here, maybe he isn't in the publishing industry. I'm not sure why I don't want him to be in the publishing industry. I just have no idea who my meeting is with, and I'm hoping it has nothing to do with him after the morning we've already had. "Does that mean you don't work in this building?"

He pulls out his identification and hands it to the security guard. "No, I don't work here. I have a meeting on the fourteenth floor."

Of course he does.

"So do I," I say.

A fleeting smile appears on his mouth and disappears just as quickly, as if he remembered what happened across the street and realized it's still too soon to not be affected. "What are the chances we're heading to the same meeting?" He takes his identification back from the guard who points us in the direction of the elevators.

"I wouldn't know," I say. "I haven't been told exactly why I'm here yet." We walk onto the elevator, and he presses the button for the fourteenth floor. He faces me as he pulls his tie out of his pocket and begins to put it on.

I can't stop staring at his wedding ring.

"Are you a writer?" he asks.

I nod. "Are you?"

"No. My wife is." He pulls at his tie until it's secured in place. "Have you written anything I would know?"

"I doubt it. No one reads my books."

His lips turn up. "There aren't many Lowens in the world. I'm sure I can figure out which books you've written."

Why? Does he actually want to read them? He looks down at his phone and begins to type.

"I never said I write under my real name."

He doesn't look up from his phone until the elevator doors open. He moves toward them, turning in the doorway to face me. He holds up his phone and smiles. "You don't write under a pen name. You write under Lowen Ashleigh, which, funny enough, is the name of the author I'm meeting at nine thirty."

I finally get that smile, and as gorgeous as it is, I don't want it anymore.

He just Googled me. And even though my meeting is at nine, not nine thirty, he seems to know more about it than I do. If we really are headed to the same meeting, it makes our chance meeting on the street seem somewhat suspicious. But I guess the odds of us both being in the same place at the same time aren't all that inconceivable, considering we were headed in the same direction to the same meeting, and therefore, witnessed the same accident.

Jeremy steps aside, and I exit the elevator. I open my mouth, preparing to speak, but he takes a few steps, walking backward. "See you in a few."

I don't know him at all, nor do I know how he relates to the meeting I'm about to have, but even without being privy to any details of what's happening this morning, I can't help but like the guy. The man literally gave me the shirt off his back, so I doubt he has a vindictive nature.

I smile before he rounds the corner. "Alright. See you in a few."

He returns the smile. "Alright."

I watch him until he makes a left and disappears. As soon as I'm out of his line of sight, I'm able to relax a little. This morning has just been...a lot. Between the accident I witnessed and being in enclosed spaces with that confusing man, I'm feeling so strange. I press my palm against the wall and lean into it. What the hell—

"You're on time," Corey says. His voice startles me. I spin around, and he's walking up to me from the opposite hallway. He leans in and kisses me on the cheek. I stiffen.

"You're never on time."

"I would have been here sooner, but..." I shut up. I don't explain what prevented me from being early. He seems disinterested as he heads in the same direction as Jeremy.

"The actual meeting isn't until nine thirty, but I figured you'd be late, so I told you nine."

I pause, staring at the back of his head. *What the hell, Corey?* If he'd told me nine thirty rather than nine, I wouldn't have witnessed the accident across the street. I wouldn't have been subjected to a stranger's blood.

"You coming?" Corey asks, pausing to look back at me.

I bury my irritation. I'm used to doing that when it comes to him.

We make it to an empty conference room. Corey closes the door behind us, and I take a seat at the conference table. He sits next to me at the head of the table, positioning himself so that he's staring at me. I try not to frown as I take in the sight of him after our months-long hiatus, but he hasn't changed. Still very clean, groomed, wearing a tie, glasses, a smile. Always such a stark contrast to myself.

"You look terrible." I say it because he doesn't look terrible. He never does, and he knows it.

"You look refreshed and ravishing." He says it because I never look refreshed and ravishing. I always look tired, and maybe even perpetually bored. I've heard of Resting Bitch Face, but I relate more to Resting *Bored* Face.

"How's your mother?"

"She died last week."

He wasn't expecting that. He leans back in his chair and tilts his head. "Why didn't you tell me?"

Why haven't you bothered asking until now? I shrug. "I'm still processing."

My mother had been living with me for the past nine months—since she was diagnosed with stage four colon cancer. She passed away last Wednesday after three months on hospice. It was difficult to leave the apartment in those last few months because she relied on me for everything—from drinking, to eating, to turning her over in her bed. When she took a turn for the worse, I wasn't able to leave her alone at all, which is why I didn't step foot outside of my apartment for weeks. Luckily, a Wi-Fi connection and a credit card make it easy to live life completely indoors in Manhattan. Anything and everything a person could possibly need can be delivered.

Funny how one of the most populated cities in the world can double as a paradise for agoraphobics.

"You okay?" Corey asks.

I mask my disquiet with a smile, even if his concern is only a formality. "I'm fine. It helps that it was expected." I'm only saying what I think he wants to hear. I'm not sure how he'd react to the truth—that I'm relieved she's gone. My mother only ever brought guilt into my life. Nothing less, nothing more. Just consistent guilt.

Corey heads for the counter lined with breakfast pastries, bottles of water, and a coffee carafe. "You hungry? Thirsty?"

"Water's fine."

He grabs two waters and hands one to me, then returns to his seat. "Do you need help with the will? I'm sure Edward can help."

Edward is the lawyer at Corey's literary agency. It's a small agency, so a lot of the writers use Edward's expertise in other areas. Sadly, I won't be needing it. Corey tried to tell me when I signed the lease on my two-bedroom last year that I wouldn't be able to afford it. But my mother insisted she die with dignity—in her own room. Not in a nursing home. Not in a hospital. Not in a hospital bed in the middle of my efficiency apartment. She wanted her own bedroom with her own things.

She promised what was left in her bank account after her death would help me catch up on all the time off I had to take from my writing career. For the past year, I've lived off what little advance I had left over from my last publishing contract. But it's all gone now, and apparently, so is my mother's money. It was one of the last things she confessed to me before she finally succumbed to the cancer. I would have cared for her regardless of her financial situation. She was my mother. But the fact that she felt she needed to lie to me in order for me to agree to take her in proves how disconnected we were from one another.

I take a sip of my water and then shake my head. "I don't really need a lawyer. All she left me was debt, but thanks for the offer."

Corey purses his lips. He knows my financial situation because, as my literary agent, he's the one who sends my royalty checks. Which is why he's looking at me with pity now. "You have a foreign royalty check coming soon," he says, as if I'm not aware of every penny coming in my direction for the next six months. *As if I haven't already spent it.*

"I know. I'll be fine." I don't want to talk about my financial issues with Corey. With anyone.

Corey shrugs a little, unconvinced. He looks down and straightens up his tie. "Hopefully this offer will be good for both of us," he says.

I'm relieved the subject is changing. "Why are we meeting in person with a publisher? You know I prefer to do things over email."

"They requested the meeting yesterday. Said they have a job they'd like to discuss with you, but they wouldn't give me any details over the phone."

"I thought you were working on getting another contract with my last publisher."

"Your books do okay, but not well enough to secure another contract without sacrificing some of your time. You have to agree to engage in social media, go on tour, build a fan base. Your sales alone aren't cutting it in the current market."

I was afraid of this. A contract renewal with my current publisher was all the financial hope I had left. The royalty checks from my previous books have dwindled along with my book sales. I've done very little writing this past year because of my commitment to my mother, so I have nothing to sell to a publisher.

"I have no idea what Pantem will offer, or if it's even something you'll be interested in," Corey says. "We have to sign a non-disclosure agreement before they'll give us more details. The secrecy has me curious, though. I'm trying not to get my hopes up, but there are a lot of possibilities and I have a good feeling. We need this."

He says *we* because whatever the offer is, he gets fifteen percent if I accept. It's the agent-client standard. What *isn't* the agent-client standard would be the six months we spent in a relationship and the two years of sex that followed our breakup.

Our sexual relationship only lasted as long as it did because he wasn't serious about anyone else and neither was I. It was convenient until it wasn't. But the reason our *actual* relationship was so short-lived is because he was in love with another woman.

Never mind that the other woman in our relationship was also me.

It has to be confusing, falling in love with a writer's words before you meet the actual writer. Some people find it difficult to separate a character from the individual who created them. Corey, surprisingly, is one of those people, despite being a literary agent. He met and fell in love with the female protagonist of my first novel, Open Ended, before he ever spoke to me. He assumed my character's personality was a close reflection of my own, when in fact, I couldn't be more opposite from her.

Corey was the only agent to respond to my query, and even that response took months to receive. His email was only a few sentences long, but enough to breathe life back into my dying hope.

I read your manuscript, Open Ended, in a matter of hours. I believe in this book. If you're still looking for an agent, give me a call.

His email came on a Thursday morning. We were having an in-depth phone conversation about my manuscript two hours later. By Friday afternoon, we had met for coffee and signed a contract.

By Saturday night, we had fucked three times.

I'm sure our relationship broke a code of ethics somewhere, but I'm not sure that contributed to how short-lived it was. As soon as Corey figured out that I wasn't the person my character was based on, he realized we weren't compatible. I wasn't heroic. I wasn't simple. I was difficult. An emotionally challenging puzzle he wasn't up for solving.

Which was fine. I wasn't in the mood to be solved.

As difficult as it was being in a relationship with him, it is surprisingly easy being his client. It's why I chose not to switch agencies after our breakup, because he's been loyal and unbiased when it comes to my career.

"You look a little frazzled," Corey says, breaking me out of my thoughts. "Are you nervous?"

I nod, hoping he'll accept my behavior as nerves because I don't want to explain why I'm frazzled. It's been two hours since I left my apartment this morning, but it feels like more has happened in that two hours than in the entire rest of this year. I look down at my hands...my arms...searching for traces of blood. It's no longer there, but I can still feel it. *Smell* it.

My hands haven't stopped shaking, so I keep hiding them under the table. Now that I'm here, I realize I probably shouldn't have come. I can't pass up a potential contract, though. It's not like offers are pouring in, and if I don't secure something soon, I'll have to get a day job. If I get a day job, it'll barely leave me time to write. But at least I'll be able to pay my bills.

Corey pulls a handkerchief out of his pocket and wipes sweat from his forehead. He only sweats when he's nervous. The fact that he's nervous is now making me even more nervous. "Do we need a secret signal if you aren't interested in whatever the offer is?" he asks.

"Let's listen to what they have to say, and then we can request to speak in private."

Corey clicks his pen and straightens in his chair as though he's cocking a gun for battle. "Let me do the talking."

I planned to anyway. He's charismatic and charming. I'd be hard-pressed to find someone who could categorize me as either of those things. It's best if I just sit back and listen.

"What are you *wearing*?" Corey is staring down at my shirt, perplexed, just now noticing it despite having spent the last fifteen minutes with me.

I look down at my oversized shirt. For a moment, I forgot how ridiculous I look. "I spilled coffee on my other shirt this morning and had to change."

"Whose shirt is that?"

I shrug. "Probably yours. It was in my closet."

"You left your house in that? There wasn't something else you could have worn?"

"It doesn't look high fashion?" I'm being sarcastic, but he doesn't catch it.

He makes a face. "No. Is it supposed to?"

Such an ass. But he's good in bed, like most assholes.

I'm actually relieved when the conference room door opens and a woman walks in. She's followed, almost comically, by an older man walking so closely behind her, he bumps into the back of her when she stops.

"Goddammit, Barron," I hear her mumble.

I almost smile at the idea of *Goddammit Barron* actually being his name.

Jeremy enters last. He gives me a small nod that goes unnoticed by everyone else.

The woman is dressed more appropriately than I am on my best day, with short black hair and lipstick so red, it's a little jarring at nine thirty in the morning. She seems to be the one in charge as she reaches for Corey's hand, and then mine, while Goddammit Barron looks on. "Amanda Thomas," she says. "I'm an editor with Pantem Press. This is Barron Stephens, our lawyer, and Jeremy Crawford, our client."

Jeremy and I shake hands, and he does a good job of pretending we didn't share an extremely bizarre morning. He quietly takes the seat across from me. I try not to look at him, but it's the only place my eyes seem to want to travel. I have no idea why I'm more curious about him than I am about this meeting.

Amanda pulls folders out of her briefcase and slides them in front of Corey and me.

"Thank you for meeting with us," she says. "We don't want to waste your time, so I'll cut right to the chase. One of our authors is unable to fulfill a contract due to medical reasons, and we're in search of a writer with experience in the same genre who may be interested in completing the three remaining books in her series."

I glance at Jeremy, but his stoic expression doesn't hint at his role in this meeting.

"Who is the author?" Corey asks.

"We're happy to go over the details and terms with you, but we do ask that you sign the non-disclosure agreement. We would like to keep our author's current situation out of the media."

"Of course," Corey says.

I acquiesce, but I say nothing as we both look over the forms and then sign them. Corey slides them back to Amanda.

"Her name is Verity Crawford," she says. "I'm sure you're familiar with her work."

Corey stiffens as soon as they mention Verity's name. *Of course* we're familiar with her work. Everyone is. I hazard a glance in Jeremy's direction. *Is Verity his wife?* They share a last name. He said downstairs that his wife is a writer. But why would he be in a meeting about her? A meeting she isn't even here for?

"We're familiar with the name," Corey says, holding his cards close.

"Verity has a very successful series we would hate to see go unfinished," Amanda continues. "Our goal is to bring in a writer who is willing to step in, finish the series, complete the book tours, press releases, and whatever else is normally required of Verity. We plan to put out a press release introducing the new co-writer while also preserving as much of Verity's privacy as possible."

Book tours? Press releases?

Corey is looking at me now. He knows I'm not okay with that aspect. A lot of authors excel in reader interaction, but I'm so awkward I'm afraid once my readers meet me in person, they'll swear off my books forever. I've only done one signing, and I didn't sleep for the week leading up to it. I was so scared during the signing that it was hard for me to speak. The next day, I received an email from a reader who said I was a stuck-up bitch to her and she'd never read my books again.

And that's why I stay at home and write. I think the idea of me is better than the reality of me.

Corey says nothing as he opens the folder Amanda hands him. "What is Mrs. Crawford's compensation for three novels?"

Goddammit Barron answers this question. "The terms of Verity's contract will remain the same with her publisher and, understandably, won't be disclosed. All royalties will go to Verity. But my client, Jeremy Crawford, is willing to offer a flat payment of seventy-five thousand per book."

My stomach leaps at the mention of that kind of payout. But as quickly as the excitement lifts my spirits, they sink again when I accept the enormity of it all. Going from being a nobody writer to co-author of a literary sensation is too much of a jump for me. I can already feel my anxiety sinking in just thinking about it.

Corey leans forward, folding his arms over the table in front of him. "I'm assuming the pay is negotiable."

I try to catch Corey's attention. I want to let him know that negotiations aren't necessary. There's no way I'm accepting an offer to finish a series of books that I'd feel too nervous to write.

Goddammit Barron straightens up in his chair. "With all due respect, Verity Crawford has spent the past over a decade building her brand. A brand that wouldn't exist otherwise. The offer is for three books. Seventy-five thousand per book, which comes to a total of two hundred and twenty-five thousand dollars."

Corey drops a pen on the table, leaning back in his chair, appearing to be unimpressed. "What's the time frame for submission?"

"We're already behind, so we're looking to have the first book submitted six months from the contract signing date."

I can't stop staring at the red lipstick smeared across her teeth as she speaks.

"The timeline for the other two is up for discussion. Ideally, we would like to see the contract completed within the next twenty-four months."

I can sense Corey doing the math in his head. It makes me wonder if he's calculating to see what his cut would be or what *my* cut would be. Corey would get fifteen percent. That's almost thirty-four thousand dollars, simply for representing me in this meeting as my agent. Half would go to taxes. That's just under one hundred thousand that would end up in my bank account. Fifty grand per year.

It's more than double the advance I've received for my past novels, but it's not enough to convince me to attach myself to such a successful series. The conversation moves back and forth pointlessly, since I already know I'll be declining. When Amanda pulls out the official contract, I clear my throat and speak up.

"I appreciate the offer," I say. I look directly at Jeremy so he'll know I'm being sincere. "Really, I do. But if your plan is to bring in someone to become the new face of the series, I'm sure there are other authors who would be a much better fit."

Jeremy says nothing, but he is looking at me with a lot more curiosity than he was before I spoke up. I stand up, ready to leave. I'm disappointed in the outcome, but even more disappointed that my first day outside of my apartment has been a complete disaster in so many ways. I'm ready to go home and take a shower.

"I'd like a moment with my client," Corey says, standing quickly.

Amanda nods, closing her briefcase as they both stand. "We'll step out," she says. "The terms are detailed in your folders. We have two other writers in mind if this doesn't seem like it would be a good fit for you, so try to let us know something by tomorrow afternoon at the latest."

Jeremy is the only one still seated at this point. He hasn't said a single word this entire time. Amanda leans forward to shake my hand. "If you have any questions, please reach out. I'm happy to help."

"Thank you," I say. Amanda and Goddammit Barron walk out, but Jeremy continues to stare at me. Corey looks back and forth between us, waiting for Jeremy to exit. Instead, Jeremy leans forward, focusing on me.

"Could we possibly have a word in private?" Jeremy asks me. He looks at Corey, but not for permission—it's more of a dismissal.

Corey stares back at Jeremy, caught off guard by his brazen request. I can tell by the way Corey slowly turns his head and narrows his eyes that he wants me to decline. He's all but saying, *"Can you believe this guy?"*

What he doesn't realize is that I'm craving to be alone in this room with Jeremy. I want them all out of this room, especially Corey, because I suddenly have so many more questions for Jeremy. About his wife, about why they reached out to me, about why she's no longer able to finish her own series.

"It's fine," I say to Corey.

The vein in his forehead protrudes as he attempts to hide his irritation. His jaw hardens, but he yields and eventually exits the conference room.

It's just Jeremy and me.

Again.

Counting the elevator, this is the third time we've been alone in a room together since we crossed paths this morning. But this is the first time I've felt this much nervous energy. I'm sure it's all mine. Jeremy somehow looks as calm as he did while he was helping me clean pieces of a pedestrian off of myself less than an hour ago.

Jeremy leans back in his chair, dragging his hands down his face. "Jesus," he mutters. "Are meetings with publishers always this stiff?"

I laugh quietly. "I wouldn't know. I usually do these things over email."

"I can see why." He stands and grabs a bottle of water. Maybe it's because I'm sitting now and he's so tall, but I don't remember feeling this small in his presence earlier. Knowing he's married to Verity Crawford makes me feel intimidated by him even more than when I was standing in front of him in my skirt and bra.

He remains standing as he leans against the counter, crossing his legs at the ankles. "You okay? You didn't really have much time to adjust to what happened across the street before walking into this."

"Neither did you."

"I'm alright." *There's that word again.* "I'm sure you have questions."

"A ton," I admit.

"What do you want to know?"

"Why can't your wife finish the series?"

"She was in a car accident," he says. His response is mechanical, as if he's forcing himself to detach from any emotion right now.

"I'm sorry. I hadn't heard." I shift in my seat, not knowing what else to say.

"I wasn't on board with the idea of someone else finishing out her contract at first. I had hope she would fully recover. But—" He pauses. "Here we are."

His demeanor makes sense to me now. He seemed a little reserved and quiet, but now I realize all the quiet parts of him are just grief. Palpable grief. I'm not sure if it's because of what happened to his wife, or what he told me in the bathroom earlier—that his daughter passed away several months ago. But this man is obviously out of his element here as he's challenged with making decisions heavier than anything most people ever have to face. "I'm so sorry."

He nods, but he offers nothing further. He returns to his seat, which makes me wonder if he thinks I'm still contemplating the offer. I don't want to waste his time any more than I already have.

"I appreciate the offer, Jeremy, but honestly, it's not something I'm comfortable with. I'm not good with publicity. I'm not even sure why your wife's publisher reached out to me as an option in the first place."

"Open Ended," Jeremy says.

I stiffen when he mentions one of the books I've written.

"It was one of Verity's favorite books."

"Your wife read one of my books?"

"She said you were going to be the next big thing. I'm the one who gave her editor your name because Verity thinks your writing styles are similar. If anyone is going to take over Verity's series, I want it to be someone whose work she respects."

I shake my head. "Wow. I'm flattered, but...I can't."

Jeremy watches me silently, probably wondering why I'm not reacting as most writers would to this opportunity. He can't figure me out. Normally, I would be proud of that. I don't like being easily read, but it feels wrong in this situation. I feel like I should be more transparent, simply because he showed me courtesy this morning. I wouldn't even know where to start, though.

Jeremy leans forward, his eyes swimming with curiosity. He stares at me a moment, then taps his fist on the table as he stands. I assume the meeting is over and start to stand as well, but Jeremy doesn't walk toward the door. He walks toward a wall lined with framed awards, so I sink back into my chair. He stares at the awards, his back to me. It isn't until he runs his fingers over one of them that I realize it's one of his wife's. He sighs and then faces me again.

"Have you ever heard of people referred to as *Chronics*?" he asks.

I shake my head.

"I think Verity might have made up the term. After our daughters died, she said we were Chronics. Prone to chronic tragedy. One terrible thing after another."

I stare at him a moment, allowing his words to percolate. He said he'd lost a daughter earlier, but he's using the term in plural form. "Daughters?"

He inhales a breath. Releases it with defeat. "Yeah. Twins. We lost Chastin six months before Harper passed. It's been..." He isn't detaching himself from his emotions as well as he was earlier. He runs a hand down his face and then returns to his chair. "Some families are lucky enough to never experience a single tragedy. But then there are those families that seem to have tragedies waiting on the back burner. What can go wrong, goes wrong. And then gets worse."

I don't know why he's telling me this, but I don't question it. I like hearing him speak, even if the words coming out of his mouth are dismal.

He's twirling his water bottle in a circle on the table, staring down at it in thought. I'm getting the impression he didn't request to be alone with me to change my mind. He just wanted to be alone. Maybe he couldn't stand another second of discussing his wife in that manner, and he wanted them all to leave. I find that comforting—that being alone with me in the room still feels like being alone to him.

Or maybe he always feels alone. Like our old next-door neighbor who, from what it sounds like, was definitely a Chronic.

"I grew up in Richmond," I say. "Our next-door neighbor lost all three members of his family in less than two years. His son died in combat. His wife died six months later of cancer. Then his daughter died in a car wreck."

Jeremy stops moving the water bottle and slides it a few inches away from him. "Where's the man now?"

I stiffen. I wasn't expecting that question.

The truth is, the man couldn't take losing everyone that meant anything to him. He killed himself a few months after his daughter died, but to say that out loud to Jeremy, who is still grieving the deaths of his own daughters, would be cruel.

"He still lives in the same town. He remarried a few years later. Has a few stepkids and grandchildren."

There's something in Jeremy's expression that makes me think he knows I'm lying, but he seems appreciative that I did.

"You'll need to spend time in Verity's office going through her things. She has years of notes and outlines—stuff I wouldn't know how to make sense of."

I shake my head. *Did he not hear anything I said?* "Jeremy, I told you, I can't—"

"The lawyer is lowballing you. Tell your agent to ask for half a million. Tell them you'll do it with no press, under a pen name, with an ironclad non-disclosure. That way, whatever it is you're trying to hide can stay hidden."

I want to tell him I'm not trying to hide anything other than my awkwardness, but before I can say anything, he's moving toward the door.

"We live in Vermont," he continues. "I'll give you the address after you sign the contract. You're welcome to stay for however long it takes to go through her office."

He pauses with his hand on the door. I open my mouth to object again, but the only word that comes out is a very unsure "*Alright.*"

He stares at me a moment, as if he has more to say. Then he says, "Alright."

He opens the door and walks out into the hallway where Corey is waiting. Corey slips past him, back into the conference room where he closes the door.

I look down at the table, confused by what just happened. Confused as to why I'm being offered such a substantial amount of money for a job I'm not even sure I can do. *Half a million dollars? And I can do it under a pen name with no tour or publicity commitment? What on earth did I say that led to that?*

"I don't like him," Corey says, plopping down in his seat. "What did he say to you?"

"He said they're lowballing me and to ask for half a million with no publicity."

I turn in time to watch Corey choke on air. He grabs my bottle of water and takes a drink. "Shit."

3

I had a boyfriend in my early twenties named Amos, who liked being choked.

It's why we broke up—because I refused to choke him. But sometimes I wonder where I'd be had I entertained his urge. Would we be married now? Would we have children? Would he have moved on to even more dangerous sexual perversions?

I think that's what worried me the most with him. In your early twenties, vanilla sex should satisfy a person without the need to introduce fetishes so early on in a relationship.

I like to think about Amos when I find myself disappointed with the current state of my life. As I stare at the pink eviction notice in Corey's hand, I remind myself that it could be worse—*I could still be with Amos.*

I open my apartment door farther, allowing Corey to step inside. I wasn't aware he was coming over, or I would have made sure there were no eviction notices taped to my door. It's the third day in a row I've received one. I take it from him and shove it into a drawer.

Corey holds up a champagne bottle. "Thought we could celebrate the new contract," he says, handing me the bottle. I'm appreciative he doesn't mention the eviction. It's not as dire now that I have a paycheck on the horizon. What I'll do until then...I'm not sure. I might have enough money for a few days in a hotel.

I can always pawn what's left of my mother's things.

Corey has already taken off his coat and is loosening his tie. This used to be our routine, before my mother moved in. He'd show up and begin losing pieces of his clothing until we were under the covers in my bed.

That came to a complete halt when I found out through social media that he had been on a few dates with a girl named Rebecca. I didn't stop our sexual relationship out of jealousy—I stopped it out of respect for the girl who wasn't aware of it.

"How's Becca?" I ask as I open the cabinet to find two glasses. Corey's hand pauses on his tie, as if he's shocked I'm aware of what's going on in his love life. "I write suspense novels, Corey. Don't be so surprised that I know all about your girlfriend."

I don't watch for his reaction. I open the bottle of champagne and pour two glasses. When I go to hand one to Corey, he's seated at the bar. I stay on the opposite side and we raise our glasses. But I lower mine before he can make a toast. I stare down at my champagne flute, finding it impossible to think of anything to toast about other than the money.

"It's not my series," I say. "They aren't my characters. And the author responsible for the success of these books is injured. It feels wrong to toast to this."

Corey's glass is still paused mid air. He shrugs and then downs his entire glass in one sip, handing it back to me. "Don't focus on why you're playing the game. Just focus on the finish line."

I roll my eyes as I set his empty glass in the sink.

"Have you ever even read one of her books?" he asks.

I shake my head and turn on the water. I should probably do dishes. I have forty-eight hours to be out of this apartment, and my dishes are something I want to take with me when I go. "Nope. Have you?" I pour dish soap into the water and grab a sponge.

Corey laughs. "No. She's not my style."

I look up at him, just as he realizes that his words double as an insult to my own writing, considering I was offered this job because of our supposed similar writing styles, according to Verity's husband.

"Not what I meant," he says. He stands up and walks around the bar, standing next to me at the sink. He waits for me to finish scrubbing a plate, and then he takes it from me and begins rinsing it off. "It doesn't look like you've packed anything. Have you found a new apartment yet?"

"I have a storage building and plan to have most of it out by tomorrow. I've put in an application at a complex in Brooklyn, but they won't have anything for two weeks."

"The eviction notice says you have two days to be out."

"I'm aware of that."

"So where are you going? A hotel?"

"Eventually. I'm leaving Sunday for Verity Crawford's house. Her husband says I'll need to go through her office for a day or two before I start the series."

Immediately upon signing the contract this morning, I received an email from Jeremy with directions to their house. I requested to come on Sunday, and luckily he agreed.

Corey takes another dish from me. I can feel him staring at me. "You're staying at their *house?*"

"How else am I supposed to get her notes for the series?"

"Have him mail them to you."

"She has over a decade years' worth of notes and outlines. Jeremy said he wouldn't even know where to begin, and it would be easier if I sorted through it myself."

Corey doesn't say anything, but I can sense he's biting his tongue. I slide the sponge down the length of the knife in my hand and then hand it to him.

"What aren't you saying?" I ask.

He rinses the knife in silence, sets it in the strainer, then grips the edge of the sink and turns his head toward me. "The man lost two daughters. Then his wife gets injured in a car wreck. I'm not sure I'm all that comfortable with you being in his home."

The water suddenly seems too cold for me. Chills run down both arms. I turn off the water and dry my hands, leaning my back against the sink. "Are you suggesting he had something to do with any of it?"

Corey shrugs. "I don't know enough about what happened to suggest *anything*. But has that thought not crossed your mind? That maybe it's not the safest thing to do? You don't even know them."

I'm not ignorant. I've been digging up as much as I can find about them online. Their first child was at a sleepover fifteen miles away when she had an allergic reaction. Neither Jeremy nor Verity was there when it happened. And the second daughter drowned in the lake behind their home, but Jeremy didn't arrive home until the search for her body was already in place. Both were ruled accidents. I can see why Corey is concerned, because I was, too, honestly. But the more I dig, the less I can find to be concerned about. Two tragic, unrelated accidents.

"And what about Verity's car wreck?"

"It was an accident," I say. "She hit a tree."

Corey's expression suggests he isn't convinced. "I read there weren't any skidmarks. Which means she either fell asleep or she did it on purpose."

"Can you blame her?" I'm irritated that he's making baseless claims. I turn around to finish the dishes. "She lost both of her daughters. Anyone who suffers through something like that would want to find a way out."

Corey dries his hands on the dish towel and then grabs his jacket off the barstool. "Accidents or not, the family obviously has shit luck and a hell of a lot of emotional damage, so you need to be careful. Get in, get what you need, and leave."

"How about you worry about the contractual details, Corey? I'll worry about the research and writing part of it."

He slips on his jacket. "Just looking out for you."

Looking out for me? He knew my mother was dying, and he hasn't checked in with me in two months. He's not looking out for me. He's an ex-boyfriend who thought he was going to get laid tonight, but instead, was quietly rejected right before finding out I'll be staying in another man's home. He's disguising his jealousy as concern.

I walk him to the door, relieved he's leaving this soon. I don't blame him for wanting to escape. This apartment has had a weird vibe in it since my mother moved in. It's why I haven't even bothered fighting the lease, or informing the landlord that I'll have the money in two weeks. I want out of this place more than Corey does right now.

"For what it's worth," he says, "congratulations. Whether you created this series or not, your writing led you to it. You should be proud of that."

I hate it when he says nice things at the height of my irritation. "Thank you."

"Text me as soon as you get there Sunday."

"I will."

"And let me know if you need any help moving."

"I won't."

He laughs a little. "Okay, then." He doesn't hug me goodbye. He salutes me as he backs away, and we've never parted more awkwardly. I have a feeling our relationship is finally as it should be: Agent and author. Nothing more.

4

I could have chosen anything else to do on this six-hour drive. I could have listened to "Bohemian Rhapsody" over sixty times. I could have called my old friend Natalie and played catch-up, especially since I haven't even spoken to her in over six months. We text occasionally, but it would have been nice to hear her voice. Or maybe I could have used the time to mentally prep myself for all the reasons I'm going to stay far away from Jeremy Crawford while I'm in his home.

But instead of doing any of that, I chose to listen to the audiobook of the first novel in Verity Crawford's series.

It just ended. My knuckles are white from gripping the steering wheel so tightly. My mouth is parched from forgetting to hydrate on the drive over. My self-esteem is somewhere back in Albany.

She's good. Really good.

Now I'm regretting having signed the contract. I'm not sure I can live up to that. And to think she's already written six of these novels, all from the villain's point of view. *How can one brain hold that much creativity?*

Maybe the other five suck. I can hope. That way, there won't be much expectation for the final three books in the series.

Who am I kidding? Every time one of Verity's novels releases, it hits number one on the *Times*.

I just made myself twice as nervous than when I left Manhattan.

I spend the rest of the drive ready to go back to New York with my tail between my legs, but I stick it out because thinking I'm not good enough is part of the writing process. It's part of mine, anyway. For me, there are three steps to completing each of my books.

1) Start the book and hate everything I write.

2) Keep writing the book despite hating everything I write.

3) Finish the book and pretend I'm happy with it.

There's never a point in my writing process where I feel like I've accomplished what I set out to accomplish, or when I believe I've written something everyone needs to read. Most of the time, I cry in my shower and stare at my computer screen like a zombie, wondering how so many other authors can promote their books with so much confidence. *"This is the greatest thing since the last book I wrote! You should read it!"*

I'm the awkward writer who posts a picture of my book and says, "It's an okay book. There are words in it. Read it if you want."

I'm afraid this particular writing experience will be even worse than I imagined. Hardly anyone reads my books, so I don't have to suffer through too many negative reviews. But once my work is out there with Verity's name on it, it's going to be read by hundreds of thousands of readers with built-in expectations for this series. And if I fail, Corey will know I failed. The publishers will know I've failed. Jeremy will know I've failed. And...depending on her mental state...*Verity* may know I've failed.

Jeremy didn't clarify the extent of Verity's injuries when we were in the meeting, so I have no idea if she's injured beyond the point of communication. There was very little online about her car wreck other than a couple of vague articles. The publisher released a statement shortly after the wreck stating Verity received non-life-threatening injuries. Two weeks ago, they released another statement that said she was recovering peacefully at home. But her editor, Amanda, said they wanted to keep the extent of her injuries out of the media. So, it's a possibility they downplayed it all.

Or, maybe, after all the loss she's experienced over the past two years, she simply doesn't want to write again.

I guess it's understandable they'd need to ensure the completion of the series. The publishers don't want to see their biggest source of income crash and burn. And while I'm honored I was asked to complete it, I don't necessarily want to be thrown into that kind of spotlight. When I started writing, it wasn't my goal to become famous. I dreamt of a life where enough people would buy my books and I could pay my bills and never be propelled into a life of riches and fame. Very few authors reach that level of success, so it was never a concern that it would happen to me.

I realize attaching my name to this series would boost sales of my past books and ensure more opportunity in the future, but Verity is extremely successful. As is this series I'm taking over. By attaching my real name to her series, I would be subjecting myself to the kind of attention I've spent most of my life fearing.

I'm not looking for my fifteen minutes of fame. I'm looking for a paycheck.

It's going to be a long wait for that advance. I spent most of the rest of my money renting this car and putting my things in storage. I paid a deposit for an apartment, but it won't be ready until next week, or maybe even the week after, which means what little I have left will need to go to a hotel once I leave the Crawford home.

This is my life. Sort of homeless, living out of a suitcase just one and a half weeks after the last of my immediate family members passes away. Can it get worse?

I could be married to Amos right now, so life could *always* be worse.

"Jesus, Lowen." I roll my eyes at my inability to realize how many writers would kill for this kind of opportunity, and here I am thinking my life has hit rock bottom.

Ungrateful, party of one.

I have to stop looking at my life through my mother's glasses. Once I get the advance on these novels, everything will start looking up. I'll no longer be between apartments.

I took the exit for the Crawford home a few miles back. The GPS is leading me down a long, windy road flanked by flowering dogwood trees and houses that keep getting bigger and more spread apart.

When I finally reach the turn-in, I put the rental in park to stop and admire the entrance. Two tall brick columns loom on both sides of the driveway—a driveway that never seems to end. I crane my neck, trying to see the length of it, but the dark asphalt snakes between the trees. Somewhere up there is the house, and somewhere inside of that house lies Verity Crawford. I wonder if she knows I'm coming. My palms start to sweat, so I lift them off the steering wheel and hold them in front of the air vents to dry them.

The security gate is propped open, so I put the car in drive and slowly amble past the sturdy wrought iron. I tell myself not to freak out, even as I notice that the repetitive pattern on top of the iron gate resembles spider webs. I shiver as I follow a curve, the trees getting denser and taller until the house comes into view. I spot the roof first as I climb the hill: slate gray like an angry storm cloud. Seconds later, the rest of it appears, and my breath snags in my throat. Dark stone works its way across the front of the house, broken only by the blood red door, the only relief of color in this sea of gray. Ivy covers the left side of the house, but instead of charming, it's threatening—like a slow-moving cancer.

I think of the apartment I left behind: the dingy walls and too-small kitchen with the olive green refrigerator circa 1970. My entire apartment would probably fit into the entrance hall of this monster. My mother used to say that houses have a soul, and if that is true, the soul of Verity Crawford's house is as dark as they come.

The online satellite images did not do this property justice. *I stalked the home before showing up.* According to a realtor website, they purchased the home five years ago for two and a half million. It's worth over three million now.

It's overwhelming and huge and secluded, but it doesn't have the typical formal vibe of homes of this caliber. There isn't an air of superiority clinging to the walls.

I edge the car along the driveway, wondering where I'm supposed to park. The lawn is lush and manicured, at least three acres deep. The lake behind the house stretches from one edge of the property to the other. The Green Mountains paint a picturesque backdrop so beautiful, it's hard to believe the awful tragedy its owners have experienced.

I sigh in relief as I spot a concrete parking area next to the garage. I put my car in park and then kill the engine.

My car doesn't fit in with this house at all. I'm kicking myself for selecting the cheapest car I could possibly rent. *Thirty bucks a day.* I wonder if Verity has ever sat in a Kia Soul. In the article I read about her wreck, she was driving a Range Rover.

I reach to the passenger seat to grab my phone so I can text Corey to let him know I made it. When I put my hand on the driver's side door handle, I stiffen, stretching my spine against the back seat. I turn and look out my window.

"Shit!"

What the fuck?

I slap my chest to make sure I still have a heartbeat as I stare back at the face staring into my car window. Then, when I see that the figure at my door is only a child, I cover my mouth, hoping he's heard his fair share of curse words. He doesn't laugh. He just stares, which seems even creepier than if he'd have scared me on purpose.

He's a miniature version of Jeremy. The same mouth, the same green eyes. I read in one of the articles that Verity and Jeremy had three children. This must be their little boy.

I open the door, and he takes a step back as I get out of the car.

"Hey." The child doesn't respond. "Do you live here?"

"Yes."

I look at the house behind him, wondering what that must be like for a child to grow up in such a home. "Must be nice," I mutter.

"Used to be." He turns and begins walking up the driveway, toward the front door. I instantly feel bad for him. I'm not sure I've given much thought to the situation this family is in. This little boy, who can't be more than five years old, has lost both of his sisters. And who knows what that kind of grief has done to his mother? I know it was apparent in Jeremy.

I save my suitcase for later and shut my door, following the little boy. I'm only a few feet behind him when he opens the front door and walks into the house, then closes the door in my face.

I wait a moment, wondering if maybe he has a sense of humor. But I can see through the frosted window of the front door, and he continues through the house and doesn't come back to let me in.

I don't want to call him an asshole. He's a little kid, and he's been through a lot. *But I think he might be an asshole.*

I ring the doorbell and wait.

And wait.

And wait.

I ring the doorbell again but get no answer. Jeremy put his contact information in the email he sent me, so I pull up his number and text him. *"It's Lowen. I'm at your front door."*

I send the text and wait.

A few seconds later, I hear steps descending the stairs. I can see Jeremy's shadow through the frosted glass grow larger as he approaches the door. Right before it opens, I see him pause like he's taking a breath. I don't know why, but that pause reassures me that maybe I'm not the only one nervous about this whole situation.

Weird how his potential discomfort brings me comfort. I don't think that's how it's supposed to work.

He opens the door, and although he's the same man I met a few days ago, he's...different. No suit or tie, no air of mystery about him. He's in sweatpants and a blue Bananafish T-shirt. Socks, no shoes. "Hey."

I don't like the buzz rushing through me right now. I ignore it and smile at him. "Hi."

He stares for a second and then steps aside, opening the door wider, waving me in with his arm. "Sorry, I was upstairs. I told Crew to get the door. Guess he didn't hear me."

I step into the foyer.

"Do you have a suitcase?" Jeremy asks.

I spin around to face him. "Yeah, it's in my back seat, but I can get it later."

"Is the car unlocked?"

I nod.

"Be right back." He slips on a pair of shoes next to the door and walks outside. I spin in a slow circle, checking out my surroundings. Not much is different from the pictures I saw of the home online. It feels odd because I've seen all the rooms in the house already, thanks to the realtor website. I feel like I already know my way around, and I'm only five feet into the house.

There's a kitchen to the right and living room to the left. They're separated by an entryway with a staircase that leads to the second floor. The kitchen in the pictures was trimmed with dark cherry cabinetry, but it's been updated, and all the old cabinets have been ripped out, replaced mostly by shelves and a few cabinets above the countertop that are a blonder wood.

There are two ovens, and a refrigerator with a glass door. I'm staring at it from several feet away when the little boy comes bounding down the stairs. He runs past me and opens the refrigerator, pulling out a bottle of Dr. Pepper. I watch as he struggles to twist open the lid.

"Want me to open it for you?" I ask him.

"Yes, please," he says, looking up at me with those big green eyes. *I can't believe I thought he was an asshole.* His voice is so sweet and his hands are so tiny, they can't even open a bottle of soda yet. I take it from him and twist open the bottle with ease. The front door opens as I'm handing the soda back to Crew.

Jeremy narrows his eyes in Crew's direction. "I just told you no sodas." He leaves my suitcase against the wall and walks over to Crew, pulling the soda out of his hands. "Go get ready for your shower. I'll be there in a minute."

Crew rolls his head and stalks back toward the stairs.

Jeremy cocks an eyebrow. "Never trust that kid. He's smarter than both of us put together." He takes a sip of the soda before returning it to the refrigerator. "You want something to drink?"

"No, I'm fine."

Jeremy grabs my suitcase and carries it down the hallway. "I hope it's not weird, but I'm giving you the master bedroom. We all sleep upstairs now, and I thought it would be easier because it's the closest room to her office."

"I'm not even sure I'm staying the night," I say as I follow behind him. The place gives mc an eerie vibe, so it would be nice if I could grab what I need and find a hotel. "I was planning to check out her office and assess the situation."

He laughs, pushing the bedroom door open. "Trust me. You'll need at least two days. Maybe more." He lays the suitcase on a chest at the foot of the bed, then opens the master closet and points to an empty area. "I made some space in case you need to hang anything." He points toward the bathroom. "Bathroom is all yours. I'm not sure if there are toiletries, so let me know if you need anything. I'm sure we have it."

"Thank you." I look around the room, and this all feels so bizarre. Especially that I'll be sleeping in their bed. My eyes are pulled to the headboard—specifically to the teeth marks bitten into the top edge of the headboard in the center of the bed. I immediately tear my eyes away before Jeremy catches me looking. He'll probably see all over my face that I'm wondering which one of them had to bite the headboard in order to keep quiet during sex. *Have I ever had sex that intense?*

"You need a minute alone in here, or would you like to go ahead and see the rest of the house?" Jeremy asks.

"I'm good," I say, following him. He walks into the hallway, but I pause, eyeing the bedroom door. "Does this door lock?"

He takes a step back inside the bedroom, looking at the door handle. "I don't know that we've ever locked it." He jiggles the handle. "I'm sure I can find a lock if it's important to you."

I haven't slept in a bedroom without a lock since I was ten. I want to *beg* him to find a lock, but I also don't want to be even more intrusive than I already am.

"No, it's fine."

He lets go of the door, but before stepping back out into the hallway, he says, "Before I take you upstairs, do you know what name you'll be writing this series under?"

I hadn't thought about it since finding out Pantem agreed to the demands Jeremy told me to make.

I shrug. "I haven't really thought about it."

"I'd like to introduce you to Verity's nurse using your pen name, in case you never want anyone attaching you to the series."

Her injuries are bad enough that she needs a nurse?

"Okay. I guess..." I'm clueless as to what name I should use.

"What street did you grow up on?" Jeremy asks.

"Laura Lane."

"What was the name of your first pet?"

"Chase. He was a Yorkie."

"Laura Chase," he says. "I like it."

I tilt my head, recognizing that pattern of questioning from Facebook quizzes. "Isn't that how people figure out their pornstar name?"

He laughs. "Pen name, pornstar name. Works across the board." He motions for me to follow him. "Come meet Verity first, and then I'll take you to her office."

Jeremy takes the stairs two at a time. There's an elevator that looks newly installed right past the kitchen. Verity must be in a wheelchair now. *God, the poor woman.*

Jeremy is waiting for me when I reach the top of the stairs. The hallway splits, with three doors on one end and two on the other. He turns left.

"This is Crew's bedroom," he says, pointing toward the first room. "I sleep in that room." He points to the door next to Crew's.

Across the hall from those two bedrooms is another room. The door is shut, so he taps on it gently and then pushes it open.

I'm not sure what I was expecting, but I certainly wasn't expecting this.

She's on her back on the bed, staring up at the ceiling, her blonde hair spilled over her pillow. A nurse in blue scrubs is at the foot of her bed, putting socks on her feet. Crew is lying next to Verity on the bed, holding an iPad. Verity's eyes are vacant, uninterested in her surroundings.

She's unaware of the nurse. Unaware of me. Of Crew. Of Jeremy as he leans over and brushes hair from her forehead. She blinks, but there's nothing else there. No recognition that the man she had three children with is trying to be affectionate with her. I try to cover the chills that have appeared on my arms.

The nurse addresses Jeremy. "She seemed tired, so I thought I'd put her to bed early tonight." She pulls a blanket over Verity.

Jeremy moves to the window and closes the curtains. "Did she take her after-dinner meds?"

The nurse lifts Verity's feet, tucking the blanket beneath them. "Yeah, she's good until midnight."

The nurse is older than Jeremy, maybe in her mid-fifties, with short red hair. She glances at me, then back at Jeremy, waiting for an introduction.

Jeremy shakes his head like he forgot I'm even here. He waves toward me while looking at the nurse. "This is Laura Chase, the author I was telling you about. Laura, this is April, Verity's nurse."

I shake April's hand, but feel her judgment as she eyes me up and down. "I thought you'd be older," she says.

What do I even say to that? Coupled by the way she looks at me, her comment feels like a dig. Or an accusation. I ignore it and smile. "It's good to meet you, April."

"You too." She grabs her purse off the dresser, directing her attention to Jeremy. "I'll see you in the morning. Should be an easy night." She reaches down and pinches Crew's thigh. He giggles and scoots away from her. I step aside as April exits the bedroom.

I glance at the bed. Verity's eyes are still open, connecting with nothing. I'm not sure she's even aware her nurse left. *Is she aware of anything?* I feel terrible for Crew. For Jeremy. For Verity.

I don't know that I'd want to live in this condition. And knowing Jeremy is tied to this life... It's all so depressing. This house, the tragedies in this family's past, the struggles in their present.

"Crew, don't make me do it. I told you to shower."

Crew looks up at Jeremy and smiles, but fails to get off the bed.

"I'm gonna count to three."

Crew sets his iPad beside him, but continues to defy Jeremy.

"Three...two..." And then, at the count of one, Jeremy lunges at Crew, gripping his ankles and pulling him up in the air. "Upside down night it is!"

Crew is laughing and squirming. "Not again!"

Jeremy looks over at me. "Laura, how many seconds can a kid hang upside down before their brain flips over and they start talking backward?"

I laugh at their interaction. "I heard twenty seconds. But it could be fifteen."

Crew says, "No, Daddy, I'll go shower! I don't want my brain to be upside down!"

"And you'll clean out your ears? Because they clearly weren't working before when I told you to take a shower."

"I swear!"

Jeremy tosses him over his shoulder, turning him right side up before placing him back on his feet. He ruffles his hair and says, "Go."

I watch as Crew rushes out the door and into his bedroom across the hall. Watching Jeremy interact with Crew makes the house seem a little more welcoming. "He's cute. How old is he?"

"Five," Jeremy says. He reaches down to the side of Verity's hospital bed and raises it a bit. He grabs a remote off the table next to her bed and turns on the TV.

We both exit the bedroom, and he pulls the door slightly shut. I'm standing in the middle of the hallway when he faces me. He slides his hands into the pockets of his grey sweatpants. He acts like he wants to say more—explain more. But he doesn't. He sighs and looks back at Verity's bedroom.

"Crew was scared to sleep up here by himself. He's been a trooper, but nights are rough for him. He wanted to be closer to her, but he didn't like sleeping downstairs. I moved us both up here to make it easier on him." Jeremy makes his way back down the hallway. "Which means you have the run of the downstairs at night." He flips off the hallway light. "Want to see her office?"

"Of course."

I follow him downstairs, to the double doors near the stairwell landing. He pushes open one of the double doors, revealing the most intimate part of his wife.

Her office.

When I step inside, it feels like I'm rummaging around her underwear drawer. There are floor-to-ceiling bookshelves with books tucked into every vacant crevice. Boxes of papers line the walls. The desk... *My God*, her desk. It extends from one end of the room to the other, stretching along a wall lined with huge window panes overlooking the entirety of the backyard. There isn't an inch of desk that isn't covered with a stack of pages or files.

"She's not the most organized person," Jeremy says.

I smile, recognizing a kinship with Verity. "Most writers aren't."

"It'll take time. I would attempt to organize it myself, but it's all Greek to me."

I walk to one of the shelves closest to me and run my hand over some of the books. They're foreign editions of her work. I pluck a German copy from the shelf and examine it.

"She has her laptop and a desktop," Jeremy says. "I wrote the passwords on sticky notes for you." He picks up a notebook next to her computer. "She was constantly taking notes. Writing down thoughts. She'd write ideas down on napkins. Dialogue in the shower on a waterproof notepad." Jeremy drops the notepad back onto the desk. "She once used a Sharpie to write down character names on the bottom of Crew's diaper. We were at the zoo, and she didn't have a notepad."

He does a full, slow circle as he looks around at her office like it's been a while since he's stepped foot in here. "The world was her manuscript. No surface was safe."

My insides warm at the way he seems to appreciate her creative process. I spin in a circle, taking it all in. "I had no idea what I was getting into."

"I didn't want to laugh when you said you might not need to stay the night. But in all honesty, this might take you more than two days. If it does, you're welcome to stay as long as you need. I'd rather you take your time and make sure you have everything you need than go back to New York unsure of how to tackle this."

I look at the shelves containing the series I'm taking over. There are to be nine total books in the series. Six have been published, and three are still to be delivered. The series title is *The Noble Virtues*, and each book is a different virtue. The three that are left up to me are Courage, Truth, and Honor.

All six books are on her shelves, and I'm relieved to see extras. I pull a copy of the second novel off the shelf and skim through it.

"Have you read the series yet?" Jeremy asks.

I shake my head, not wanting to reveal I listened to the audiobook. He might ask me questions about it. "I haven't yet. I didn't have time between signing the contract and coming here." I place the book back on the shelf. "Which is your favorite?"

"I haven't read any of them, either. Not since her first book."

I spin and look at him. "Really?"

"I didn't like being inside her head."

I hold back my smile, but he sounds a little bit like Corey right now. Unable to separate the world his wife creates from the one she lives in. At least Jeremy seems to be a little more self-aware than Corey ever was.

I look around the room, slightly overwhelmed, but I'm not sure if it's because Jeremy is standing here or because of the chaos I'm about to have to sort through. "I don't even know where to start."

"Yeah, I'll let you get to that." Jeremy points to the office door. "I should probably go check on Crew. Make yourself at home. Food...drinks...the house is yours."

"Thank you."

Jeremy closes the door, and I settle in at Verity's desk. Her desk chair alone probably cost more than a month's rent in my apartment. I wonder how much easier writing is for someone who has money to burn on things I've always dreamt of having at my disposal while I write. Comfortable furniture, enough money to have an on-call masseuse, more than one computer. I imagine it would make the writing process a lot easier and a lot less stressful. I have a laptop with a missing key and Wi-Fi when a neighbor forgets to password protect theirs. I sit on an old dining room table chair at a makeshift desk that's really just a plastic folding table I ordered from Amazon for twenty-five bucks.

Most of the time, I don't even have enough money for printer ink and computer paper.

I guess being here in her office for a few days will be one way to test my theory. The richer you are, the more creative you're able to be.

I take the second book of the series off the shelf. I open it, only intending to glance at it. See how she picked up from where book one left off.

I end up reading for three hours straight.

I haven't moved from my spot, not even once. Chapter after chapter of intrigue and fucked up characters. *Really* fucked up characters. It's going to take me time to work myself into that mindset while writing. No wonder Jeremy doesn't read her work. All her books are from the villain's point of view, so that's new to me. I really should have read all these books before arriving.

I stand up to stretch out my spine, but it doesn't even really hurt; the desk chair I've been sitting in is the most comfortable piece of furniture my ass has ever pressed against.

I look around, wondering if I should go through computer files next or printed files.

I decide to check out her desktop. I browse several files in Microsoft Word, which seems to be the program she prefers. All the files I find are related to books she's already written. I'm not too worried about those yet. I want to find any plans she had for the books yet to be written. Most of the files on her laptop are the same as the files on her desktop.

Maybe Verity was the type of author who hand-wrote her outlines. I turn my attention to the stacks of boxes on the back wall, near a closet. A thin layer of dust coats the tops of them. I go through several boxes, pulling out versions of manuscripts at various stages in the writing process, but they're all versions of books in her series that she's already written. Nothing hinting at what she planned to write next.

I'm on the sixth box, rummaging through the contents, when I find something with an unfamiliar title. This one is called *So Be It*.

I flip through the first few pages, hoping I'll get lucky and find that it's an outline for the seventh book in the series. Almost immediately, I can tell that it isn't. This seems...*personal.* I flip back to the first page of chapter one and read the first line.

I sometimes think back on the night I met Jeremy and wonder, had we not made eye contact, would my life still end the same?

As soon as I see Jeremy's name mentioned, I scan a little more of the page. *It's an autobiography.*

It's not at all what I'm searching for. An autobiography isn't what the publishers are paying me to turn in, so I should just move on. But I look over my shoulder to make sure the door is shut because I'm curious. Besides, reading some of this is research. I need to see how Verity's mind works to understand her as a writer. *That's my excuse, anyway.*

I carry the manuscript to the couch, make myself comfortable, and begin reading.

So Be It
by
Verity Crawford

Author's note:

The thing I abhor most about autobiographies are the counterfeit thoughts draped over every sentence. A writer should never have the audacity to write about themselves unless they're willing to separate every layer of protection between the author's soul and their book. The words should come directly from the center of the gut, tearing through flesh and bone as they break free. Ugly and honest and bloody and a little bit terrifying, but completely exposed. An autobiography encouraging the reader to like the author is not a true autobiography. No one is likable from the inside out. One should only walk away from an autobiography with, at best, an uncomfortable distaste for its author.

I will deliver.

What you read will taste so bad at times, you'll want to spit it out, but you'll swallow these words and they will become part of you, part of *your* gut, and you will hurt because of them.

Yet...even with my generous warning...you're going to continue to ingest my words, because here you are.

Human.

Curious.

Carry on.

Chapter One

"Find what you love and let it kill you."
- Charles Bukowski

I sometimes think back on the night I met Jeremy and wonder, had we not made eye contact, would my life still end the same? Was it my destiny from the beginning to suffer such a tragic end? Or is my tragic end a result of poor choices rather than fate?

Of course, I haven't met a tragic end yet, or I wouldn't be able to recount what led to it. Nevertheless, it's coming. I can sense it, just as I sensed Chastin's death. And just as I embraced her fate, I will embrace my own.

I wouldn't say I was lost before the night I met Jeremy, but I had certainly never been found until the moment he laid eyes on me from across the room.

I'd had boyfriends before. One-night stands, even. But I'd never come close to imagining life with someone else until that moment. When I saw him, I pictured our first night together, our wedding, our honeymoon, our children.

Until that moment, the idea of love had always felt very manufactured to me. A Hallmark ploy. A marketing scheme for greeting card companies. I had no interest in love. My only goal that night was to get drunk on free booze and find a rich investor to fuck. I was already halfway there, having downed three Moscow Mules. And judging by the look of Jeremy Crawford, I was going to leave that party an overachiever. He looked rich, and it *was* a charity event, after all. Poor people don't show up to charity events unless they're *serving* the rich.

Present company not included.

He was talking with a few other men, but every time he'd glance in my direction, I felt like we were the only two people in the room. Every now and then, he would smile at me. Of course he did. I had on my red dress that night, the one I stole from Macy's. *Don't judge me. I was a starving artist and it was ridiculously expensive.* I intended to make up for the theft when I had the money. I'd donate to a charity or save a baby or something. The good thing about sins is they don't have to be atoned for immediately, and that red dress was too perfect for me to pass up.

It was a fuckable dress. The kind of dress a man can easily bypass when he wants between your legs. The mistake women make when they choose their clothes for events like the one I was at, is that they don't think about them from the man's perspective. A woman wants her breasts to look good, her figure to be hugged. Even if that means sacrificing comfort and wearing something impossible to remove. But when *men* look at dresses, they aren't admiring the way it hugs the hips or the cinch at the waist or the fancy tie up the back. They're sizing up how easy it will be to remove. Will he be able to slip his hand up her thigh when they're seated next to each other at a table? Will he be able to fuck her in a car without the awkward mess of zippers and Spanx? Will he be able to fuck her in the bathroom without having to remove her clothes completely?

The answers to my stolen red dress were yes, yes, and *hell* yes.

I realized, with that dress on, there was no way he would be able to leave the party without approaching me. I chose to stop paying attention to him. It made me seem desperate. I was not the mouse, I was the cheese. I was going to stand there until he came to me.

He did, eventually. I was standing at the bar, my back to him, when he put his hand on my shoulder and leaned forward, motioning for the bartender. Jeremy didn't look at me in that moment. He simply kept his hand on my shoulder, as if he were laying claim to me. When the bartender approached, I watched in fascination. Jeremy nudged his head toward me and said, "Make sure you only serve her water for the rest of the evening."

I hadn't been expecting that. I turned, leaning an arm on the bar, and faced him. He dropped his hand from my shoulder, but not before his fingers grazed all the way down to my elbow. A flicker of electricity flashed through me, mixed with a surge of anger.

"I'm perfectly capable of deciding when I've had enough to drink."

Jeremy smirked at me and even though I hated the arrogance behind that smirk, he was good-looking. "I'm sure you are."

"I've only had three drinks all evening."

"Good."

I stood up straight and called the bartender back over. "I'll have another Moscow Mule, please."

The bartender glanced at me, then Jeremy. Then back at me. "I'm sorry, ma'am. I've been asked to serve you water."

I rolled my eyes. "I *heard* him ask you to serve me water, I'm standing right here. But I don't know this man, and he doesn't know me, and I'd like another Moscow Mule."

"She'll take a water," Jeremy said.

I was definitely attracted to him, but his looks were quickly fading with that chauvinistic attitude. The bartender lifted his hands and said, "I don't want to get involved in whatever this is. If you want a drink, go order it from the bar over there." He pointed to the bar across the room. I grabbed my purse, tipped my chin up in the air, and walked away. When I reached the other bar, I found a stool and waited for the bartender to finish with his customer. In that time, Jeremy appeared again, this time leaning his elbow across the bar.

"You didn't even give me a chance to explain why I'd like you to have water."

I rolled my head in his direction. "I'm sorry, I didn't realize I owed you my time."

He laughed, moving until his back was against the bar, and stared at me with a tilted head and a crooked smile. "I've been watching you since the moment I walked through the door. You've had three drinks in forty-five minutes, and if you keep going at that rate, I won't feel comfortable asking you to leave with me. I'd much rather you make that choice while you're sober."

His voice sounded like his throat was coated in honey. I held eye contact with him, wondering if it was an act. Could a man that good looking and presumably rich *also* be considerate? It felt more presumptuous than anything, but I was drawn in by his gall.

The bartender approached with impeccable timing. "What can I get for you?"

I straightened up, breaking eye contact with Jeremy. I turned and faced the bartender. "I'll have a water."

"Make it two," Jeremy said.

And that was that.

It's been years since that night, and it's difficult to recall every detail, but I do remember being drawn to him in those first few moments in a way I'd never been drawn to a man. I liked the sound of his voice. I liked his confidence. I liked his teeth, perfect and white. I liked the stubble on his jaw. It was the perfect length to scratch my thighs. Maybe even scar them if he stayed down there long enough.

I liked that he wasn't afraid to touch me while we talked, and every time he did, the graze of his fingers made my skin tingle.

After we both finished our waters, Jeremy led me to the exit, his hand on my lower back, his fingers caressing my dress.

We walked to his limousine, and he held the back door open for me as I climbed inside. He took the seat across from me rather than next to me. The car smelled like a bouquet, but I knew it was perfume. I quite liked it, despite knowing another woman had been in the limousine. My eyes fell to a bottle of champagne that was half empty next to two wine glasses, one lined with red lipstick.

Who is she? And why did he leave the party with me and not her?

I didn't care to ask those questions out loud, because he was leaving with me. That's really all that mattered.

We sat in silence for a minute or two, staring at each other with anticipation. He knew he had me in that moment, which is why he felt confident enough to reach forward and lift my leg, draping it across the seat next to him. He left his hand on my ankle, caressing it, watching as my chest began to rise and fall in response to his touch.

"How old are you?" he asked. The question made me pause because he looked older than I was, maybe late twenties, early thirties. I didn't want to scare him off with the truth, so I lied and said I was twenty-five.

"You look younger."

He knew I was lying. I kicked off my shoe and ran my toes across the outside of his thigh. "Twenty-two."

Jeremy laughed and said, "A liar, huh?"

"I stretch truths where I see fit. I'm a writer."

His hand moved to my calf.

"How old are *you*?"

"Twenty-four," he said with as much truth as I'd given him.

"So...twenty-eight?"

He smiled. "Twenty-seven."

His hand was on my knee at this point. I wanted it even higher. I wanted it on my thigh, between my legs, exploring me from the inside. I wanted him, but not here.

I wanted to *go* with him, see where he lived, judge the comfort of his bed, smell his sheets, taste his skin.

"Where's your driver?" I asked.

Jeremy glanced behind him, toward the front of the limousine. "I don't know," he replied, looking back at me. "This isn't my limousine." His expression was mischievous, and I couldn't tell if he was lying.

I narrowed my eyes, wondering if this man had really led me to a limousine that didn't even belong to him. "Whose limousine *is* this?"

Jeremy's eyes had left mine and were focused on his hand. The one tracing circles over my knee. "I don't know." I expected my desire to wane at the realization that he may *not* be rich, but instead, his admission made me smile. "I'm an entry-level scrub," he said. "I drove my car here. Honda Civic. Parked it myself because I'm too cheap to pay the ten bucks for valet."

I was surprised by how much I loved that he had brought me to a limo that wasn't even his. He wasn't rich. He wasn't rich, *yet I still wanted to fuck him.*

"I clean office buildings in the city," I admitted. "I stole an invitation to this party out of a trash can. I'm not even supposed to be here."

He smiled, and I've never wanted to taste a grin like I wanted to taste the one that spread across his face. "Aren't you resourceful?" he asked. His hand slipped behind my knee and he pulled me toward him. I slid across the seat and onto his lap because that's what dresses like mine were for. I could feel him growing hard between my legs as he pressed a thumb against my bottom lip. I swiped my tongue across the pad of his thumb, and it made him sigh. Not groan. Not moan. He *sighed*, like it was the sexiest thing he'd ever felt.

"What's your name?" he asked.

"Verity."

"Verity." He said it twice. "*Verity*. That's really pretty." His eyes were on my mouth, and he was about to lean in and kiss me, but I pulled back.

"What's yours?"

His eyes flickered back to mine. "Jeremy." He said it fast, like it was a waste of his time, an inconvenient interruption to our kiss. As soon as the word left his mouth, his lips touched mine, and as soon as they touched mine, the interior light kicked on above our heads and we both froze, our lips grazing, our bodies suddenly stiff as someone climbed into the driver's seat of the limousine.

"Shit," Jeremy whispered against my mouth. "What an untimely return." He pushed me off of him and opened the door. He ushered me out of the car just as the driver realized someone else was in the car with him.

"Hey!" he yelled into the backseat.

Jeremy grabbed my hand and began to pull me after him, but I needed out of my shoes. I tugged on his arm, and he stopped as I slipped my shoes off my feet. The driver started heading in our direction. "Hey! What the hell were you doing in my car?"

Jeremy grabbed my shoes in one hand, and we ran down the street, laughing in the dark, out of breath when we finally reached his car. He hadn't been lying about it. It was a Honda Civic, although it was a newer model, so that counted for something. He pushed me against the passenger door, dropped my shoes on the concrete, and then swept a hand into my hair.

I looked over my shoulder at the car we were leaning against. "Is *this* really your car?"

He smiled as he reached into his suit pocket and pulled out his key fob. He unlocked the doors to prove it was his, which made me laugh.

He stared down at me, our mouths *thisclose*, and I could swear he was already imagining what life with me would be like. You can't look at someone the way he looked at me—with the entirety of his past—without also imagining the future.

He closed his eyes and kissed me. The kiss was full of both desire and respect—two things a lot of men didn't seem to know could go hand in hand.

His fingers felt good in my hair, and his tongue felt good in my mouth. I felt good to him, too. I could feel how good I felt to him in the way he kissed me. We knew very little about each other in that moment, but it was almost better that way. Sharing a kiss that intimate with a stranger was like saying, *"I don't know you, but I believe I would like you if I did."*

I liked that he believed he could like me. It almost made me believe I was likeable.

When he pulled away from me, I wanted to go with him. I wanted my mouth to follow his, my fingers to stay wrapped around his. It was torture remaining in the passenger seat of his car as we drove. I was burning inside for him. He had lit a fire in me, and I was determined to make sure it didn't go out.

He fed me before he fucked me.

Took me to a Steak 'n Shake, and we sat on the same side of the booth, eating French fries and sipping chocolate shakes between kisses. The restaurant was mostly empty, so we were in a quiet corner booth, far enough away that no one noticed when Jeremy's hand slid up my thigh and disappeared between my legs. No one heard me when I moaned. No one cared when he pulled his hand away and whispered that he wasn't going to give me an orgasm in a Steak 'n Shake.

I wouldn't have minded.

"Take me to your bed, then," I said.

He did. His bed was in the middle of a studio apartment in Brooklyn. Jeremy wasn't rich. He could barely afford the Steak 'n Shake he had bought me. But I didn't care. I was on his bed, lying on my back, watching him undress, when I realized I was about to make love for the first time. I'd had sex before, but never with more than just my body.

There was so much more of me invested in that moment than my body. My heart felt full—of what, I don't know. But my heart had felt empty with the men who came before Jeremy.

It was amazing how different sex felt when a person used more than their body. I involved my heart and my gut and my mind and my hope. I fell in that moment. Not in love. I just...*fell.*

It was as if I'd been standing on the edge of a cliff my whole life, and finally, after meeting Jeremy, I felt confident enough to jump. Because—for the first time in my life—I felt confident that I wouldn't land. I would keep flying.

Looking back, I realize how crazy it is that I fell for him so fast. But it was only crazy because it never stopped. Had I woken up the next morning and slipped out of his apartment, it would have ended as a fun one-night stand, and I wouldn't even be recalling any of this all these years later. But I didn't leave the next morning, so it became more. With every day that passed, that first night with him was further validated. And that's what love at first sight is. It isn't really love at first sight until you've been with the person long enough for it to *become* love at first sight.

We didn't leave his apartment for three days.

We ate Chinese takeout. We fucked. We ordered pizza. We fucked. We watched TV. We fucked.

We both called in sick to work that Monday, and by Tuesday, I was obsessed. I was obsessed with his laugh, with his cock, with his mouth, with his skill, with his stories, with his hands, with his confidence, with his gentleness, with a new and intense need to please him.

I *needed* to please him.

I *needed* to be what made him smile, breathe, wake up in the mornings.

And for a while, I was. He loved me more than he loved anything or anyone. I was his sole reason for living.

Until he discovered the one thing that meant more to him than I did.

5

It's like I have surpassed opening Verity's underwear drawer, and now I'm rummaging around among the silk and lace. I am well aware that I shouldn't be reading this. This is not why I came here. But...

I slide the manuscript onto the couch next to me, and I stare at it. I have so many questions about Verity. Questions I can't ask her and questions Jeremy probably doesn't feel like answering. I need to get to know her better to see how her mind works, and you can't get more answers from any other source like you can from an autobiography. One this brutally honest.

I can see myself getting sidetracked by this, and I really shouldn't. I'm here to find what I need and get out of this family's hair. They've been through enough and don't need an intruder touching their underwear.

I walk over to the monster desk and pick up my phone. It's already after eleven. I arrived around seven this evening, but I didn't expect it to be this late already. I didn't even hear anything outside of this office. Like it's soundproof.

Hell, it probably is. If I could afford to work in a soundproof office, I would.

I'm hungry.

It's an awkward feeling, being hungry in a house you aren't familiar with. I know Jeremy said to help myself, so I head for the kitchen.

I don't make it far. I pause right when I open the office door.

The office is definitely soundproof, or I would have heard this noise. It's coming from upstairs, and I have to still myself completely to focus on it. To pray it's not at all what it sounds like.

I move quietly and cautiously to the foot of the stairs, and sure enough, the sound seems to be coming from the direction of Verity's room. It's the creaking of a bed. *Repetitive* creaking, like the sound a bed would make if a man were on top of a woman.

Oh, my God. I cover my mouth with unsteady fingers. *No, no, no!*

I read an article about this once. A woman was injured in a car wreck and was in a coma. She lived in a nursing facility and her husband came to visit her every day. The staff became suspicious that he was having sex with her despite her being in a coma, so they set up hidden cameras. The man was arrested for rape because his wife was unable to give consent.

Much like Verity.

I should do something. *But what?*

"It's noisy, I know."

I gasp and spin around, coming face to face with Jeremy.

"I can turn it off if it bothers you," he says.

"You scared me." My voice is full of breath. I blow out a sigh of relief, knowing that whatever I'm hearing is not at all what I thought it was. Jeremy looks over my shoulder, up at where the noise is coming from.

"It's her hospital bed. It's on a timer every two hours to lift different parts of her mattress. Takes weight off her pressure points."

I can feel the embarrassment creeping up my neck. I pray to God he doesn't know what I thought that noise was. I cover my chest with my hand to hide the redness I know is there. I'm fair skinned, and anytime I get nervous or worked up or embarrassed, my skin tells on me, erupting in angry red splotches. I wish I could sink into the lush, rich-people carpet and disappear.

I clear my throat. "They make beds like that?" I could have used one when my mother was on hospice. It was hell trying to move her on my own.

"Yeah, but they're obscenely expensive. Several thousand for a brand new one, and insurance wouldn't even cover it."

I choke on that price.

"I'm heating up leftovers," he says. "You hungry?"

"I was just on my way to the kitchen, actually."

Jeremy walks backward. "It's pizza."

"Perfect." *I hate pizza.*

The microwave timer goes off right when Jeremy reaches it. He pulls out a plate of pizza and hands it to me, then makes himself another plate. "How's it going in there?"

"Good," I say. I grab a bottle of water out of the fridge and take a seat at the table. "You were right, though. There's a lot. It's gonna take me a couple of days."

He leans against the counter as he waits for his pizza to finish. "Do you work better at night?"

"Yeah. I stay up pretty late and then sleep in most mornings. I hope that's not an issue."

"Not at all. I'm actually a night owl, too. Verity's nurse leaves in the evenings and comes back at seven in the morning, so I stay up until midnight and give Verity her nighttime medications. Nurse takes over when she gets here." He grabs his plate from the microwave and sits across from me at the table.

I can't even make eye contact with him. All I can think of when I look at him is the part of Verity's manuscript I read where she mentioned his hand was between her legs at the Steak 'n Shake. *God, I shouldn't have read that.* Now I'll be blushing every time I look in his direction. He has really nice hands, too, which doesn't help the situation.

I need to change the direction of my thoughts.

Like *now*.

"Did she ever talk with you about the series she was writing? Like what she had planned for the characters? The ending?"

"If she did, I can't remember," he says, looking down at his plate. He absentmindedly moves around a slice of pizza. "Before her car wreck, it had been a while since she'd written anything. Or even *talked* about writing."

"How long ago was her wreck?" *I already know the answer, but I don't want him to know I Googled his family's history.*

"Not long after Harper died. She was in a medically induced coma for a while, then went into an intense rehabilitation center for several weeks. She's only been home for a few weeks now." He takes another bite. I feel bad for talking about it, but he doesn't seem put off by the conversation.

"Before my mother died, I was her only caregiver. I don't have any siblings, so I know it isn't easy."

"It *isn't* easy," he says in agreement. "I'm sorry about your mother, by the way. I'm not sure I said that when you told me about it in the coffee shop bathroom."

I smile at him, but say nothing else about it. I don't want him to ask about her. I want the focus to remain on him and Verity.

My mind keeps going back to the manuscript, because even though I know very little about the man sitting across from me, I almost feel as though I know him. At the very least, I know him the way Verity described him.

I'm curious to know what kind of marriage they had, and why she ended the first chapter with the sentence she chose. *"Until he discovered the one thing that meant more to him than I did."*

The sentence is ominous. It's almost as if she were setting up the next chapter to reveal some terrible, dark secret about this man. Or maybe it was a writing strategy, and she's going to say he's a saint and that their children mean more to him than she did.

Whatever it means, I'm dying to read the next chapter now that I'm staring at him. And I hate that I have so many other things that should be my focus right now, but all I want to do is curl up and read about Jeremy and Verity's marriage. It makes me feel a little pathetic.

It's probably not even about them. I know a writer who admitted she uses her husband's name in every manuscript until she can come up with a name for her character. Maybe that's what Verity does. Maybe it was just another work of fiction, and Jeremy's name was only there as a placeholder.

I guess there's only one way to find out if what I read was true.

"How did you and Verity meet?"

Jeremy pops a pepperoni in his mouth and grins. "At a party," he says, leaning back in his chair. Finally, he doesn't look sad for once. "She was wearing the most amazing dress I'd ever seen. It was red, and so long that it dragged on the floor a little bit. *God*, she was beautiful," he says with a hint of wistfulness. "We left the party together. When I walked outside, I saw a limousine parked out front, so I opened the door and we climbed inside and talked a little. Until the driver showed up and I had to admit the limousine wasn't mine."

I'm not supposed to know any of this, so I force a laugh. "It wasn't yours?"

"No. I just wanted to impress her. We had to make an escape after that because the driver was pretty pissed." He's still smiling, like he's right back in that night with Verity and her fuckable red dress. "We were inseparable after that."

It's hard for me to smile for him. For *them*. Seeing how happy they seemed back then, and then looking at what their life turned into. I wonder if her autobiography explains in detail how they got from point A to point B. At the beginning of it, she mentions Chastin's death. Which means she wrote it, or at least *added* to it, after that first huge tragedy. I wonder how long she's been working on it?

"Was Verity already an author when you met her?"

"No, she was still in grad school. It was later, when I had to take a temporary position in Los Angeles for a few months, that she wrote her first book. I think it was her way of passing the time until I came back home. She was passed up by a couple of publishers at first, but once she sold that first manuscript, everything just... It all happened so fast. Our lives changed practically overnight."

"How did she handle the fame?"

"I think it was harder for me than it was for her."

"Because you like being invisible?"

"Is it that obvious?"

I shrug. "Fellow introvert, here."

He laughs. "Verity isn't your typical author. She loves the spotlight. The fancy events. It all makes me uncomfortable. I like being here with the kids." There's a very subtle shift in his expression when he realizes he spoke of his girls in the present tense. "With *Crew*," he says, correcting himself. He shakes his head and then clasps his hands behind his neck, leaning back like he's stretching. Or uncomfortable. "It's hard sometimes—remembering they aren't here anymore." His voice is quiet, and he's staring past me, at nothing. "I still find their hairs on the sofa. Their socks in the dryer. Sometimes I yell out their names when I want to show them something, forgetting they aren't going to come running down the stairs."

I watch him closely, because not all of me is convinced yet. I write suspense novels. I know when there are suspicious situations, suspicious people almost always accompany those situations. I'm torn between wanting to find out more about what happened to his girls, and getting out of here as fast as I can.

But right now, I'm not looking at a man who is putting on a show to garner sympathy. I'm looking at a man who's sharing his thoughts out loud for the first time.

It makes me want to do the same.

"My mother hasn't been gone that long, but I know what you mean. Every morning that first week, I'd get up and make her breakfast, only to remember she wasn't there to eat it."

Jeremy drops his arms to the table. "I wonder how long it lasts. Or if it'll always be this way."

"I think time will definitely help, but it probably wouldn't hurt to entertain the idea of moving. If you're in a house they've never been in, the reminders of them might fade. Not having them around would become your new normal."

He runs a hand across the stubble on his jaw. "I'm not sure I want a normal where there aren't traces of Harper and Chastin."

"Yeah," I say in agreement. "I wouldn't either."

His eyes remain on me, but it's quiet. Sometimes a look between two people can last so long, it shakes you. Forces you to look away.

So I do.

I look at my plate and run my finger along the scalloped edge of it. His stare felt like it was going far past my eyes, into my thoughts. And even though he doesn't mean for it to, it feels intimate. When Jeremy's eyes are on mine, it feels like an exploration of the deepest parts of me.

"I should get back to work," I say, my voice barely above a whisper.

He's unmoving for a few seconds, but then sits up straight, quickly scooting back his chair as if he just broke out of a trance. "Yeah," he says, reaching for our plates as he stands. "I should get Verity's meds ready." He walks our plates to the sink, and as I'm exiting the kitchen, he says, "Goodnight, Low."

When I hear him call me that, my *goodnight* gets stuck in my throat. I release a flicker of a smile and then walk out of the kitchen, in a hurry to get back to Verity's office.

The more time I spend in Jeremy's presence, the more eager I am to dive back into that manuscript and get to know him even better.

I grab it from the couch, turn off the lights in Verity's office, and take the manuscript to the bedroom with me. There isn't a lock on the door, so I push a wooden chest from the foot of the bed all the way to the door, blocking it off.

I'm exhausted after traveling the entire day, and I still need to shower, but I can fit in at least one more chapter before I sleep.

I *have* to.

Chapter Two

I could write entire novels about the first two years we dated, but they wouldn't sell. There wasn't enough drama between Jeremy and me. Hardly any fighting at all. No tragedies to write about. Just two years of saccharine love and adoration between the two of us.

I. Was. *Taken*. By. Him.

Addicted to him.

I'm not sure it was healthy—how codependent I was. *Still* am, really. But when a person finds someone who makes all the negativity in their lives disappear, it's hard not to feed off that person. I fed off Jeremy in order to keep my soul alive. It was starving and shriveled before I met him, but being in his presence nourished me. Sometimes I felt if I didn't have him, I couldn't function.

We had been dating almost two years when he was temporarily transferred to Los Angeles. We had recently moved in together, unofficially. I say unofficially because there was a point when I just stopped going back to my place. Stopped paying the bills, the rent. It wasn't until two months after I'd completely moved out that Jeremy found out I didn't have my own apartment anymore.

He had suggested I move in with him one night, during sex. He does that sometimes. Makes huge decisions about our lives together while he's fucking me.

"Move in with me," he said, thrusting slowly into me. He lowered his mouth to mine. "Break your lease."

"I can't," I whispered.

He stopped moving and pulled back to look down on me. "Why not?"

I lowered my hands to his ass and made him start moving again. "Because I broke my lease two months ago."

He stilled inside me, staring down at me with those intense green eyes and lashes so black, I expected to taste licorice when I kissed them. "We already *live* together?" he asked.

I nodded, but realized he wasn't reacting the way I'd hoped he'd react. He seemed blindsided.

I needed to fix things—to take over and sidetrack him. Make him realize it wasn't that big of a deal. "I thought I told you."

He pulled out of me, and it felt like a punishment. "You did *not* tell me we're living together. That's something I would have remembered."

I sat up and positioned myself so that I was on my knees right in front of him, face to face with him. I ran my fingernails across both sides of his jaw and brought my mouth close to his. "Jeremy," I whispered. "I haven't spent a night away from you in six months. We've lived together for a while now." I grabbed his shoulders and then pushed him onto his back. His head met the pillow, and I wanted to lie on top of him and kiss him, but he seemed a little angry with me. Like he wanted to talk about this subject I considered closed.

I didn't *want* to talk anymore. I just wanted him to make me come.

So, I straddled his face and lowered myself onto his tongue. When I felt his hands grip my ass, pulling me closer to his mouth, my head rolled back for a delicious moment. *This is why I moved in with you, Jeremy.*

I leaned forward, gripped his headboard, and then bit down on it, stifling my screams.

And that was that.

I was happier than I'd ever been until he was transferred. Sure, it was only temporary, but you can't take away someone's only means of survival and expect them to function on their own.

That's how I felt, anyway—like the only nourishment for my soul had been ripped from me. Sure, I got small bouts of replenishment when he'd call me or video chat with me, but those nights alone in our bed were grueling.

Sometimes, I would straddle my pillow and bite down on the headboard while I touched myself, pretending he was beneath me. But then, after I came, I'd fall back onto an empty bed and stare up at the ceiling, wondering how I'd survived all the years of my life that he hadn't been a part of.

Those were thoughts I couldn't admit to him, of course. I might have been obsessed with him, but a woman knows if she wants to keep a man forever, she has to act like she could get over him in a day.

And that is when I became a writer.

My days were filled with thoughts of Jeremy, and if I didn't figure out how to fill them with thoughts of something else until he returned, I was afraid I wouldn't be able to hide how much his absence gutted me. I created a fictional Jeremy and called him Lane. When I was missing Jeremy, I'd write a chapter about Lane. My life over those next few months became less about Jeremy and more about my character. Who was, in a sense, still Jeremy. But writing about it instead of obsessing about it felt more productive.

I wrote an entire novel in the few months he was gone. When he showed up at our front door to surprise me with his return home, I had just finished editing the final page.

It was kismet.

I congratulated him with a blowjob. It was the first time I swallowed. That's how happy I was to see him.

I acted like a lady after I swallowed, smiling up at him. He was still standing by the front door, fully clothed, other than the jeans that were now down to his knees. I stood up and kissed him on the cheek and said, "Be right back."

When I got to the bathroom, I locked the door, turned on the water in the sink, and then puked in the toilet. When I let him come in my mouth, I had no idea how much there would be. How long I would have to continue swallowing. Keeping my composure was tough while his dick was in my throat, drowning me.

I brushed my teeth and then returned to the bedroom, where I found him sitting at my desk. He had a couple of pages of my manuscript in his hands.

"Did you write this?" he asked, spinning in my desk chair to face me.

"Yes, but I don't want you to read it." I could feel my palms beginning to sweat, so I wiped them across my stomach and walked toward him. He stood up as I launched myself forward to snatch the pages from him. He held them over his head, too high for me to reach.

"Why can't I read it?"

I jumped, trying to pull his arm down so I could reach the pages. "It needs work."

"That's fine," he said, backing up a step. "But I still want to read it."

"I don't want you to read it."

He gathered the rest of the manuscript and tucked it to his chest. He was going to read it, and all I could think about was stopping him. I didn't know if it was any good, and I was scared—*terrified*—that it would make him love me less if he thought I was a bad writer. I dove across the bed to try and reach him faster, but he slipped into my bathroom and locked the door.

I beat on it.

"Jeremy!" I yelled.

No answer.

He ignored me for ten minutes as I tried to pry open the door with a credit card. A bobby pin. Promises of another blowjob.

Fifteen more minutes went by before he made a noise.

"Verity?"

I was on the floor at this point, my back pressed against the bathroom door. "What?"

"It's good."

I didn't respond.

"Really good. I am so proud of you."

I smiled.

It was my first taste of what it felt like for a reader to enjoy what I had created for them. That one comment—that sweet, simple comment—made me want him to finish reading it. I left him alone after that. I went to our bed, crawled under the covers, and fell asleep with a smile on my face.

He woke me up two hours later. His lips were skimming my shoulder, his fingers tracing an invisible line down my waist, over my hip. He was behind me, curved around me, molded to me. I had missed him so much.

"Are you awake?" he whispered.

I made a soft moaning sound to let him know I was.

He kissed a spot below my ear, and then he said, "You're fucking brilliant." I don't think I've ever smiled so big. He rolled me onto my back and swept my hair out of my face. "I hope you're ready."

"For what?" I asked.

"Fame."

I laughed, but he didn't. He pulled off his pants and removed my panties. After he pushed into me, he said, "Do you think I'm kidding?" He kissed me, then continued. "Your writing is going to make you famous. Your mind is incredible. If I could fuck it, I would."

My laughter was mixed with a moan as he continued to make love to me. "Are you saying that because you believe it? Or because you love me?"

He didn't answer right away. His moves became slow and deliberate. His stare was intense. "Marry me, Verity."

I didn't react, because I thought maybe I had misheard him. *Did he really just ask me to marry him?* I could tell by the intensity in his expression that he was more in love with me in that moment than he'd ever been before. I should have said yes immediately, because that's where my heart was. But instead, I said, "Why?"

"Because," he said, grinning. "I'm your biggest fan."

I laughed, but then his smile disappeared and he started to fuck me. Hard, fast thrusts that he knew would drive me crazy. The headboard was slapping against the wall, and the pillow beneath my head was slipping. "Marry me," he pleaded again, and then his tongue was in my mouth, and it was the first real kiss we'd shared in months.

We needed each other so badly in that moment, our bodies were making it difficult for our mouths to stay aligned, so the kiss was sloppy and painful and "Okay," I whispered.

"Thank you," he said in the middle of a sigh, his words full of more breath than voice. He continued to fuck me, *his fiancée*, until we were covered in sweat, and I could taste blood in my mouth where he had accidentally bitten my lip. Or maybe I'd bitten his. I wasn't sure, but it didn't matter because his blood was my blood now.

When he finally came, he did it inside me, without a condom, while his tongue was in my mouth and his breath was sliding down my throat and my eternity was entwined with his.

When he was finished, he reached to the floor for his jeans. He crawled back on top of me and lifted my hand, then slipped a ring on my finger.

He'd planned to ask me all along.

I didn't even look at the ring. I brought my hands up over my head and closed my eyes, because his hand was between my legs and I knew he wanted to watch me come.

So I did.

For two months, we looked back on that night as the night we got engaged. For two months, I would grin every time I looked at my ring. For two months, I would tear up when I thought about what our wedding would be like. What our wedding *night* would be like.

But then the *night we got engaged* became *the night we conceived.*

And here is where it gets real. The guts of my autobiography. This is the point when other authors would paint themselves in a better light, rather than throw themselves into an X-ray machine.

But there is no light where we're going. This is your final warning.

Darkness ahead.

6

The upside to Verity's office is the view from these windows. The glass starts at the floor and rises all the way up to the ceiling. And there aren't any obstructions. Just huge panes of solid glass, so I can see everything. *Who cleans these?* I study the panes of glass for a spot, a smudge—anything.

The downside to Verity's office is *also* the view from these windows. The nurse has parked Verity's wheelchair on the back porch, right in front of the office. I can see her entire profile as she faces west of the back porch. It's a nice day out, so the nurse is sitting in front of Verity, reading her a book. Verity is staring off into space, and I wonder, does she comprehend anything? And if so, how much?

Her fine hair lifts in the breeze, like the fingers of a ghost are playing with the strands.

When I look at her, my empathy magnifies. Which is why I don't want to look at her, but these windows make it impossible. I can't hear the nurse reading to her, presumably because these windows are as soundproof as the rest of this office. But I know they're there, so it's hard to concentrate on work without glancing up every few minutes.

I've had issues finding any notes so far for the series, but I've only been able to wade through a portion of the stuff in here. I decided my time would be better spent this morning skimming the first and second books, making notes about every character. I'm creating a filing system for myself because I need to know these characters as well as Verity knows them. I need to know what motivates them, what moves them, what sets them off.

I see movement outside the window. When I look up, the nurse is walking away, toward the back door. I stare at Verity for a moment, wondering if she'll react now that the nurse has stopped reading to her. There's no movement at all. Her hands are in her lap, and her head is tilted to the side, as if her brain can't even send a signal to let her know she needs to straighten up her posture before it causes her neck to ache.

The clever and talented Verity is no longer in there. Was her body the only thing that survived that wreck? It's as if she were an egg, cracked open and poured out, and all that's left are the tiny fragments of hard shell.

I glance back down at the desk and try to focus. I can't help but wonder how Jeremy is handling all this. He's a concrete pillar on the outside, but the inside *has* to be hollow. It's disappointing, knowing this is his life now. Caring for an egg shell with no yolk.

That was harsh.

I'm not trying to be harsh. I'm just... I don't know. I feel like it would have been better for everyone if she hadn't survived the wreck. I immediately feel guilty for thinking that, but it reminds me of the last few months I spent caring for my mother. I know my mother would have preferred death over being as severely incapacitated as the cancer made her. But that was just a few months of her life...of my life. This is Jeremy's *whole* life now. Caring for a wife who is no longer his wife. Tied to a home that's no longer a home. And I can't imagine this is how Verity would want him to live. I can't imagine this is how *she* would want to live. She can't even play with or speak to her own child.

I pray she isn't in there, for her own sake. I can't imagine how difficult it would be if her mind were still there, but the brain damage had left her with no physical way to express herself, robbing her of any ability to react or interact or verbalize what she's thinking.

I lift my head again.

She's staring straight at me.

I jump up, and the desk chair moves backward across the wood floor. Verity is looking right at me through the window, her head turned toward me, her eyes locked on mine. I bring my hand up to my mouth and step back; I feel threatened.

I want out of her line of sight, so I creep to my left, toward the office door. For a moment, I can't escape her gaze. She's the Mona Lisa, following me as I move across the room. But when I reach her office door, we're no longer making eye contact.

Her eyes didn't follow me.

I drop my hand and lean against the wall, watching as April walks back outside with a towel. She wipes Verity's chin and then takes a small pillow from Verity's lap and lifts her head, placing it between her shoulder and her cheek. With her head adjusted, she's no longer staring into the window.

"Shit," I whisper to no one.

I'm scared of a woman who can barely move and can't even speak. A woman who can't willingly turn her head to look at someone, much less make intentional eye contact.

I need water.

I open the office door, but let out a yelp when my cell phone rings behind me on the desk.

Dammit. I hate adrenaline. My pulse is racing, but I blow out a breath and try to calm down as I answer the phone. It's an unknown number.

"Hello?"

"Ms. Ashleigh?"

"This is she."

"This is Donovan Baker from Creekwood apartments. You put in an application a few days ago?"

I'm relieved to have a distraction. I walk back over to the window, and the nurse has moved Verity's chair so that I'm only looking at the back of her head now. "Yes, how can I help you?"

"I'm calling because the application you submitted was processed today. Unfortunately, there was a recent eviction that showed up in your name, so we can't approve you for the apartment."

Already? I just moved out a couple of days ago. "But my application was already approved with you guys. I'm supposed to move in next week."

"Actually, you were only *pre*-approved. Your application wasn't fully processed until today. We can't approve applications with recent evictions. I hope you understand."

I squeeze the back of my neck. I won't get my money for another two weeks. "Please," I say to him, trying not to sound as pathetic as I feel right now. "I've never been late on my rent until now. I was just hired for another job, and in two weeks, if you let me move in now, I can pay you an entire *year's* rent. I swear."

"You can always appeal the decision," he says. "It might take a few weeks, but I've seen applications get approved due to extenuating circumstances."

"I don't have a few weeks. I already moved out of my last apartment."

"I'm sorry," he says. "I'll email you our decision, and at the bottom of the email, contact that number for an appeal. Have a good day, Ms. Ashleigh."

He ends the call, but I still have the phone pressed to my ear as I squeeze my neck. I'm hoping I'll wake up from this nightmare any second now. *Thank you, Mother.* What the hell am I going to do now?

There's a soft knock on the office door. I spin around, startled again. *I can't deal with today.* Jeremy is standing in the office entryway, looking at me with a face full of empathy.

I left the door open when my phone rang. He probably heard that entire conversation. I can tack mortified onto the list of adjectives that describe today.

I set my phone on Verity's desk, then fall into her desk chair. "My life wasn't always this much of a hot mess."

He laughs a little, stepping into the room. "Neither was mine."

I appreciate that comment. I look down at my phone. "It's fine," I say, spinning my phone around in a circle. "I'll figure it out."

"I can loan you money until your advance is processed through your agent. I'll have to pull it from our mutual fund, but it can be here in three days."

I have never been this embarrassed, and I know he can see it because I practically curl into myself as I lean forward on the desk and drop my face into my hands.

"That's really sweet, but I'm not taking a loan from you."

He's quiet for a moment, then chooses to take a seat on the couch. He sits casually, leaning forward, clasping his hands in front of him. "Then stay here until your advance hits your account. It'll only be a week or two." He looks around the office, seeing how much progress I *haven't* made since I arrived yesterday. "We don't mind. You aren't in the way at all."

I shake my head, but he interrupts.

"Lowen. This job you've taken on is not easy. I'd rather you spend too much time in here prepping for it than get back to New York tomorrow and realize you should have stayed longer."

I do need more time. But two weeks in *this* house? With a woman who scares me, a manuscript I shouldn't be reading, and a man I know way too many intimate details about?

It's not a good idea. None of it is good.

I start to shake my head again, but he holds up a hand. "Stop being considerate. Stop being embarrassed. Just say *alright*."

I look past him, at all the boxes lining the walls behind him. The things I haven't even touched yet. And then I think about how, with two weeks in here, I would have time to read every book in her backlist, make notes on each of them, and possibly outline the three new ones.

I sigh, conceding with a little bit of relief. "Alright."

He smiles a little, then stands up and walks toward the door.

"Thank you," I say.

Jeremy turns back around and faces me. I wish I had let him walk out the door, because I swear I can see a trace of regret in his expression. He opens his mouth, like he wants to say, "You're welcome," or "No problem." But he just closes his mouth and forces a smile, and then shuts the door behind him when he leaves.

•••

Jeremy told me earlier this afternoon that I needed to be outside before the sun disappeared behind the mountains. *"You'll see why Verity wanted an unobstructed view from her office."*

I brought one of her books with me to read on the back porch. There are about ten chairs to choose from, so I take a seat at a patio table. Jeremy and Crew are down by the water, tearing old pieces of wood out of their fishing dock. It's cute, watching Crew grab the pieces of wood Jeremy's handing to him. He carries them to a huge pile, then grabs another from his dad. Jeremy has to wait for him each time, because it takes Crew longer to dispose of the wood than it does for Jeremy to rip it out of the wooden frame. It proves how much patience he has as a father.

He reminds me a little of my father. He died when I was nine, but I'm not sure I ever saw him angry. Not even at my mother, with her prickly comments and frequent hot temper. I grew to resent that about him, though. Sometimes I perceived his patience as weakness when it came to her.

I watch Crew and Jeremy a little longer, in between attempts at finishing my chapter. But I'm finding it hard to comprehend anything because Jeremy took his shirt off a few minutes ago and, while I've seen him take his shirt off before, I've never seen him without an undershirt. His skin is slick from the sweat he's worked up over the past two hours of being down at the dock. When he yanks at the wood with the hammer, his muscles stretch across his back, and I immediately recall the last chapter Verity wrote. There were so many intimate details about their sex life, and from what I read, it was very active. More so than any of my relationships have been.

It's hard looking at him and *not* thinking about sex now. Not that I want to have sex with him. *And not that I don't*. It's just that, as a writer, I know he was her inspiration for several of the men in her books. And it makes me wonder if I need to view him as my inspiration as I tackle the rest of this series. I mean...it's not the worst thing. Being forced to step into Verity's shoes and visualize Jeremy for the next twenty-four months as I write.

The back door slams shut, and I tear my eyes away from Jeremy. April is standing on the patio, staring at me. Her gaze follows the path of mine, and then she cuts her eyes back to me. She saw. She saw me eyeing my new boss. Pathetic.

How long was she watching me stare at him? I want to cover my face with this book, but instead, I smile like I was doing nothing wrong. I mean, *I wasn't*.

"I'm heading out," April says. "I put Verity in bed and turned on her television. She's had dinner and her meds, in case he asks."

I don't know why she's telling me this, since I'm not in charge. "Okay. Have a good night."

She doesn't tell me to have a good night in return. She walks back into the house and lets the door fall shut again. A minute later, I hear the hum of her engine as her car pulls out of the driveway, disappearing between the trees. I glance back at Jeremy and Crew, and Jeremy is ripping up another piece of wood.

Crew is staring at me, standing near the pile of discarded fishing dock. He smiles and waves. I lift my hand to wave back, but curl my fingers into a soft fist when I realize Crew isn't waving at me. He's looking above me, to the right.

He's looking up at Verity's bedroom window.

I spin around and look up, just as her bedroom curtain falls shut. I drop her book onto the patio table, knocking over my bottle of water in the process. I stand up and take three steps farther back to get a better look at the window, but there's no one there. My mouth falls open. I look back at Crew, but he's retreating back to the dock to grab another piece of wood from Jeremy.

I'm seeing things.

But why was he waving at her window? If she wasn't there, why was he waving?

It doesn't make sense. If she was looking out her window, Crew would have had a much bigger reaction, considering she hasn't been able to speak or walk on her own since her wreck.

Or maybe he doesn't understand that his mother walking to her window would be a miracle. He's only five.

I look down at the book, now covered in water, and pick it up and shake the liquid from it. I blow out an unsteady breath because it feels like I've been on edge all day. I'm sure I'm still a little shaken from thinking she was staring at me earlier, and that's why I assumed I saw the curtain move.

Part of me wants to forget it and lock myself in the office and work the rest of the night. But I know I won't be able to if I don't check on her. Make sure I didn't see what I thought I saw.

I lay the book open on the patio table to dry and make my way into the house, toward the stairs. I'm quiet. I'm not sure why I feel the need to be quiet as I work to sneak a peek at her. I know she probably can't process much, so what would it matter if I made my approach known? Even still, I remain quiet as I make my way up the stairs, down the hallway, and to her bedroom door.

It's slightly ajar, and I can see the window that overlooks the backyard. I press my palm to the door and begin to open it. I'm biting my bottom lip as I peek my head in.

Verity is in her bed, eyes closed, hands to her sides on top of the blanket.

I breathe a quiet sigh of relief, and then feel even more relief when I open the door a little wider, revealing an oscillating fan moving back and forth from Verity's bed to the window overlooking the backyard. Every time the fan points toward the window, the curtain moves.

My sigh is louder this time. *It was the damn fan. Get a grip, Lowen.*

I turn off the fan because it's a little too chilly in here for it. I'm surprised April left it on to begin with. I cut my eyes toward Verity again, but she's still asleep. When I get to the door, I pause. I look at the dresser—at the remote sitting on top of it. I look up at the TV mounted to the wall.

It isn't on.

April said she turned on the TV before she left, but the TV is not on.

I don't even look back at Verity. I pull the door shut and rush down the stairs.

I'm not going back up there again. I'm scaring myself. The most helpless person in this house is the one I'm the most afraid of. It doesn't even make sense. She *wasn't* staring at me through the office window. She *wasn't* standing at her window, looking at Crew. And she *didn't* turn off her own TV. It's probably on a timer, or April accidentally hit the power button twice and assumed she turned it on.

Regardless of the fact that I'm aware this is all in my head, I still walk back to Verity's office, close the door, and pick up another chapter of her autobiography. Maybe reading more from her point of view will reassure me that she's harmless and *I need to chill the fuck out.*

Chapter Three

I knew I was pregnant because my breasts looked better than they had ever looked.

I'm very aware of my body, what goes into it, how to nourish it, how to keep it toned. Growing up watching my mother's waistline expand with her laziness, I work out daily, sometimes twice a day.

I learned very early on that a human is not merely comprised of only one thing. We are two parts that make up the whole.

We have our conscience, which includes our mind, our soul, and all the intangible parts.

And we have our physical being, which is the machine that our conscience relies on for survival.

If you fuck with the machine, you will die. If you neglect the machine, you will die. If you assume your conscience can outlive the machine, you will die shortly after learning you were wrong.

It's very simple, really. Take care of your physical being. Feed it what it *needs*, not what the conscience tells you it wants. Giving in to cravings of the mind that ultimately hurt the body is like a weak parent giving in to her child. *"Oh, you had a bad day? Do you want an entire box of cookies? Okay, sweetie. Eat it. And drink this soda while you're at it."*

Caring for your body is no different from caring for a child. Sometimes it's hard, sometimes it sucks, sometimes you just want to give in, but if you do, you'll pay for the consequences eighteen years down the road.

It's fitting when it comes to my mother. She cared for me like she cared for her body. *Very little.* Sometimes I wonder if she's still fat—if she's still neglecting that machine. I wouldn't know. I haven't spoken to her in years.

But I'm not interested in speaking about a woman who chose never to speak of me again. I'm here to discuss the first thing my baby ever stole from me.

Jeremy.

I didn't notice the theft at first.

At first, after we found out that *the night we got engaged* became *the night we conceived*, I was actually happy. I was happy because Jeremy was happy. And at that point, other than my breasts looking better than ever, I didn't realize how detrimental the pregnancy was going to be to the machine I had worked so hard to maintain.

It was around the third month, a few weeks after I found out I was pregnant, that I started to notice the difference. It was a small little pooch, but it was there. I had just gotten out of the shower, and I was standing in front of the mirror, looking at my profile. My hand was flat on my stomach and I felt something foreign, and my stomach was slightly protruding.

I was disgusted. I vowed to start working out three times a day. I'd seen what pregnancy could do to women, but I also knew most of the damage was done in that last trimester. If I could somehow figure out how to deliver early...maybe around thirty-three or thirty-four weeks, I could avoid the most detrimental part of pregnancy. There have been so many advances in medical care, babies born that early are almost always fine.

"Wow."

I dropped my hand and looked at the doorway. Jeremy was leaning against the doorframe, his arms folded over his chest. He was smiling at me. "You're starting to show."

"I am not." I sucked in.

He laughed and closed the distance between us, wrapping his arms around me from behind. He placed both hands on my stomach and looked at me in the mirror. He kissed my shoulder. "You've never looked more beautiful."

It was a lie to make me feel better, but I was grateful. Even his lies meant something to me. I squeezed his hands and he spun me around to face him, then he kissed me, walking me backward until I reached the bathroom counter. He lifted me onto it, then stood between my legs.

He was fully clothed, just returning from work. I was completely naked, fresh from the shower. The only thing between us were his pants and the pooch I was still trying to suck in.

He started fucking me on the counter, but we finished in bed.

His head was on my chest, and he was tracing circles over my stomach when it rumbled loudly. I tried to clear my throat to hide the noise, but he laughed. "Someone's hungry."

I started to shake my head, but he lifted off my chest to look at me. "What's she craving?"

"Nothing. I'm not hungry."

He laughed again. "Not you. *Her*," he said, patting my stomach. "Aren't pregnant women supposed to get weird cravings and eat all the time because of the babies? You barely eat. And your stomach is growling." He sits up on the bed. "I need to feed my girls."

His *girls*.

"You don't even know if it's a girl yet."

He smiled at me. "It's a girl. I have a feeling."

I wanted to roll my eyes, because technically, it was nothing. Not a boy, not a girl. It was a blob. I wasn't that far along yet, so assuming the thing growing inside me was actually hungry or craving any particular type of food was absurd. But it was hard for me to state my case because Jeremy was so ecstatic about the baby, I didn't really care if he treated it like it was more than it was.

Sometimes his excitement excited *me*.

For the next few weeks, his excitement helped me cope. The more my stomach grew, the more attentive he became. The more he would kiss it when we were in bed together at night.

In the mornings, he would hold my hair while I puked. When he was at work, he would text me potential baby names. He became as obsessed with my pregnancy as I was with him. He went to my first doctor's visit with me.

I'm thankful he was at the second doctor's visit, too, because that was the day my world shifted.

Twins.

Two of them.

I was quiet when we left the doctor's office that day. I had already feared becoming the mother of one baby. Being forced to love the one thing Jeremy loved more than me. But when I found out there were two, and that they *were* girls, I was suddenly not okay with being the third most important thing in Jeremy's life.

I tried to force my smile when he'd talk about them. I would act like it filled me with joy when he rubbed my stomach, but it repulsed me, knowing he was only doing it because they were in there. Even if I delivered early, it didn't matter. Now that there were two of them, my body would suffer even more damage. I shuddered daily at the thought of them both growing inside me, stretching my skin, ruining my breasts, my stomach, and god forbid the temple between my legs where Jeremy worshipped nightly.

How could Jeremy still want me after this?

During the fourth month of my pregnancy, I started hoping for a miscarriage. I prayed for blood when I went to the bathroom. I imagined how, after losing the twins, Jeremy would make me his priority again. He would dote on me, worship me, care for me, worry for me, and not because of what was growing inside me.

I took sleeping pills when he wasn't looking. I drank wine when he wasn't around. I did anything I could to destroy the things that were going to push him away from me, but nothing worked. They kept growing. My stomach continued to stretch.

In my fifth month, we were lying on our sides in the bed. Jeremy was fucking me from behind. His left hand gripped my breast, and his right hand was against my stomach. I didn't like it when he touched my stomach during sex. It made me think of the babies and ruined my mood.

I thought maybe he had reached orgasm when he stopped moving, but I realized he'd stopped moving because he'd felt *them* move. He pulled out of me and then rolled me onto my back, pressing his palm against my stomach.

"Did you feel that?" he asked. His eyes were dancing with excitement. He wasn't hard anymore. He was excited for reasons that had nothing to do with me. He pressed his ear to my stomach and waited for one of them to move again.

"Jeremy?" I whispered.

He kissed my stomach and looked up at me.

I reached down and teased at strands of his hair with my fingers. "Do you love them?"

He smiled because he thought I wanted him to say yes. "I love them more than anything."

"More than me?"

He stopped smiling. He kept his hand on my stomach, but he scooted up, sliding an arm under my neck. "Different from you," he said, kissing my cheek.

"Different, yes. But more? Is your love for them more intense than your love for me?"

His eyes scanned mine, and I was hoping he would laugh and say, "Absolutely not." But he didn't laugh. He looked at me with nothing but honesty and said, "Yes."

Really? His reply crushed me. Suffocated me. Killed me.

"But that's how it should be," he said. "Why? Do you feel guilty because you love them more than me?"

I didn't answer. Did he really think I loved them more than I loved *him?* I don't even *know* them.

"Don't feel guilty," he said. "I *want* you to love them more than you love me. Our love for each other is conditional. Our love for them isn't."

"My love for you is unconditional," I said.

He smiled. "No, it isn't. I could do things you would never forgive me for. But you'll always forgive your children."

He was wrong. I didn't forgive them for existing. I didn't forgive them for forcing him to put me third. I didn't forgive them for taking *the night we got engaged* from us.

They weren't even born yet, but they were already taking things that had once belonged to me.

"Verity," Jeremy whispered. He wiped a tear that had fallen from my eye. "Are you okay?"

I shook my head. "I just can't believe how much you already love them and they aren't even born yet."

"I know," he said, smiling.

I didn't mean it as a compliment, but he took it that way. He laid his head back on my chest and touched my stomach again. "I'll be a fucking mess when they're born."

He's going to cry?

He had *never* cried for me. Over me. About me.

Maybe we haven't fought enough.

"I have to go to the bathroom," I whispered. I didn't have to go, I just needed to get away from him and all the love he was aiming in every direction but mine.

He kissed me, and when I climbed off the bed, he rolled over, his back to me, and forgot we'd never even finished fucking.

He fell asleep while I was in the bathroom, attempting to abort his daughters with a wire hanger. I tried for half an hour, until my stomach started to cramp and blood was running down my leg. I was certain more would follow.

I climbed into bed, waiting for the miscarriage. My arms were shaking. My legs were numb from the squatting. My stomach hurt and I wanted to puke, but I didn't move because I wanted to be in the bed with him when it happened. I wanted to wake him up, frantic, and show him the blood. I wanted him to panic, to worry, to feel bad for me, to cry for me.

To cry for *me*.

7

I drop the last page of the chapter.

It flutters to the polished wood floor and disappears under the desk, like its trying to get away from me. I immediately drop to my knees, searching for it, arranging it back into the pile of pages I'm determined to hide. I'm... I don't even...

I'm still on my knees in the middle of Verity's office when the tears come. They don't spill; I hold them off with deep breaths, focusing on the grinding pain in my knees to distract my thoughts. I don't even know if it's sadness or anger. I only know this was written by a very disturbed woman—a woman whose house I currently inhabit. Slowly, I lift my head until my eyes are fixed to the ceiling. She's there right now, on the second floor, sleeping, or eating, or staring blankly into space. I can feel her lurking, disapproving of my presence.

Suddenly, I know, without a doubt, that it's true.

A mother wouldn't write that about herself—about her daughters—if it weren't the truth. A mother who never had those feelings or thoughts would never even dream of them. I don't care how good of a writer Verity is; she would never compromise herself as a mother by writing something so horrid if she didn't actually experience that.

My mind begins to spin with worry, sadness, fear. If she did that—if she actually tried to take their lives over a streak of maternal jealousy—what else was she capable of?

What actually happened to those girls?

After a while of processing it, I put the manuscript in a drawer, beneath a slew of other things. I don't ever want Jeremy to come across that. And before I leave here, I will destroy it. I can't imagine how he would feel if he read that. He's already grieving the deaths of his daughters. Imagine if he knew what they endured at the hands of their own mother.

I pray she was a better mother after they were born, but I'm honestly too shaken to continue reading. I'm not sure if I want to read more at *all*.

I want a drink. Not water or soda or fruit juice. I walk to the kitchen and open the refrigerator, but there's no wine. I open the cabinets above the refrigerator, but there's no liquor. I open the cabinet below the sink and it's bare. I open the refrigerator again, but all I see are small boxes of fruit juice for Crew and bottles of water that aren't going to help me shake this feeling.

"Are you okay?"

I spin around, and Jeremy is sitting at the dining room table with papers strewn out in front of him. He looks concerned for me.

"Do you have anything alcoholic at all in the house?" I plant my hands firmly on my hips, attempting to hide the trembling in my fingers. *He has no idea what she was truly like.*

Jeremy studies me for a moment, then heads for the pantry. On the top shelf is a bottle of Crown Royal. "Sit down," he says, concern still embedded in his expression. He watches me as I take a seat at the table and drop my head in my hands.

I hear him open a can of soda and mix it with the liquor. A few moments later, he sets it in front of me. I bring it to my lips so fast, a few drops spill onto the table. He's back in his chair now, watching me closely.

"Lowen," he says, watching as I try to swallow the Crown and Coke with a straight face. I squint because it burns. "What happened?"

Oh, let's see, Jeremy. Your brain-damaged wife made eye contact with me. She walked to her bedroom window and waved at your son. She tried to abort your babies while you were asleep in your bed.

"Your wife," I say. "Her books. I just... There was a scary part and it freaked me out."

He watches me for a moment, expressionless. Then he laughs. "Seriously? A book did this to you?"

I shrug and take another sip. "She's a great writer," I say, setting the glass on the table. "I'm easily spooked, I guess."

"Yet you write in the same genre as her."

"Even my own books do this to me sometimes," I lie.

"Maybe you should switch to romance."

"I'm sure I will once this contract is over."

He laughs again, shaking his head as he begins gathering the papers in front of him. "You missed dinner. It's still warm if you want some."

"I do. I need to eat." Maybe that will help me calm down. I carry my drink to the stove, where there's a chicken casserole covered in tinfoil. I make myself a plate and grab a water out of the refrigerator, then take a seat at the table again. "Did you make this?"

"Yep."

I take a bite. "It's really good," I say with a mouthful.

"Thanks." He's still staring at me, but now he looks more amused than concerned. I'm happy to see the amusement take over. I wish I could find this entertaining, but everything I just read makes me question Verity. Her condition. Her honesty.

"Can I ask you a question?"

Jeremy nods.

"Just tell me if I'm being too nosey. But is there a chance Verity could make a full recovery?"

He shakes his head. "The doctor doesn't believe she'll ever walk or talk again since she hasn't already made that kind of progress."

"Is she paralyzed?"

"No, there wasn't any damage to her spinal cord. But her mind...it's similar to the mind of an infant now. She has basic reflexes. She can eat, drink, blink, move a little. But none of it is intentional. I'm hoping with continued therapy, she'll be able to improve a little, but—"

Jeremy looks away from me, toward the kitchen entryway, when he hears Crew coming down the stairs.

Crew rounds the corner in his footed Spiderman pajamas and then jumps onto Jeremy's lap.

Crew. I forgot about Crew while I was reading. If Verity actually despised those girls after they were born as much as she despised them in utero, there's no way she would have agreed to have another child.

That can only mean she must have bonded with them. That's probably why she wrote what she wrote, because in the end, she fell just as in love with them as Jeremy was. Maybe writing about her thoughts during pregnancy was like a release for Verity. Like a Catholic going to confession.

That thought calms me, along with Jeremy's explanation of her injuries. She has the physical and mental capabilities of a newborn. My mind is making all of this more than it is.

Crew leans his head back against Jeremy's shoulder. He's holding his iPad, and Jeremy is scrolling through his phone. They're cute together.

I've been so focused on the negative things that have happened in this family, I need to remember to focus more on the positive that still remains. And that is definitely Jeremy's bond with his son. Crew loves him. Laughs around him. He's comfortable with his dad. And Jeremy isn't afraid to show him affection, because he just kissed the side of Crew's head.

"Did you brush your teeth?" Jeremy asks.

"Yep," Crew says.

Jeremy stands up and lifts Crew with him, effortlessly. "That means it's bedtime." He throws Crew over his shoulder. "Tell Laura goodnight."

Crew waves at me as Jeremy rounds the corner and disappears with him upstairs.

I take note of how he calls me by the pen name I'll be using in front of everyone else, but he calls me Lowen when it's just us. I also take note of how much I like it. I don't *want* to like it.

I eat the rest of my dinner and wash the dishes in the sink while Jeremy remains upstairs with Crew. When I'm finished, I feel somewhat better. I'm not sure if it was the alcohol, the food, or the realization that Verity probably wrote that horrific chapter because a much better one follows it up. One where she realizes what a blessing those girls were to her.

I walk out of the kitchen, but my eye is drawn to several family photos that hang on the hallway wall. I pause to look at them. Most of them are of the kids, but a few of them have Verity and Jeremy in them. They bear a striking resemblance to their mother, while Crew takes after Jeremy.

They were such a beautiful family. So much so that these photos are depressing to look at. I take them all in, noticing how easy it is to distinguish the girls from each other. One of them has a huge smile and a small scar on her cheek. One of them rarely smiles.

I lift my hand to touch a photo of the girl with the scar on her cheek and wonder how long she'd had it. Where it came from. I move down the line of pictures to a much older photo of the girls when they were toddlers. The smiling one even has the scar in that picture, so she got it at a young age.

Jeremy walks down the stairs as I'm looking at the photos. He pauses next to me. I point at the twin with the scar. "Which one is this?"

"Chastin," he says. He points to the other one. "This is Harper."

"They look so much like Verity."

I'm not looking at him, but I can see him nod out of the corner of my eye.

"How did Chastin get that scar?"

"She was born with it," Jeremy says. "The doctor said it was scarring from fibrous tissue. It's not uncommon, especially with twins because they're cramped for room."

I look at him this time, wondering if that's actually where Chastin's scar came from. Or if maybe—somehow—it was a result of Verity's failed abortion attempt.

"Did both the girls have the same allergy?" I ask.

As soon as I ask it, I bring a hand up and squeeze my jaw in regret. The only way I know one of them even had a peanut allergy is because of what I read about her death. And now he knows I was reading about the death of his daughter.

"I'm sorry, Jeremy."

"It's fine," he says quietly. "And no, just Chastin. Peanuts."

He doesn't elaborate, but I can feel him staring at me. I turn my head, and our eyes meet. He holds my gaze for a moment, but then his eyes drop to my hand. He lifts it with delicate fingers, flipping it over. "How'd you get this one?" he asks, running his thumb over the scar across my palm.

I make a fist, not because I'm trying to hide it. It's faded, and I rarely think about it anymore. I've trained myself not to think about it. But I cover it because of how my skin felt when he touched it, like his finger burned a hole right through my hand.

"I can't remember," I say quickly. "Thank you for dinner. I'm gonna go shower." I point past him, toward the master bedroom. He steps out of my way. When I get to the room, I open the door quickly and close it just as fast, pressing my back against the door, willing myself to relax.

It's not that he makes me uncomfortable. Jeremy Crawford is a good man. Maybe it's the manuscript that makes me uncomfortable, because I have no doubt that he would have shared his love equally with his three children and his wife. He doesn't hold back, even now. Even when his wife is virtually catatonic, he still loves her selflessly.

He's the sort of man a woman like Verity could easily become addicted to, but I don't think I'll ever understand how Verity could be so consumed and obsessed with him, to the point that creating a child with him would ignite that kind of jealousy in her.

But I do understand her attraction to him. I understand it more than I want to.

When I push off the door, something pulls my hair, and I end up back against it. What the hell? My hair is tangled in something. I pull at my hair until I break free, and then turn around to see what I got hung up in.

It's a lock.

He must have installed it today. He really is considerate. I reach up and lock the door.

Does Jeremy think I wanted a lock on the inside of this bedroom door because I don't feel safe in this house? I hope not because that's not why I wanted the lock at all. I wanted a lock so they would all be safe from *me*.

I walk to the bathroom and turn on the light. I look down at my hand, trailing my fingers across the scar.

After the first few times my mother caught me sleepwalking, she became concerned. She put me in therapy, hoping it would help more than the sleeping pills did. My therapist said it was important to unfamiliarize myself with my surroundings. He said it would help if I created obstacles that would be hard for me to move past while I was sleepwalking. A lock on the inside of my bedroom door was one of those obstacles.

And, while I'm almost certain I locked it before I fell asleep all those years ago, it doesn't explain why I woke up the next morning with a broken wrist and covered in blood.

8

I choose not to read more of Verity's manuscript. It's been two days since I read about the attempted abortion, and the manuscript is still at the bottom of her desk drawer, hidden and untouched by me. I can feel it, though. It exists with me in Verity's office, breathing shallowly beneath the junk I covered it with. The more I read, the more unsettled I become. The more unfocused I become. I'm not saying I'll never finish it, but until I make progress on what I'm here to do, I can't get sidetracked by it again.

I've noticed, now that I've stopped reading it, being in Verity's presence doesn't creep me out as much as it did a few days ago. I actually came up for air after working all day yesterday in the office to find Verity and her nurse seated at the dinner table with Crew and Jeremy. In the first couple of days I was here, I was in the office while they had dinner, so I wasn't aware that they brought her to the table when they ate together. I didn't want to intrude, so I went back to my office.

There's a different nurse today. Her name is Myrna. She's a little older than April, round and cheerful with two rosy spots on her cheeks that make her look like an old-fashioned Kewpie doll. Right off the bat, she's a lot more pleasant than April. And honestly, it's not that April is *un*pleasant. But I get the vibe she doesn't trust me around Jeremy. Or Jeremy around me. I'm not sure why she dislikes my presence, but I can see how being protective of her patient would mean judging another woman who is staying in her invalid patient's home. I'm sure she thinks Jeremy and I lock ourselves in the master bedroom together after she leaves every evening. *I wish she were right.*

Myrna works on Fridays and Saturdays, while April takes the rest of the week. Today is Friday and, while I expected to be moving into my apartment today, I'm relieved it's all worked out the way it has. I would have left here unprepared. The extra time I've been given has been a lifesaver. I've knocked out reading two more books in the series in the past two days, and I actually enjoyed them a lot. It was fascinating, seeing how Verity always writes from the antagonist's point of view. And I have a good sense of the direction I need to take with the series. But just in case, I still search for notes now that I know what I'm actually looking for.

I'm on the floor, digging through a box when Corey texts me.

Corey: Pantem did a press release this morning, announcing you as the new co-author of Verity's series. Sent a link to your email if you want to take a look.

As soon as I open my email, there's a knock on the door of the office.

"Come in."

Jeremy opens the door, peeking his head in. "Hey. I'm headed to Target to get a few groceries. If you make me a list, I can grab whatever you need."

There are a few things I need. Tampons being one of them, even though I only have a day or two left of my period. I just wasn't expecting to be here this long, so I didn't pack enough. I'm not sure I want to tell Jeremy that, though. I stand up, dusting off my jeans. "Actually, do you mind if I go with you? Might be easier."

Jeremy opens the door a little wider and says, "Not at all. Leaving in about ten minutes."

•••

Jeremy drives a dark grey Jeep Wrangler with jacked-up tires, covered in mud. I've never actually seen it because it's been in the garage, but it's not what I expected him to drive. I assumed he'd drive a Cadillac CTX or an Audi A8. Something a man in a suit would drive. I don't know why I keep picturing him as the professional, clean-cut businessman I met that first day. The man wears jeans or sweatpants every day, is always outside working, and has a rotating stock of muddy boots he leaves by the back door. A Jeep Wrangler actually fits him better than any other vehicle I've been picturing him in.

We're out of his driveway, about half a mile down the road, when he turns down his radio.

"Did you see Pantem's press release today?" he asks.

I grab my phone from my purse. "Corey sent me the link, but I forgot to read it."

"It's only one sentence long in Publishers Weekly," Jeremy says. "Short and sweet. Just how you wanted it."

I open the email and read the link. It's not a link to Publishers Weekly, though. Corey sent me a link to the announcement made on Verity Crawford's social media page, via her publicity team.

> *Pantem Press is excited to announce that the remaining novels in The Virtue Series, made successful by Verity Crawford, will now be co-written with author Laura Chase. Verity is ecstatic to have Laura on board, and the two are looking forward to the co-creation of an unforgettable conclusion to the series.*

Verity is ecstatic? Ha! At least I know never to trust another publicity announcement. I start reading the comments below the announcement.

-Who the heck is Laura Chase?
-WHY IS VERITY HANDING OVER HER BABY TO SOMEONE ELSE?
-Nope. Nope, nope, nope.

-That's how it usually works, right? Mediocre
author gets successful, hires shittier author to do
her job?

I set down my phone, but it's not enough. I turn off the
ringer and put it in my purse, then zip it shut. "People are
brutal," I mutter under my breath.

Jeremy laughs. "Never read the comments. Verity
taught me that years ago."

I've never really had to deal with comments because
I've never really put myself out there. "Good to know."

When we arrive at the store, Jeremy hops out of the
Jeep and runs around to open my door for me. It makes
me uneasy because I'm not used to this kind of treatment,
but it would probably make Jeremy even more uneasy if he
allowed me to open the door myself. He is just the type of
guy Verity describes him to be in her autobiography.

This is the first time I've ever had a guy open a door for
me. *Dammit.* How messed up is that?

When he grabs my hand to help me out of the Jeep, I
tense up because I can't prevent my reaction to his touch. I
want more of it when I shouldn't want any of it.

Does he feel the same around me?

Sex for him has been out of the picture for quite a
while now, which leads me to wonder if he misses it.

That has to be a hard adjustment. To have a marriage
that seemed to revolve around sex in the beginning, only to
have sex ripped out of the marriage overnight.

*Why am I thinking about his sex life as we're walking
into Target?*

"Do you like to cook?" Jeremy asks.

"I don't *dis*like it. I've just always lived alone, so I don't make meals very often."

He grabs a shopping cart, and I go with him to the produce section. "What's your favorite meal?"

"Tacos."

He laughs. "Simple enough." He grabs all the vegetables he'll need to make tacos. I offer to make spaghetti for them one night. It's really the only thing I cook that I can honestly say I'm good at.

He's on the juice aisle when I tell him I'll be back, that I need a few things outside of the grocery department. I get the tampons, but grab other things to throw in the cart with them, like shampoo, socks, and a few shirts since I didn't really bring any with me.

I have no idea why I'm embarrassed to buy tampons. It's not like he's never seen them. And, knowing Jeremy, he's probably purchased them for Verity a few times. He seems like the type of husband who wouldn't think twice about it.

I find Jeremy in the grocery section, and as I walk toward him, I notice he's flanked by two women who have abandoned their carts to talk to him. His back is pressed against the ice cream cooler, giving the impression that he wishes he could melt right into it and escape. I can only see the backs of their heads as I approach, but when Jeremy's eyes meet mine, an attractive blonde turns around to see what he's looking at. The brunette seems more my speed, but only until she looks at me. Her glare changes my mind instantly.

I approach the cart as if it's a wild animal, cautiously, timidly. Do I place my items into the cart or will that make this awkward? I decide to set my things in the upper basket, a clear line in the red-cart sand: *We are together but not together*. The women both look at me, simultaneously, their eyebrows climbing higher with each item I set in the basket. The one standing closest to Jeremy, the blonde, is staring at my tampons. She looks back up at me and tilts her head.

"And you are?"

"This is Laura Chase," Jeremy answers. "Laura, this is Patricia and Caroline."

The blonde looks like she's been handed a warm cup of gossip tea. "We're friends of Verity's," Patricia says. She gives me a very noticeable condescending look. "Speaking of, Verity must be feeling better if she's got a friend in town." She looks at Jeremy for more explanation. "Or is Laura *your* friend?"

"Laura is here from New York. She's working with Verity."

Patricia smiles at the same time she makes an *mhm* sound and looks back at me. "How does one work with a writer, exactly? I assumed it would be more of a solitary job."

"That's usually what non-literary people assume," Jeremy says. He nods at them, dismissing us from the conversation. "Have a good afternoon, ladies." He begins to move the shopping cart, but Patricia places her hand on it.

"Tell Verity I said hello and we hope she's recovering well."

"I'll share the message," Jeremy says, walking past her. "Give my best to Sherman."

Patricia makes a face. "My husband's name is William."

Jeremy nods once. "Oh. That's right. I get them confused."

I hear Patricia scoff as we walk away. When we make it to the next aisle, I say, "Um. Who is Sherman?"

"The guy she fucks behind her husband's back."

I look at him, shocked. He's smiling.

"Holy shit," I say, laughing. When we get to the register, I can't stop smiling. I don't know that I've ever seen that kind of epic burn in person.

Jeremy begins placing things on the conveyor belt. "I probably shouldn't have stooped to her level, but I can't stand hypocrites."

"Yes, but without hypocrites, there would be no epic karmic moments like the one I just witnessed."

Jeremy grabs the rest of the things from the cart. I try to keep mine separate, but he refuses to let me pay for it myself.

I can't stop staring at him as he runs his credit card. I feel something. I'm not sure what. A crush? That would make complete sense. I *would* develop a crush on a man who is so devoted to his ailing wife that he's too blind to see anyone or anything else. He's too blind to even see who his own wife was.

Lowen Ashleigh, falling for an unavailable man with more baggage than even she has.

Now *that's* karma.

9

I only arrived here five days ago, but it seems like longer. The days here drag, whereas in New York, well, *New York minute.*

I heard Myrna tell Jeremy this morning that Verity had a fever, which is why she didn't bring Verity down at all today before she left for the evening. I wasn't sad about that. It meant I didn't have to be in her presence, or look at her from my office window during their outdoor breaks.

I'm looking at Jeremy, though. He's sitting alone on the back porch, staring out at the lake, leaning back in a rocking chair that he hasn't rocked in over ten minutes. He's sitting completely still. Every now and then, he remembers to blink. He's been out there for a while now.

I wish I knew what thoughts were going through his head right now. Is he thinking of the girls? Of Verity? Is he thinking about how much his life has changed in the past year? He hasn't shaved in a few days, so his stubble is getting thicker. It looks good on him, but I'm not sure much could look *bad* on him.

I lean forward on Verity's desk and drop my chin in my hand. I immediately regret moving, because Jeremy notices. He turns his head and looks at me through the window. I want to look away, force myself to appear busy, but it's obvious I've been staring at him, now that I'm leaned forward on the desk with my head propped on my hand. It would look worse if I tried to hide it at this point, so I just smile gently at him.

He doesn't return the smile, but he doesn't look away. We hold eye contact for several seconds, and I feel his stare stirring things up inside me. It makes me wonder if it does anything to him when I look at *him*.

He inhales a slow breath and then lifts up from his chair and walks away, toward the dock. When he reaches it, he picks up his hammer and begins ripping at the remaining few slabs of wood.

He was probably craving a moment of peace, without Crew or Verity or a nurse or myself invading his privacy.

I need a Xanax. I haven't taken one in over a week. It makes me groggy, which makes it difficult for me to focus on writing or research. But I'm tired of the moments in this house that send my pulse racing like it is right now. Once the adrenaline kicks in, I can't seem to reel it in. Whether it's Jeremy, Verity, or Verity's books, there's always something wreaking havoc on my anxiety levels. My reaction to this house and the people in it are more distracting than a little grogginess would be.

I walk to the bedroom to sift through my bag for the Xanax. As soon as I get the bottle open, I hear a scream come from upstairs.

Crew.

I drop my unopened bottle of pills on the bed and rush out of the room and up the stairs. I can hear him crying. It sounds like it's coming from Verity's room.

As much as I want to turn around and run in the other direction, I also realize he's a little boy who might be in trouble, so I keep walking.

When I reach the door, I push it open without knocking. Crew is on the floor, holding his chin. There's blood on his hands and fingers. A knife next to him on the floor. "Crew?" I reach down and pick him up, then rush him to the bathroom down the hall. I set him on the counter.

"Let me see." I pull his shaky fingers from his chin to assess the injury. It's seeping blood, but it doesn't look to be very deep. It's a cut right underneath his chin. He must have been holding the knife when he fell. "Did you cut yourself with the knife?"

Crew is wide-eyed, looking up at me. He shakes his head, probably trying to hide that he had a knife. I'm sure Jeremy wouldn't approve of that. "Mommy said I'm not supposed to touch her knife."

I freeze. "Your mommy says that?"

Crew doesn't respond.

"Crew," I say, grabbing a washcloth. It feels like my heart is stuck in my throat as I speak to him, but I try to hide my fear as I wet the washcloth. "Does your mommy talk to you?"

Crew's body is rigid, and the only thing that moves is his head when he shakes it. I press the washcloth to his chin right before I hear Jeremy's footsteps bounding up the stairs. He must have heard Crew scream.

"Crew!" he yells.

"We're in here."

Jeremy's eyes are full of worry when he reaches the door. I step out of his way while still holding the washcloth to Crew's chin.

"You okay, buddy?"

Crew nods, and Jeremy takes the washcloth from me. He bends down and looks at the injury on Crew's chin and then at me. "What happened?"

"I think he cut himself," I say. "He was in Verity's bedroom. There was a knife on the floor."

Jeremy looks at Crew, his eyes full of more disappointment than fear now. "What were you doing with a knife?"

Crew shakes his head, sniffling as he tries to stop crying. "I didn't have a knife. I just fell off the bed."

Part of me feels bad, like I tattled on the poor kid. I try to cover for him. "He wasn't holding it. I saw it on the floor and assumed that's what happened."

I'm still shaken from what Crew said about Verity and the knife, but I remind myself that everyone talks about Verity in present tense. The nurse, Jeremy, Crew. I'm sure Verity told him not to play with knives in the past, and now my imagination is turning it into more than it is.

Jeremy opens the medicine cabinet behind Crew and grabs a first-aid kit. When he closes the mirror, he's staring at my reflection. "Go check," he mouths, motioning toward the door with his head.

I leave the bathroom, but pause in the hallway. I don't like going in that room, no matter how helpless Verity is. But I also know Crew doesn't need to have access to a knife, so I trudge forward.

Verity's door is still wide open, so I tiptoe in, not wanting to wake her. *Not that I could.* I round the bed, to where Crew was on the floor.

There's no knife.

I turn around, wondering if maybe I kicked it somewhere when I picked him up. When I still don't see it, I lower myself to the floor to check under the bed. It's completely empty beneath the frame, other than a thin layer of dust. I slide my hand beneath the nightstand next to the hospital bed, but find nothing.

I know I saw a knife. I'm not going crazy.

Am I?

I put my hand on the mattress to lift myself up off the floor, but immediately shift backward onto my palms when I catch Verity watching me. Her head is in a different position, turned to the right, her eyes on mine.

Holy shit! I choke on my fear as I scoot myself backward, away from her bed. I end up several feet away from her, and even though her head is the only thing different about her from when I walked into the room, my fear is telling me to run for my life. I pull myself up, using the dresser for support, and keep my eyes fixated on her as I move back toward the door, facing her the whole time. I'm trying to suppress my terror, but I'm not convinced she isn't about to lunge at me with the knife she picked up from the floor.

I close her door behind me and stand there, gripping the doorknob, until I can control my panic. I breathe in and out, steadily, five times, hoping Jeremy doesn't see the terror in my eyes when I walk back to tell him there was no knife.

But there *was* a knife.

My hands are shaking. I don't trust her. I don't trust this house. As much as I know I need to stay in order to do the best job, I'd much rather sleep in my rental car on the streets of Brooklyn for the next week than sleep in this house another night.

I squeeze the tension from my neck as I return to the bathroom. Jeremy is bandaging up Crew's chin.

"You're lucky you don't need stitches," Jeremy says to Crew. He's helping Crew wash the blood from his hands, and then tells him to go play. Crew brushes past me and returns to Verity's room.

I find it odd that sitting on her bed while he plays his iPad is fun for him. But then again, I'm sure he just wants to be near his mother. *Have at it, buddy. I don't want to be near her at all.*

"Did you grab the knife?" Jeremy asks, drying his hands on a towel.

I try to refrain from sounding as scared as I still feel. "I couldn't find it."

Jeremy eyes me for a second and then says, "But you saw one?"

"I thought I did. Maybe I didn't. It wasn't there."

Jeremy brushes past me. "I'll look around." He walks toward Verity's room, but turns around and pauses as he reaches her door. "Thanks for helping him." He smiles, but it's a playful grin. "I know how busy you've been today." He winks at me before walking into Verity's room.

I close my eyes and allow the embarrassment to sink in. *I deserved that*. He probably thinks all I do is stare out that office window.

I should probably take *two* Xanax at this point.

When I get back to Verity's office, the sun is beginning to set, which means Crew will shower and go to bed soon. Verity will remain in her room for the night. And I'll feel somewhat safe, because for whatever reason, I'm only scared of Verity in this house. And I don't have to be around her at nighttime. In fact, nighttime has become my favorite time around here because it's when I see the least of Verity and the most of Jeremy.

I'm not sure how much longer I can try to convince myself that I don't have a serious crush on that man. I'm also not sure how much longer I can try to convince myself that Verity is a better person than she really is. I think, after reading every book in her series, I'm beginning to understand the reason her suspense novels do so well is because of how she writes them from the villain's point of view.

Critics love that about her. When I listened to her first audiobook on the drive over, I loved that her narrator seemed a little psychotic. I wondered how Verity got in the mind of her antagonists like she did. But that was before I knew her.

I still don't technically know her, but I know the Verity who wrote the autobiography. It's apparent that the way she wrote the rest of her novels wasn't a unique approach for her. After all, they say *write what you know*. I'm beginning to think Verity writes from a villainous point of view because she's a villain. Being evil is all she knows.

I feel a little evil myself as I open the drawer and do exactly what I swore to myself I wouldn't do again: read another chapter.

Chapter Four

They were determined to live, I'll give them that.

Nothing I tried worked. The attempted self-abortion, the random pills, the "accidental" fall down a flight of stairs. The only thing any of my attempts resulted in was a small scar on one of the baby's cheeks. A scar I'm sure I'm responsible for. A scar Jeremy couldn't shut up about.

A few hours after they brought me to the room after their birth—*cesarean, thank god*—their pediatrician came by to check on the girls. I closed my eyes, pretending to nap, but really I was just scared to interact with their pediatrician. I feared he would see right through me and know I had no idea how to be a mother to these things.

Jeremy asked the doctor about the scar before he left the room. The doctor brushed it off, said it's not uncommon for identical twins to accidentally scratch each other in utero. Jeremy disagreed. "It's too deep to be a simple scratch, though."

"Could be scarring from fibrous tissue," the doctor said. "No worries. It'll fade with time."

"I'm not worried about the way it *looks*," Jeremy said, almost defensively. "I'm worried it could be something more serious."

"It's not. Your daughters are perfectly healthy. Both of them."

Figures.

The doctor left and the nurse was gone and it was just Jeremy, the girls, and me. One of them was asleep in the glass bed thing—I don't know what it's called. Jeremy was holding the other one. He was smiling down at her when he noticed my eyes were open.

"Hey, Momma."

Please don't call me that.

I smiled at him anyway. He looked good as a dad. Happy. Never mind that his happiness had little to do with me. But even in my jealousy, I could appreciate him. He was probably going to be the type of dad to change their diapers. To help with feedings. I knew I'd appreciate that side of him even more with time. I just needed to get used to this. To being a mother.

"Bring me the scarred one," I said.

Jeremy made a face, indicating he was disappointed in my choice of words. I guess that was a weird way to put it, but we hadn't named them yet. The scar was her only identifier.

He carried her to me and placed her in my arms. I looked down at her. I waited for the flood of emotions, but there wasn't even a trickle. I touched her cheek, ran my finger down the scar. *I guess the wire hanger wasn't strong enough.* I probably should have used something that didn't give so easily under pressure. A knitting needle? I'm not sure it would have been long enough.

"The doctor said the scarring could be a scratch." Jeremy laughed. "Fighting before they were even born."

I smiled down at her. Not because I felt like smiling, but because it's probably what I was supposed to do. I didn't want Jeremy to think I wasn't in love with her like he was. I took her hand and wrapped it around my pinky. "Chastin," I whispered. "You can have the better name since your sister was so mean to you."

"Chastin," Jeremy said. "I love it."

"And Harper," I said. "Chastin and Harper."

They were two of the names he had sent me. I liked them okay. I chose them because he mentioned them both more than once, so I gathered they were at the top of his list. Maybe if he could see how much I was trying to love him, he wouldn't notice the two areas in which my love lacked.

Chastin started to cry. She was wriggling in my arms, and I wasn't sure what to do about that. I started bouncing her, but that hurt, so I stopped. Her cries continued to grow louder.

"She might be hungry," Jeremy suggested.

I was so sold on the thought of them not actually surviving their birth with all I had put them through, what I would do beyond that wasn't given much thought. I knew breastfeeding them would be the best choice, but I had absolutely no desire to do that kind of damage to my breasts. Especially since there were two of them.

"Sounds like someone is hungry," a nurse said as she pranced into the room. "Are you breastfeeding?"

"No," I said immediately. I wanted her to prance right back out of there.

Jeremy looked at me, concerned. "Are you sure?"

"There are *two* of them," I replied.

I didn't like the look on Jeremy's face—like he was disappointed in me. I hated to think this was how it was going to be. Him taking their side. Me not mattering anymore.

"It's not any more difficult than bottle-feeding them," Prancing Nurse said. "It's actually more convenient. Do you want to try it? See how it goes?"

I couldn't take my eyes off Jeremy as I waited for him to dismiss me of that kind of torture. It killed me to know that he wanted me to breastfeed them when there were so many other perfectly adequate alternatives. But I nodded and pulled the sleeve of my gown down because I wanted to please him. I wanted him to be happy that I was the mother of his children, even though *I* wasn't happy about it.

I removed my breast and brought Chastin toward my nipple. Jeremy was watching the whole thing. He saw her latch on to my nipple. He saw her head move back and forth, her little hand press into my skin. He watched her begin to suck.

It felt wrong.

This infant, sucking on something Jeremy had sucked on before. I didn't like it. How would he find my breasts attractive after seeing babies feed from them every day?

"Does it hurt?" Jeremy asked.

"Not really."

He put a hand on my head and brushed back my hair. "You look like you're in pain."

Not in pain. Just disgusted.

I watched as Chastin continued to feed from me. My stomach clenched as I tried my hardest not to show him how repulsed I was. I'm sure some mothers found this beautiful. I found it disturbing.

"I can't do it," I whispered, my head falling back against the pillow.

Jeremy reached down and pulled Chastin from my breast. I sighed with relief when I was free of her.

"It's fine," Jeremy said reassuringly. "We'll use formula."

"Are you sure?" the nurse asked him. "She seemed to be taking to it."

"Positive. We'll use formula."

The nurse conceded and said she'd grab a can of Similac as she left the room.

I smiled because my husband still supported me. He had my back. He put me first in that moment, and I reveled in it. "Thank you," I said to him.

He kissed Chastin's forehead and then sat down on the edge of my bed with her. He stared at her and shook his head in disbelief. "How can I already feel so protective over them, and I've only known them a couple of hours?"

I wanted to remind him that he's always been protective of *me*, but it didn't feel like the right moment. I almost felt as if I were intruding on something I wasn't a part of. This father-daughter bond I was never going to be included in. He already loved them more than he had ever loved me. He was eventually going to take their side, even if I wasn't in the wrong. This was so much worse than I had imagined it would be.

He lifted a hand to his face and wiped away a tear.

"Are you *crying*?"

Jeremy snapped his head in my direction, shocked at my words. I panicked. Recovered. "That came out weird," I said. "I meant it in a good way. I love how much you love them."

His sudden tension disappeared with my quick recovery. He looked back down at Chastin and said, "I've never loved anything this much. Did you think you were capable of loving someone so much?"

I rolled my eyes and thought to myself, *I have loved someone this much, Jeremy. You. For four years. Thanks for noticing.*

10

I don't know why I'm surprised when I set the manuscript back in the drawer. The contents of the drawer rattle as I slam it shut angrily. *Why am I angry?* This isn't my life or my family. I'd trolled Verity's reviews before coming here, and in nine out of ten of them, the reviewer referenced wanting to throw their Kindles or books across the room.

I kind of want to do the same with her autobiography. I was hoping she'd have seen the light with the birth of the girls, but she didn't. She only saw more darkness.

She seems so cold and hard, but I'm not a mother. Do a lot of mothers feel this way about their children at first? If so, they certainly aren't honest about it. It's probably similar to when a mother claims she doesn't have a favorite child, but they probably do. It's an unspoken thing between mothers. One I suppose you don't become aware of until you are one.

Or maybe Verity just didn't deserve to be a mother. I think about having children sometimes. I'll be thirty-two soon and I'd be lying if I said I didn't worry the opportunity might never present itself. But if I ever do find myself in a relationship with a man I'd want to father my child, it would be someone like Jeremy. Rather than appreciate the wonderful father he seemed to be, Verity resented him.

Jeremy's love for his girls seemed genuine from the very beginning. It still seems genuine. And it hasn't been that long since he lost them. I keep losing sight of that. He's still probably moving through the stages of grief, while dealing with Verity and being there for Crew and ensuring the income they've gotten used to as a family doesn't come to a complete halt. Just a fraction of what he's been through would be too much for some people. But he's dealing with all of it at once.

I found boxes of pictures in Verity's office closet this week as I was rummaging through her things. I pulled a box down, but haven't gone through the pictures yet. It seems like another invasion of privacy on my part. This family, at least Jeremy, has entrusted me to finish this series, and I keep getting sidetracked by my obsession with Verity.

But if Verity is putting so much of herself into her series, I really do need to get to know her as well as possible. This really isn't snooping. It's research. There you go. Justification complete.

I take the box of pictures to the kitchen table, pry open the lid, and then pull a handful of the pictures out, wondering who had them developed. People don't really have a lot of physical pictures on hand nowadays, thanks to the invention of smartphones. But there are so many pictures of the kids in here. Someone went through the trouble of making sure every picture they took was in physical form. My bet is on Jeremy.

I pick up a picture of Chastin. A close-up. I stare at her scar for a moment. I couldn't stop thinking about it yesterday, so I Googled to find out if attempted abortions could actually cause damage in utero.

That's something I'll never Google again. Sadly, a lot of babies survive the attempts and are born disfigured in much worse ways than just a small scar. Chastin was really lucky. She and Harper both were.

Well...until they weren't.

Jeremy's footsteps approach the stairs. I don't try to hide the pictures, because I'm not sure he would mind that I'm down here looking at them.

When he walks into the kitchen, I smile at him and continue sorting through them. He hesitates on his way to the refrigerator, his eyes falling to the box on the table.

"I feel like getting to know her helps put me in her headspace," I explain. "Helps with the writing." I look away from him, down at a picture of Harper, the one who rarely smiles in pictures.

Jeremy takes a seat next to me and picks up one of the pictures of Chastin.

"Why did Harper never smile?"

Jeremy leans over, taking the picture of Harper from my hand. "She was diagnosed with Asperger's when she was three. She wasn't very expressive."

He runs a finger over her picture and then puts it aside, pulling another from the box. This one is of Verity and the girls. He hands it to me. The three of them are dressed alike, in matching pajamas. If Verity didn't love the girls in this photo, she was certainly good at faking it.

"Our last Christmas before Crew was born," he says, explaining the photo. He pulls a handful out and begins flipping through them. He pauses every now and then on pictures of the girls, but flips past pictures of Verity.

"Here," he says, pulling one out of the stack. "This is my favorite picture of them. A rare smile from Harper. She was obsessed with animals, so we had a zoo come in and set up in the backyard for their fifth birthday."

I smile down at the picture. But mostly because Jeremy is in the photo with a rare look of joy spread across his face. "What were they like?"

"Chastin was a protector. A little spitfire. Even when they were young, she could sense Harper was different from her. She mothered her. She'd try to tell me and Verity how to parent. And God, when Crew came along, we thought we were going to have to hand him over to her. She was obsessed." He puts a picture of Chastin in the pile of pictures he's already looked at. "She would have made a great mother someday."

He picks up a picture of Harper. "Harper was special to me. Sometimes I'm not sure Verity understood her like I did, but it's almost as if I could sense her needs, you know? She had trouble expressing her emotions, but I knew what made her tick, what made her happy, what made her sad, even when she didn't quite know how to reveal that to the world. She was mostly happy. She didn't have an immediate interest in Crew, though. Not until he turned three or four and could actually play with her. Before that, he might as well have been another piece of furniture." He picks up a picture of the three of them. "He hasn't asked about them. Not even once. Hasn't even mentioned their names."

"Does that worry you?"

He looks at me. "I don't know if I should be relieved or worried."

"Probably both," I admit.

He picks up a picture of Verity and Crew, right after Crew's birth. "He went to therapy for a few months. But I was scared it was just a weekly reminder of the tragedies, so I pulled him out. If he shows signs that he needs it when he's older, I'll take him back. Make sure he's okay."

"And you?"

He looks at me again. "What about me?"

"How are *you*?"

He doesn't break eye contact. Doesn't skip a beat. "My world was turned upside down when Chastin died. And then when Harper died, it ended completely." He looks back down at the box of pictures. "When I got the call about Verity...the only thing left in me to feel was anger."

"Toward who? God?"

"No," Jeremy says, his voice quiet. "I was angry at Verity."

He looks back at me, and he doesn't even have to say why he was angry at her. *He thinks she hit the tree on purpose.*

It's quiet in the room...in the house. He's not even breathing.

Eventually, he scoots back in his chair and stands. I stand up with him because I feel like that's the first time he's ever admitted this to anyone. Maybe even to himself. I can tell he doesn't want me to see what he's thinking, because he turns away from me and clasps his hands behind his head. I place my hand on his shoulder, and then I move so that I'm standing in front of him, whether he wants me to or not. I slip my arms around his waist and press my face against his chest and I hug him. His arms clasp around my back with a heavy sigh. He squeezes me, tight, and I can tell it's a hug he's needed for no telling how long.

We stand like this longer than a hug should last, until it's obvious to us both that we shouldn't still be clinging to each other. The strength in his hug eases, and at some point, we're no longer hugging. We're holding each other. Feeling the weight of how long it's been since either of us has probably felt this. It's quiet in the house, so I hear it when he tries to hold his breath. I feel all of his hesitation as his hand moves slowly up to the back of my head.

My eyes are closed, but I open them because I want to look at him. There's a pull in me, tilting my head back into his hand as I lift my face from his chest.

He's looking down at me now, and I have no idea if he's about to kiss me or pull away, but either way, it's too late. I feel everything he's been trying not to say in the way he holds me. In the way he's stopped inhaling.

I can feel him bringing me closer to his mouth. But then his eyes flicker up and his hand falls.

"Hey, buddy," Jeremy says, looking over my shoulder. Jeremy steps back. Releases me. I grip the back of the chair, feeling as if I weigh twice as much now that he's let go of me.

I glance at the doorway, and Crew is staring at us. No expression. He looks a lot like Harper right now. His eyes fall to the box of pictures on the table and he rushes toward them. *Lunges*, almost.

I step back in a hurry, shocked by his movements. He's picking up the pictures, angrily slamming them back into the box.

"Crew," Jeremy says, his voice gentle. He tries to grab his son's wrist, but Crew pulls away from him. "Hey," Jeremy says, leaning down closer to him. I can hear the confusion in Jeremy's voice, as if this is a side of Crew he's never seen before.

Crew starts crying as he's slamming all the pictures back inside the box.

"Crew," Jeremy says, unable to hide his concern now. "We're just looking at pictures." He tries to pull Crew to him, but Crew rips himself out of Jeremy's arms. Jeremy grabs Crew again, pulling him to his chest.

"Put them back!" Crew yells toward me. "I don't want to see them!"

I grab the rest of the pictures and shove them into the box. I put the lid on it and pick it up, clutching it to my chest as Crew tries to wrangle himself from Jeremy's grip. Jeremy picks him up and rushes out of the kitchen with him. They go upstairs, and I'm left standing in the kitchen, shaken, concerned.

What was that?

It's quiet upstairs for several minutes. I don't hear Crew putting up a fight or yelling, so I think that's a good sign. But my knees feel weak and my head feels heavy. I need to lie down. Maybe I shouldn't have taken two Xanax tonight. Or maybe I shouldn't have brought family pictures out and put them on display in front of a family who still hasn't recovered from their loss. Or maybe I shouldn't have almost kissed a married man. I rub at my forehead, suddenly feeling the urge to bolt—flee—and never come back to this house of sadness.

What am I still doing here?

11

Even at the height of day, when the sun is keeping watch over this part of the world, it still feels eerie inside this house. It's four o'clock in the afternoon. Jeremy is working on the dock again, and Crew is playing near him in the sand.

An unsettling energy buzzes throughout the house. It's always here, and I can't seem to shake it. It seems to be getting worse at night, nocturnal and intense. I'm sure it's mostly in my head, but that doesn't put me at ease, because the things lurking around inside the mind can be just as dangerous as tangible threats.

I woke up last night to use the restroom. I thought I heard a noise in the hallway—footsteps lighter than Jeremy's and heavier than Crew's. Then, shortly after, it sounded as though the stairs were creaking, one at a time, as if someone were creeping up them with a deliberately light foot. It took me a while to go to sleep after that because in a house this size, noises are inevitable. And with the imagination of a writer, every noise becomes a threat.

My head jerks toward the office door. I'm jumpy, even now, and all I hear is April in the kitchen talking to someone. She uses the same calming tone when she speaks to Verity, like she's trying to coax her back to life. I've never heard Jeremy speak to his wife. But he did admit to being angry at her. Does he still love her? Does he sit in her room and tell her how much he misses the sound of her voice? That seems like something he would do. Or would have done. *But now?*

He cares for her, helps feed her sometimes, but I've never actually seen him speak directly to her. It makes me wonder if he doesn't believe she's in there at all anymore. As if the person he cares for is no longer his wife.

Maybe he's able to separate his anger and disappointment toward Verity from the woman he cares for, because he no longer feels they're the same person.

I go to the kitchen because I'm hungry, but also because I'm curious to watch April as she interacts with Verity. I'm curious to see if Verity has any sort of physical response to her interaction.

April is seated at the table with Verity's lunch. I open the refrigerator and watch as she feeds her. Verity's jaw moves back and forth, almost robotically, after April feeds her a spoonful of mashed potatoes. It's always soft foods. Mashed potatoes, apple sauce, blended vegetables. Hospital foods, bland and easy to ingest. I grab a cup of Crew's pudding and then sit at the table with April and Verity. April acknowledges me with a fleeting glance and a nod, but nothing else.

After eating a few bites of the pudding, I decide to try making small talk with this woman who refuses to interact with me.

"How long have you been a nurse?"

April pulls the spoon out of Verity's mouth and dips it back into the potatoes. "Long enough to be in the single-digit countdown to retirement."

"Nice."

"You're my favorite patient, though," April says to Verity. "By far."

She's directing her answers at Verity, even though I'm the one asking the questions.

"How long have you worked with Verity?"

Again, April answers toward Verity. "How long have we been doing this now?" she asks, as if Verity is going to answer her. "Four weeks?" She looks at me. "Yeah, I was officially hired about four weeks ago."

"Did you know the family? Before Verity's accident?"

"No." April wipes Verity's mouth and then places the tray of food on the table. "Can I speak with you for a moment?" She nudges her head toward the hallway.

I pause, wondering why we need to leave the kitchen in order for her to have a conversation with me. I stand up, though, and follow her out. I lean against the wall and spoon another bite of pudding into my mouth as April shoves her hands into the pockets of her scrub top.

"I don't expect you to know this, especially if you've never been around someone in Verity's condition. But it's not respectful to discuss people like her as though they aren't right in front of you."

I'm gripping my spoon, about to pull it out of my mouth. I pause for a moment, then shove the spoon back into the pudding cup. "I'm sorry. I wasn't aware that's what I was doing."

"It's easy to do, especially if you believe the person can't acknowledge you. Verity's brain doesn't process like it used to, obviously, but we don't know how much she does process. Just watch how you word things in her presence."

I stand up straight, pulling away from my casual position against the wall. I had no idea I was being insulting.

"Of course," I say, nodding.

April smiles, and it's actually genuine for once.

Luckily, our awkward moment ends thanks to Crew. He runs through the back door, cupping something in his hands. He rushes between me and April, into the kitchen. April follows him.

"Mom," Crew says, excitedly. "Mom, Mom, I found a turtle."

He stands in front of her, holding the turtle up for her to see. He runs his fingers over its shell. "Mom, *look* at him." He's holding it up higher now, trying to get Verity to make eye contact with the turtle. Of course she doesn't. He's only five, so he probably can't even process all the reasons she can no longer speak to him or look at him or react to his excitement. I immediately hurt for him, knowing he's probably still waiting for her to fully recover.

"Crew," I say, walking over to him. "Let me see your turtle."

He turns and holds it up for me. "He's not a snapping turtle. Daddy said those kind have marks on their necks."

"Wow," I say. "That's really awesome. Let's go outside and find something to put him in."

Crew jumps with excitement, then brushes past me. I follow him out of the house and help him search around the property until he finds an old red bucket to put him in. Then Crew plops down on the grass and brings the bucket onto his lap.

I sit down next to him, partly because I'm starting to feel really bad for this kid, but also because we have a clear view of Jeremy from this spot in the yard as he works on the dock.

"Daddy said I can't have another turtle because I killed my last turtle."

I swing my head toward Crew.

"You killed him? How did you kill him?"

"Lost him in the house," he says. "Mommy found him under her couch and he was dead."

Oh. Okay. My mind was going somewhere much more sinister with that. For a second, I thought he'd murdered the turtle intentionally.

"We could let him go right here in the grass," I tell him. "That way you can watch and see which direction he crawls. He might lead you to his secret turtle family."

Crew picks him up out of the bucket. "Do you think he has a wife?"

"He might."

"He could have babies, too."

"He could."

Crew puts him down in the grass, but naturally, the turtle is too scared to move. We watch him for a while, waiting for him to come out of his shell. I can see Jeremy approaching out of the corner of my eye. When he's closer, I look up at him, shielding the sun from my eyes with my hand.

"What'd you two find?"

"A turtle," Crew says. "Don't worry, I'm not keeping him."

Jeremy shoots me an appreciative smile. Then he sits down next to Crew in the grass. Crew scoots closer to him, but when he grabs Jeremy's arm, Crew pulls away. "Gross. You're sweaty."

He is sweaty, but I don't really think it's gross.

Crew pushes off the grass. "I'm hungry. You promised we could go out to eat tonight. We haven't been to a restaurant in years."

Jeremy laughs. "Years? It's only been one week since I took you to McDonald's."

Crew says, "Yeah, but we used to go out to eat all the time before my sisters died."

I watch Jeremy's shoulders tense with that comment. He said himself that Crew hasn't mentioned the girls since they died, so this moment feels significant.

Jeremy breathes deeply and then pats Crew on the back. "You're right. Go wash your hands and get ready. We'll need to be back before April leaves tonight."

Crew rushes toward the house, forgetting all about the turtle. Jeremy watches him for a while, his eyes full of thoughts. Then he stands up and reaches out a hand to help me up. "Wanna come?" he asks.

He's asking me to a friendly dinner with his child, but my wistful heart responds like I was just asked out on a date. I smile as I brush off the backs of my jeans. "I'd love that."

•••

I haven't had a reason to make an effort with my physical appearance since I arrived at Jeremy's house. Even though I still didn't make much of an effort before we left, Jeremy must have noticed the mascara, the lip gloss, and the fact that my hair is down for the first time. When we arrived at the restaurant and he was holding the door for me, he said quietly, "You look really nice."

His compliment settled in my stomach, and I can still feel it, even though we're finished eating. Crew is sitting on the same side of the booth as Jeremy. He's been telling jokes since he finished eating his dessert.

"I have another one," Crew says. "What is E.T. short for?"

Jeremy doesn't attempt to answer Crew's jokes because he says he's heard them a million times. I smile at Crew and pretend I don't know the answer.

"Because he has little legs," Crew says, falling back into his seat with laughter. His reaction to his own jokes make me laugh more than the jokes themselves.

And then, "Why don't they play poker in the jungle?"

"I don't know, why?" I say.

"Too many cheetahs!"

I don't know that I've stopped laughing since he started telling us jokes.

"Your turn," Crew says.

"Mine?" I ask.

"Yeah, it's your turn to tell a joke."

Oh, God. I'm feeling pressure from a five-year-old. "Okay, let me think." A few seconds later, I snap my fingers. "Okay, I've got one. What is green, fuzzy, and if it fell out of a tree, it could kill you?"

Crew leans forward with his chin in his hands. "Ummmm. I don't know."

"A fuzzy green piano."

Crew doesn't laugh at my joke. Neither does Jeremy. *At first.*

Then, a few seconds later, Jeremy releases a burst of laughter that makes me smile.

"I don't get it," Crew says.

Jeremy is still laughing, shaking his head.

Crew looks up at Jeremy. "How is that funny?"

Jeremy puts his arm around Crew. "It's not," he says. "It's funny because it's *not* funny."

Crew looks at me. "That's not how jokes are supposed to work."

"Okay, I have another one," I say. "What's red and shaped like a bucket?"

Crew shrugs.

"A blue bucket painted red."

Jeremy squeezes his jaw, trying to hold back his laughter. Seeing him laugh is probably the best thing that's happened since I showed up here.

Crew scrunches up his nose. "You aren't very good at telling jokes."

"Come on. Those were so funny."

Crew shakes his head, disappointed. "I hope you don't try to make jokes in your books."

Jeremy leans back in his seat and grips his side, trying to hold back his laughter as the waitress approaches with the check. Jeremy takes it from her. "My treat," he manages to say.

When we return to the house, Crew makes it inside before we do. "Run upstairs and let April know we're back," Jeremy calls after him.

Jeremy closes the door that leads into the garage, and we both pause before moving farther into the house. We're tucked away into an unlit corner near the stairs, but a stream of light from the kitchen streaks across his face.

"Thank you for dinner. That was fun."

Jeremy pulls off his jacket. "It was." He's smiling as he hangs his jacket on a coat rack next to the door. He looks different tonight, like he's less weighed down by his life than he usually is. "I should get Crew out more often."

I nod in agreement, slipping my hands into my back pockets. The next few seconds fill with thick silence. It almost feels like that moment at the end of real dates when you can't decide between a kiss or a hug.

Of course, neither would be appropriate in this case because it wasn't a date.

Why did it feel like one?

Our eye contact is broken when Crew begins to descend the stairs. Jeremy's gaze diverts to his feet for a moment, but before he walks away, I see him release a quick breath, as if Crew interrupted something Jeremy was about to regret. Something I'm not sure *I* would have regretted.

I sigh heavily and then go straight to Verity's office and close the door. I need to distract myself. I feel an emptiness—an ache in my stomach that I don't think is going to go away. Like I need more moments with him. Moments I can't get. Moments I *shouldn't* get.

I flip through the pages of Verity's manuscript, hoping to find an intimate scene with Jeremy.

I'm not sure what kind of person that makes me in this moment, because reading this is wrong on so many levels, but it isn't as wrong as crossing that line with him physically would be.

I can't have him in real life, but I can learn what he's like in bed to aid in all my fantasies I'm probably going to have about him.

Chapter Five

I was about to have a breakdown. I could feel it. Or at least a meltdown. A temper tantrum. A hissy fit. Any of them would have been inappropriate, though.

I just couldn't take it anymore. If one of them wasn't crying, the other one was. If one of them wasn't hungry, the other one was. They rarely slept at the same time. Jeremy was a big help and did half the work with them, but if we'd only had one child, I'd at least have gotten a break. But there were two, so it was as if we each were full-time single parents of an infant.

Jeremy was still selling real estate at the time the girls were born. He took two weeks off to help me with the girls, but his two weeks were up, and he needed to go back to work. We couldn't afford a nanny because the advance I had recently received for the sale of my first manuscript was small. I was terrified of being left alone with the babies while he was away from the house for nine hours every day.

However, once Jeremy returned to work, it ended up being the best thing that ever happened to me.

He would leave at seven in the morning. I would wake up with him so he could see me caring for the girls. After he was gone, I would put them back in their cribs, unplug their monitors and go back to bed. From the day he started back to work, I began getting more sleep than I think I'd ever gotten. We were in a corner apartment, and their room didn't butt up to any other apartment, so no one could hear them cry.

I couldn't even hear them when I put my earplugs in.

After three days of Jeremy being back at work, I felt like my life was returning to normal. I was getting so much sleep during the day, but before Jeremy would come home, I'd feed them, bathe them, and start on dinner. Every night when he would walk in the door, the babies would be calm from finally being tended to, the smell of dinner would be coming from the kitchen, and he'd be blown away by how well I was tackling life.

Nighttime feedings didn't even bother me at that point, because my sleep schedule had shifted. I was doing most of my sleeping while Jeremy was at work. And the girls would sleep fairly well at night due to the exhaustion from crying all day. But the crying was probably good for them. I was able to write most nights while everyone slept, so I was even ahead career-wise.

The only place I was lacking was in the bedroom. I hadn't been cleared to have sex from my doctor yet, as it had only been four weeks since their births. But I knew if I didn't keep that part of my marriage alive, it could quickly spread into other areas of our marriage. A terrible sex life is like a virus. Your marriage can be healthy in all other aspects, but once the sex dies out, it starts to infect all the other parts of your relationship.

I was determined not to let that happen to us.

I had tried the night before to have sex with him, but Jeremy was worried he would hurt me. Even though it had been a cesarean, he still worried about the incision. He had read online that he couldn't even so much as finger me until we got the okay from my doctor, and that appointment was still two weeks away. He refused to have sex with me until a medical professional approved it.

I didn't want to wait that long, though. I couldn't. I missed him. I missed that connection with him.

Jeremy woke up that night at two in the morning because my tongue was sliding up his dick. I'm almost positive his dick was rock hard before he was even fully awake.

The only reason I knew he was awake is because his hand moved to my head and his fingers snaked through my hair. That's the only movement he made. He didn't even lift his head off his pillow to look at me, and for some reason, I liked that. I'm not even sure he opened his eyes. He remained still and silent while I drove him mad with my tongue.

I licked him, teased him, touched him for fifteen minutes without ever putting him inside my mouth. I knew how much he wanted me to, because he was growing restless and needed that relief, but I didn't want him to get relief from my mouth. I wanted him to get it by fucking me for the first time in weeks.

His hand was impatient, squeezing the back of my head, pressing me down on his dick as he silently begged me to take him in my mouth. I refused and continued to fight against the pressure of his hand as I kissed and licked him, when all he wanted to do was shove it into my mouth.

When I was certain I had driven him so crazy that his desire outweighed his concern for me, I moved away from him. He followed. I fell onto my back, spread my legs, and he was inside me without a second thought about whether or not it was too soon for him to be there. He wasn't even gentle. It was as if my tongue had driven him to a point of madness, because he was pounding into me so hard, it actually *did* hurt.

It lasted almost an hour and a half because as soon as he finished, I sucked him off until he was hard again. Both times we fucked, we never said a word. And even after it was all over and I was crushed beneath the weight of his exhausted body, we still didn't speak. He rolled off me and wrapped himself around me. Our sheets were covered in sweat and semen, but we were too consumed with sleep to care.

I knew then that it was okay. We would be okay. Jeremy still worshipped my body as much as he always had.

The girls might have taken a lot from us by then, but his desire was the one thing I knew would always be mine.

12

This chapter has been the most difficult to continue reading by far. How a mother could sleep soundly down the hall from her crying infants baffles me. She's callous.

I've been under the impression that Verity might have been a sociopath, but now I'm leaning more toward psychopath.

I put the manuscript away and use Verity's computer to refresh my memory of the exact definition for psychopath. I scroll through every personality trait. *Pathological liar, cunning and manipulative, lack of remorse or guilt, callousness and lack of empathy, shallow emotional response.*

She displays every characteristic. The only thing about her that makes me question if she was a psychopath is her obsession with Jeremy. Psychopaths find it more difficult to fall in love, and if they do, it's difficult for them to retain that love. They tend to move on quickly from one person to the next. But Verity didn't want to move on from Jeremy. He was Verity's entire focus.

The man is married to a psychopath, and he has no idea because she did everything she could to hide it from him.

There's a soft knock on the office door, so I minimize the screen on the computer. When I open the door, Jeremy is standing in the hallway. His hair is damp and he's wearing a white T-shirt with a pair of black pajama bottoms.

This is my favorite look on him. Barefoot, casual, easygoing. It's sexy as hell, and I hate how attracted to him I am. Would I even be attracted to him if it weren't for the intimate details I've read about him in that manuscript?

"Sorry to bother you. I need a favor."

"What's up?"

He motions for me to follow him. "There's an old aquarium somewhere in the basement. I just need you to hold the door open for me so I can bring it upstairs and clean it out for Crew."

I smile. "You're gonna let him have a turtle?"

"Yeah, he seemed excited today. He's a little older now, so hopefully he'll remember to feed this one." Jeremy reaches the basement door and opens it. "The door was installed backward. It's impossible to come up the stairs with your hands full or you can't open the door to get out."

Jeremy flips on a light and begins to descend the stairs. The basement doesn't feel like an extension of the house. It feels abandoned and uncared for, like a neglected child. Creaky steps and dust on the handrail attached to the wall. Normally, I would have zero desire to walk into a basement this unwelcoming. Especially in a house that already terrifies me. But their basement is the only place in this house I've yet to see, and I'm curious what's down there. What kind of things could Verity have packed away?

The stairwell leading into the basement is dark because the light switch at the top of the stairs only powered a light that was inside the actual basement. When I reach the bottom step, I'm relieved to see the room isn't at all as eerie as I had expected. To the left is an office desk that looks to have gone unused for quite some time. There are stacks of files and papers all over the desk, but it looks more like a corner used for storage than a place where a person could actually sit and get work done.

To the right are boxes of things accumulated over the years they've been together. Some with lids, some without. There's a baby video monitor sticking out of one of the boxes and I cringe, thinking about the chapter I just read and how Verity admitted to unplugging it during the day so she couldn't hear them crying.

Jeremy is sorting through a collection of things behind and in between the boxes.

"Did you used to work down here?" I ask him.

"Yeah. I owned a realty firm and brought a lot of work home most days, so this was my office." He lifts a sheet and tosses it aside, revealing an aquarium that's covered in a layer of dust. "Bingo." He begins to rummage through the contents inside the aquarium to ensure he has all the pieces.

I'm still thinking about the career he casually mentioned giving up. "You owned your own firm?"

He lifts the aquarium and walks it to the desk on the other side of the room. I make room by pushing papers and files out of the way so he can set it down.

"Yep. Started it the same year Verity started writing books."

"Did you love it?"

He nods. "I did. It was a lot of work, but I was good at it." He plugs the lid to the aquarium into an outlet, checking to see if the attached light still works. "When Verity's first book released, we both thought it was more of a hobby than an actual career. When she sold it, we still didn't take it very seriously. But then word started to get out, and more copies of her books were selling. After a couple of years, her checks started to make mine look cute." He laughs, as if it's a fond memory and not one that bothers him at all. "By the time she got pregnant with Crew, we both knew I was only working for the sake of working. Not because my income had a real impact on our lifestyle. It was the only choice, really. For me to quit, since the job required so much of my time." He unplugs the light to the aquarium, and when he does, there's a popping sound behind us, followed by the escape of the only light we had in the basement.

It's pitch black now. I know he's right in front of me, but I can no longer see him. My pulse quickens, and then I feel his hand on my arm. "Here," he says, bringing my hand to his shoulder. "Must have flipped a breaker. Walk behind me, and when we make it to the top of the stairs, just slip around me and open the door."

I feel his shoulder muscles contract as he lifts the aquarium. I keep my hand on his shoulder, following closely behind him as he makes his way toward the stairs. He takes each step slowly, probably for my benefit. When he stops, he moves so that his back is against the wall. I slip around him and feel around for the doorknob. I pull the door open and a flood of light pours in.

Jeremy walks out first, and as soon as he's out of my way, I pull the door shut quickly, causing it to slam. He laughs when I release a shaky breath.

"Not a fan of basements, huh?"

I shake my head. "Not a fan of *dark* basements."

Jeremy walks the aquarium to the kitchen table and looks at it. "That's a lot of dust." He picks it up again. "Do you mind if I wash it in the master shower? It'd be easier than trying to do it in the sink."

I shake my head. "Not at all."

Jeremy carries the aquarium to the master shower. Part of me wants to follow him and help, but I don't. I go back to the office and do my best to focus on the series I'm supposed to be working on. Thoughts of Verity continue to distract me like they do every time I finish a chapter in her autobiography. Yet, I can't stop reading it. It's like a train wreck and Jeremy doesn't even realize he was mangled in the wreckage.

I choose to work on the series rather than read more of the manuscript, but I've gotten very little done by the time Jeremy finishes up in the master bath. I decide to call it a night and head back to the bedroom.

After I've washed my face and brushed my teeth, I stare at the handful of shirts I brought with me that are hanging in the closet. I have no desire to wear any of them, so I begin to rummage through Jeremy's shirts. The shirt he lent me smelled like him the entire day I wore it. I thumb through them until I find a T-Shirt of his that's soft enough to sleep in. In small print over the left breast, it reads, "Crawford Realty."

I pull the shirt on over my head and then walk over to the bed. Before climbing into it, I focus on the bite marks on the headboard. I walk closer to them, running my thumb over them.

I look down the length of the headboard and notice there is more than one imprint of teeth. There are five or six areas where Verity bit the headboard, some not as noticeable as the others until you're up close.

I crawl onto the bed and lift up onto my knees as I face the headboard. I straddle a pillow and imagine being in this position—sprawled over Jeremy's face as I grip the headboard. I close my eyes and slide a hand up into Jeremy's T-shirt, imagining it's his hand that drags up my stomach and caresses my breast.

My lips part and I suck in air, but a noise above me breaks me out of the moment. I look up at the ceiling and listen to the sound of Verity's hospital bed as it begins to hum and move.

I pull the pillow out from under me and lie on my back as I stare up at the ceiling, wondering what—if anything—goes through Verity's mind. Is it complete darkness in there? Does she hear what people say to her? Does she sense the sunshine when it's on her skin? Does she know whose touch is whose?

I put my arms at my sides and lie still, imagining what it would be like not to be able to control my movements. I remain in the same position on the bed, even though I'm growing more and more restless with each passing minute. I need to scratch my nose, and it makes me wonder if that bothers Verity, not being able to lift a hand to scratch an itch. Or if her condition even allows her to feel an itch.

I close my eyes and all I can think about is that Verity possibly deserves the darkness, the stillness, the quiet. Yet for a psychopath, she certainly has so many still wrapped around her immobile finger.

13

The smell is different when I open my eyes. So are the noises.

I'm not confused about where I am. I know I'm in Jeremy's house. I just...I'm not in my room.

I'm staring at a wall. The wall in the master bedroom is light grey. This wall is yellow. *Yellow, like the walls in the upstairs bedrooms.*

The bed beneath me begins to move, but it isn't because someone in the bed is moving. It's different...like it's...mechanical.

I squeeze my eyes shut. Please, God. No. *No, no, no, please don't tell me I am in Verity's bed.*

I'm trembling all over now. I open my eyes, slowly, and turn my head at the slowest pace possible. When I see the door and then the dresser and then the TV mounted to the wall, I roll out of the bed, falling to the floor. I scramble to the wall and slide up it with my back against it. I squeeze my eyes shut. I can hardly hold myself up I am so hysterical.

My body is shaking so badly, I can hear it when I breathe. Whimpers at first, but as soon as I open my eyes and see Verity on her bed, I scream.

Then I slap my hand over my mouth.

It's dark outside. Everyone is asleep. I have to be quiet.

It's been so long since this has happened. Years, probably. But it's happening and I am terrified and I have no idea why I ended up here. Was it because I was thinking about her?

"Sleepwalking is patternless, Lowen. It has no meaning. It is unrelated to intention."

I hear my therapist's words, but I don't want to process them. *I need to get out of here. Move, Lowen.*

I slide across the wall, keeping as far from that bed as I can while I make my way to Verity's bedroom door. I'm flat against the door, tears streaming down my cheeks as I turn the handle and open it, then flee the bedroom.

Jeremy flings his arms around me, pulling me to a stop.

"Hey," he says, turning me to face him. He sees the tears on my face, the terror in my eyes. He loosens his grip, and as soon as he does, I run. I run down the hall, down the stairs, and I don't stop until I slam the bedroom door and I'm back on my bed.

What the fuck? What the fuck?

I curl up on top of the covers, facing the door. My wrist begins to throb, so I grip it with my other hand and tuck it against my chest.

The bedroom door opens and then closes behind Jeremy. He's shirtless, in a pair of red flannel pajama bottoms. It's all I see, a blur of red plaid as he rushes toward me. Then he's on his knees, his hand on my arm, his eyes searching mine.

"Lowen, what happened?"

"I'm sorry," I whisper, wiping at my eyes. "I'm sorry."

"For what?"

I shake my head and sit up on the bed. I have to explain it to him. He just caught me in his wife's bedroom in the middle of the night, and his head is probably swarming with questions. Questions I don't really have answers to.

Jeremy takes a seat next to me on the bed, lifting a leg so he can face me. He puts both his hands on my shoulders and lowers his head, looking at me very seriously.

"What happened, Low?"

"I don't know," I say, rocking back and forth. "Sometimes I walk in my sleep. I haven't in a long time, but I took two Xanax earlier and I think maybe... I don't know..." I sound just as hysterical as I feel. Jeremy must sense that, because he pulls me to him, putting pressure around me with his arms, trying to calm me. He doesn't ask me anything else for a couple of minutes. He runs a comforting hand over the back of my head and as good as it feels to have his support, I feel guilty. Undeserving.

When he pulls back, I can see his questions practically spilling from his mouth. "What were you doing in Verity's room?"

I shake my head. "I don't know. I woke up in there. I was scared and I screamed and..."

He grabs my hands. Squeezes them. "You're okay."

I want to agree with him, but I can't. *How am I supposed to sleep in this house after that?*

I can't count how many times I've woken up in random places. It used to happen so often, I went through a period where I had three locks on the inside of the bedroom door. I'm not unfamiliar with waking up in strange rooms, but why, out of all the rooms in this house, did it have to be Verity's?

"Is this why you wanted a lock on your door?" he asks. "To stop yourself from getting out?"

I nod, but for whatever reason, my response makes him laugh.

"Jesus," he says. "I thought it was because you were afraid of *me*."

I'm glad he finds levity in the moment, because I can't seem to.

"Hey. *Hey*," he says gently, tilting my chin up so that I'll look at him. "You're okay. It's okay. Sleepwalking is harmless."

I shake my head in profound disagreement. "No. *No*, Jeremy. It's not." I hold my hand up to my chest, still clutching my wrist. "I've woken up outside before, I've turned on stoves and ovens in my sleep. I even..." I blow out a breath. "I broke my hand in my sleep and didn't even feel it until I woke up the next morning."

A rush of adrenaline surges through my body as I think about how I can now add what just happened to the list of disturbing things I've done in my sleep. Although unconscious, I still walked up those stairs and crawled into that bed. If I'm capable of doing something that disturbing, what else am I capable of?

Did I unlock the door in my sleep or did I forget to lock it? I can't even remember.

I push off the mattress and head for the closet. I grab my suitcase and the few shirts I brought with me that are hanging up. "I should go."

Jeremy says nothing, so I continue to pack my things. I'm in the bathroom gathering my toiletries when he appears in the doorway. "You're leaving?"

I nod. "I woke up in her *room*, Jeremy. Even after you put a lock on my door. What if it happens again? What if I scare Crew?" I open the shower door to grab my razor. "I should have told you all this before I ever stayed the night here."

Jeremy takes the razor out of my hand. He places my bag of toiletries back on the counter. Then he pulls me to him, wrapping a hand around my head as he tucks me into his chest. "You sleepwalk, Low." He presses a comforting kiss into the top of my hair. "You sleepwalk. It's not that big of a deal."

Not that big of a deal?

I laugh halfheartedly against his chest. "I wish my mother would have felt that way."

When Jeremy pulls back, there's worry in his eyes. But is he worried *for* me or *because* of me? He walks me back into the bedroom, where he motions for me to sit down on my bed while he begins to hang up the shirts I shoved into my suitcase.

"Do you want to talk about it?" he asks.

"Which part, exactly?"

"Why your mother thought it was a big deal."

I don't want to talk about it. He must see my expression change because he pauses as he's reaching for another shirt. He drops it back into the suitcase and sits on the bed.

"I don't mean to sound harsh," he says, pegging me with a firm stare. "But I have a son. Seeing you this worried about what you're capable of is starting to make *me* worry. Why are you so scared of yourself?"

A small part of me wants to defend myself, but there's nothing to defend. I can't tell him I'm harmless, because I'm not sure that I am. I can't tell him I'll never sleepwalk again, because it just happened twenty minutes ago. The only thing I could probably say to defend myself is to tell him I'm not nearly as horrific as his own wife, but I'm not even sure if I believe that.

I'm not horrific *yet*, and I don't trust myself enough to say that I never will be.

I drop my eyes to the bed and swallow, preparing to tell him all about it. My wrist begins to throb again. When I look down at it, I trace the scar over my palm. "I didn't feel what happened to my wrist when it happened," I say. "I woke up one morning when I was ten. As soon as I opened my eyes, I felt this intense pain shoot up from my wrist to my shoulder. And then it was like a bright light exploded in my head. I screamed because it hurt so bad. My mother ran into my bedroom, and I remember lying on the bed in the most pain I'd ever been in, but in that second I realized my door had been unlocked. I knew I had locked it the night before."

I look up from my hand, back at Jeremy. "I couldn't remember what had happened, but there was blood all over my blanket, my pillow, my mattress, myself. And dirt on my feet, as if I'd been outside during the night. I couldn't even remember ever leaving my room. We had security cameras that monitored the front of the house and several of the rooms inside it. Before my mother checked them, she took me to the hospital because the cut on my hand needed stitches and my wrist needed an X-ray. When we got home later that afternoon, she pulled up the security footage of our front yard. We sat on the couch and watched it."

I reach to the nightstand and grab my water to ease the dryness in my throat. Before I continue, Jeremy places a hand on my knee, his thumb rubbing back and forth reassuringly. I stare at it as I finish telling him what happened.

"At three o'clock that morning, the footage showed me walking outside, onto the front porch. I climbed up on the thin porch railing and stood there. That's all I did at first. I just...stood there. For an hour, Jeremy. We watched the entire hour, waiting, hoping to see if the footage was broken because no one should be able to remain balanced for that long. It was unnatural, but I never moved. I never spoke any words. And then...I jumped. I must have hurt my wrist in the fall, but in the footage I showed no reaction. I pushed off the ground with both hands and then walked up the porch steps. You could see the blood already coming from my hand and dripping onto the porch, but my expression was dead. I walked straight back to my room and I fell asleep."

My eyes return to his. "I have no recollection of that. How can I inflict that much pain on myself and not be aware of it? How can I stand on a railing for an entire hour without swaying, not even a little bit? The video frightened me more than the injury did."

Again, he hugs me, and I am so grateful that I cling to him tightly. "My mother sent me away for a two-week psychiatric evaluation after that," I say into his chest. "When I returned home, she had moved farther down the hall, into a spare bedroom where she placed three locks on the inside of her bedroom door. My own mother was terrified of me."

Jeremy buries his face in my hair and sighs heavily. "I'm sorry that happened to you."

I squeeze my eyes shut.

"And I'm sorry your mother didn't know how to handle it. That had to have been hard for you."

Everything about him is exactly what I needed tonight. His voice is calm and caring, and his arms are protective, and his presence is comforting. I don't want him to let go of me. I don't want to think about waking up in Verity's bed. I don't want to think about how much I don't trust my own mind in my sleep, and even when I'm awake.

"We can talk more tomorrow," he says, releasing me. "I'll try to come up with a plan to make you feel more comfortable. But for now, just try to get some sleep, okay?"

He squeezes my hands reassuringly and then goes to the door. I feel panicked by the thought of him leaving me alone in here. Of going back to sleep. "What do I do about the rest of tonight? Just lock my door?"

Jeremy looks at the alarm clock. It's ten minutes to five. He stares at the clock for a moment and then walks back to me. "Lie down," he says, lifting the covers. I crawl into the bed and he scoots in behind me.

He wraps his arm around me, tucking my head under his chin. "It's almost five, I won't go back to sleep. But I'll stay until you do."

He's not rubbing my back or soothing me in any way. If anything, the arm that's holding me is stiff, like he doesn't want me to misconstrue our position on this bed in any way. But even with how uncomfortable he is right now, I appreciate he's making an effort to make *me* comfortable.

I try to close my eyes and sleep, but all I see is Verity. All I hear is the sound of her bed upstairs, moving.

It's after six when he assumes I'm asleep. His arm moves and his fingers end up in my hair for a moment. It's quick, as quick as the kiss he plants on the side of my head, but his actions linger long after he leaves the bedroom and closes the door.

14

I never fell back asleep, which is why I'm pouring my second cup of coffee and it's just after eight in the morning.

I stand at the sink, staring out the window. It started raining around five o'clock this morning while I was in my bed with Jeremy, pretending to be asleep.

April's car pulls up into the muddy drive as I'm staring out the window. *I wonder if Jeremy will tell her what happened.*

I haven't seen him this morning. I assume he's upstairs, where he usually remains until April arrives. I don't want to be in the kitchen when April walks in, so I turn to head toward my office. I unexpectedly bump into Jeremy, but he cushions the blow by taking a step back and grabbing my shoulders. Thank goodness because it saves my precious coffee from spilling.

He looks tired, but I can't judge him for that since it's my fault. "Good morning," he says it like it's anything but.

"Morning." I'm whispering. I don't know why.

He moves so that he's right next to me, leaning in as if to shield anyone from hearing what he's about to say. "How would you feel if I put a lock on your bedroom door?"

His question confuses me. "You already did."

"On the *outside* of the door," he clarifies.

Oh.

"I can lock it after you go to sleep. Open it before you wake up. If you ever need out, you can text me, call me, and I'll open it in two seconds. But I think you'll sleep better, knowing you can't leave the room."

I'm not sure how I feel about that. I don't know why it feels more drastic than a lock on the inside of the door, when they'd both be used for the same purpose: to keep me in my room. Even though the thought of it makes me uncomfortable, I'd be *more* uncomfortable knowing I could possibly get out of the room again. "I'd like that. Thank you."

April enters the house, pausing when she passes the kitchen. Jeremy is still looking at me, ignoring her presence. "I feel like you need to take a break today."

I look away from April, back to Jeremy. "I'd rather stay busy."

He regards me for a silent moment before nodding in understanding.

"Good *morning*," April says, kicking her muddy shoes off at the door.

"Morning, April." Jeremy says it so casually, as if he has nothing to hide. He walks past her, toward the back door. She doesn't move. She stares at me with her glasses at the tip of her nose.

"Morning, April." I don't look as innocent as Jeremy. I head back to Verity's office and start my day, despite not being able to get over what happened last night.

I spend the morning online, catching up on emails. Corey has forwarded a few interviews, something that's never been requested of me. A lot of the questions are similar, wanting to know why Verity hired me, what I plan to bring to the table, how my past experience has put me in the position to write for her. I copy and paste a lot of the answers.

After lunch, I focus on developing an outline for the seventh book. I've given up on finding one, so I work on building the novel from scratch. It's hard because I'm exhausted from last night. I'm unsettled. But I try not to think about last night.

It's afternoon when I smell tacos. It makes me smile, knowing he's making them because I requested them. I'm sure he'll save me a plate like he always does. I'm just not in a position where I feel comfortable eating dinner with them when April has Verity at the table.

I spend the next several minutes thinking about Verity, wondering why I'm so scared of her. I stare down at the drawer that contains her manuscript. *One more chapter and I'll stop. That's it.*

Chapter Six

It had been six months since they were born, and I still wished they didn't exist.

But they did, and Jeremy loved them. So I tried. Sometimes I wondered if it was worth it. Sometimes I wanted to pack my bags and leave and never look back. He was the only thing stopping me from going through with it. I knew a life without Jeremy was not a life I wanted to live. I had two options:

Live with him and the two girls he loved more than me.

Live without him.

They were a package deal at that point. I hate myself for not using birth control. For thinking I could do this and everything would be alright. Everything was not alright. Not with me anyway. It was like my family existed in a snow globe. Inside, everything was cozy and perfect, but I wasn't a part of them; I was just an outsider looking in.

It was snowing outside that night, but the apartment was warm. Even still, I woke up with chills. Or *tremors*, really. I couldn't stop shaking. The nightmare I'd had was so vivid, I felt the effects of it for hours after I woke up. A nightmare hangover.

I dreamt of the future, of the girls and Jeremy and me. They were eight or nine years old. I wasn't sure because I didn't know a lot about kids and what they look like at each stage. I just remember waking up and *feeling* like they were eight or nine.

In the dream, I was walking by their bedroom. I peeked inside and couldn't understand what I was seeing. Harper was on top of Chastin, covering her head with a pillow. I rushed over to the bed, terrified that it was too late. I pushed Harper off her sister and pulled the pillow away. I looked down at Chastin and then slapped my hand over my mouth with a gasp.

There was nothing there. The front of Chastin's face was smooth, like the back of a bald head. No scar. No eyes, no mouth. Nothing to smother.

I glanced at Harper, taking in her sinister expression. "What did you *do*?"

And then I woke up.

My reaction wasn't to the dream. It was to how much it felt like a premonition. And how much it gutted me.

I hugged my knees, rocking back and forth on the bed, wondering what this feeling was. Pain. It was pain. And... *heartache*.

I had felt heartache in my dream? When I thought Chastin was dead, I wanted to fall to my knees and weep. It's exactly how I felt when I thought of the possibility of Jeremy dying. I would lose all function.

I sat there and cried, the feeling was so overwhelming. Had I finally connected to them? To Chastin, at least? Was this what it felt like to be a mother? To love something so much, the thought of it being ripped away from you causes physical pain?

It was the most I had ever felt since the girls had been conceived. Even if I only felt it for one of them, it still counted for something.

Jeremy rolled over in the bed. He opened his eyes and saw me sitting up, hugging my knees. "You okay?"

I didn't want him to ask me that because Jeremy was good at getting my thoughts out. Most of them, anyway. I didn't want him to know this one. How could I admit that I'd finally fallen in love with one of our daughters without also admitting I had never loved either of them to begin with?

I had to do something. Preoccupy him so he wouldn't ask too many questions. I knew from experience that Jeremy couldn't get the truth out of me if I had his dick in my mouth.

I crawled down him, and by the time I was positioned over him, my mouth ready to work, he was already hard. I took as much of him as I could take.

I loved it when he moaned. He was a quiet lover, but sometimes, when I really caught him off guard, he wasn't so quiet. In that moment, he was euphoric. And I wondered, before I came along, how many other women had coaxed noises out of him? How many other pairs of lips had been wrapped around his dick?

I let him slide out of my mouth. "How many women have sucked your dick?"

He lifted up onto his elbows and looked down at me, perplexed. "Are you serious?"

"More like curious."

He laughed, dropping his head back to the pillow. "I don't know. I've never counted."

"That many?" I teased. I climbed up his body and straddled him. I liked it when he jerked beneath me and gripped my thighs. "If it's not an immediate answer, that means it's more than five."

"Definitely more than five," he said.

"More than ten?"

"Maybe. Possibly. *Yes.*"

It's odd how *that* didn't make me jealous, but two infants could leave me seething. Maybe it was because the girls were currently in his life, but all his past whores were just that...in the past.

"More than *twenty*?"

He raised his hands to my breasts and cupped them. Squeezed them. He was getting that look on his face that was my cue I was about to be fucked. Hard. "That's probably a good estimate," he whispered, pulling me to him. He brought his lips close to mine and stuck a hand between us, rubbing me. "How many guys have licked your pussy?"

"Two. I'm not a whore like you."

He laughed against my lips and then rolled me onto my back. "But you're in *love* with a whore."

"A *former* whore," I clarified.

I had been wrong about the look he had gotten in his eye. He didn't fuck me that night. He made love to me. Kissed every inch of my body. Made me lie still while he teased me and tortured me, when all I wanted to do was suck his dick. Every time I tried to move, to take over, he would stop me.

I don't know why I got so much pleasure out of pleasing him, but I liked it more than being pleased. That's probably defined in the love languages or some bullshit. My love language was acts of service. Jeremy's love language was getting his dick sucked. We were a perfect match.

He was moments from climax when one of the girls started crying. He groaned, and I rolled my eyes, and we both reached for the monitor. Him to look at them. Me to turn it off.

I could feel him growing softer inside me, so I pulled the plug out of the back of the monitor. We could still hear the cries coming from down the hallway, but I was certain I could drown them out if he'd just resume where we left off.

"I'll go check," he said, trying to roll off me. I pulled him back to the bed and climbed on top of him.

"I'll go when you finish. Let her cry for a few minutes. It's good for them."

He didn't seem comfortable with that, but once my mouth was back on his dick, he accepted it.

I'd gotten so much better at swallowing compared to the first time I attempted it. I could feel him ready to come, so I pretended I was gagging. I don't know why, but that always set him off, thinking I was choking on his cock. *Men*. He groaned, and I forced him farther down my throat with another gurgling sound, and then it was over. I swallowed, wiped my mouth, and then stood up. "Go to sleep. I can deal with it."

I actually *wanted* to deal with it this time. It was the first time I'd ever felt anything other than irritation at the thought of having to feed them. But I wanted to feed Chastin. Hold her, cuddle her, love her. I was excited when I approached their bedroom.

But that excitement turned to irritation as soon as I saw that it was Harper who was crying.

How disappointing.

Their cribs were head to head, and I was surprised Chastin was sleeping through Harper's screams. I walked past Harper and looked down at Chastin.

It hurt how much I felt for her in that moment. It hurt how much I wanted Harper to shut up.

I lifted Chastin out of her crib and carried her to the rocking chair. When I sat down with her, she stirred in my arms. I thought about my dream and how terrified I was to see Harper trying to hurt her. I thought I might cry just from the thought of losing her someday. At the thought of it all one day possibly coming true.

Maybe what I felt was mother's intuition. Maybe, deep down, I knew something terrible was going to happen to Chastin, and that's why I had been given that immense and sudden love for her. What if it was the universe's way of telling me to love that baby girl as much and as hard as I possibly could, because I wouldn't have her for as long as I would have Harper?

Maybe that was why I felt nothing for Harper yet. Because Chastin was the one whose life was going to be cut short. She would die, and then Harper would be the only one left.

I knew, somewhere inside me, I must have been burying the love I had for Harper. Saving it for after my time with Chastin.

I squeezed my eyes shut, getting a headache from Harper's screaming. *Shut the fuck up! Crying, crying, crying! I'm trying to bond with my baby!*

I tried to ignore it for a few more minutes, but I was afraid it would concern Jeremy. I eventually put Chastin back in her bed, surprised she was still asleep. *She really is a good baby.* I moved to Harper's crib and looked down at her, filling with anger. It somehow felt like her fault that I'd had the dream.

Maybe I was misinterpreting my dream. Maybe it wasn't a premonition. Maybe it was a *warning*. If I didn't do something about Harper before it was too late, Chastin would die.

I suddenly had this overwhelming urge to rectify what I knew was going to happen. Never in all my life had a dream been that vivid to me. I felt if I didn't do something about it in that moment, it would come true any day. For the first time, I couldn't bear the thought of losing Chastin. It hurt almost as much as the thought of losing Jeremy.

I didn't know anything about ending a life, much less the life of an infant. The one time I'd tried, it resulted in nothing more than a scratch. But I'd heard of SIDS. Jeremy had made me read about it. It's not uncommon, but I didn't know enough about it to know if they would be able to tell a difference between suffocation and SIDS.

I'd heard of people choking in their sleep on their own vomit, though. That would probably be harder to declare an intentional act.

I touched my finger to Harper's lips. Her head moved back and forth quickly, thinking it was a bottle. She latched on and began sucking the tip of my finger, but she wasn't satisfied. She released my finger and started screaming again. Kicking. I shoved my finger farther into her mouth.

She was still crying, so I continued to shove. She made a gasping sound, but was somehow still crying. *Maybe one finger wasn't enough.*

I pushed two fingers into her mouth and throat, until my knuckles were pressed against her gums and she was no longer crying. I watched her for a moment, and soon, her arms began to stiffen between each violent jerk of her little body. Her legs locked up.

This is what she would have done to her sister if I hadn't done it to her first. I'm saving Chastin's life.

"She okay?" Jeremy asked.

Fuck. Fuck, fuck, fuck.

I pulled my fingers out of Harper's mouth and picked her up, pressing her face into my chest so Jeremy couldn't hear her gasping for air. "I don't know," I said, turning to him. He was making his way across the room. My voice was frantic. "I can't make her happy. I've tried everything." I was petting the back of her head, attempting to show him how concerned I was.

That's when she puked on me. As soon as she puked, she screamed. *Wailed.* Her voice sounded hoarse, and she was gasping between screams. It was a cry like neither of us had ever heard before. Jeremy quickly grabbed her, pulling her from me so he could try to soothe her.

He didn't even care that she had puked on me. He didn't even look up at me. He was full of concern, his eyebrows drawn together, his forehead wrinkled as he inspected her. But out of all that concern he held, none of it was for me. It was only pointed in Harper's direction.

I held my breath and walked straight to the bathroom, afraid to breathe in the smell. It was the one thing I hated most about being a mother. All the *fucking* vomit.

While I was in the bathroom, Jeremy made Harper a bottle. By the time I got out of the shower, she'd already fallen back to sleep. He was in our bed, plugging the video monitor back in.

I froze as I was climbing into bed. I stared at the video monitor, at the perfect view right into Harper and Chastin's cribs.

How did I forget the fucking monitor?

If he had seen what I was doing to Harper, he would have ended it with me.

How could I have been so careless?

I slept very little that night, wondering what Jeremy would have done to me had he caught me trying to save Chastin from her sister.

15

Oh, my God. I double over in my chair, clutching my stomach. "Please...please..." I say out loud. Though I don't know why or to whom I'm saying it.

I need to get out of this house. I feel like I can't breathe. I should go sit outside and attempt to clear my head of everything I just read.

Every time I'm reading her manuscript, my stomach cramps from all the time I spend clenching it. I skimmed several more chapters beyond chapter five, but none were as horrifying as the chapter that detailed how she tried to choke her infant daughter.

In the subsequent chapters, Verity focused mainly on Jeremy and Chastin, rarely mentioning Harper at all, which grew more disturbing with each paragraph. She talked about the day Chastin turned one, and she talked about when Chastin spent the night at Jeremy's mother's house for the first time at the age of two. Everything that had initially been "the twins" in her manuscript eventually dwindled down to just "Chastin." If I didn't know any better, I would think something had happened to Harper long before it did.

It wasn't until the girls were three that she wrote about both of them again. But as soon as I start the chapter, there's a sharp rapping on the office door.

I open the desk drawer and quickly shove the manuscript inside it. "Come in."

When he opens the door, I have one hand on the mouse and the other resting casually in my lap.

"I made tacos."

I smile at him. "Is it time to eat already?"

He laughs. "It's after ten. It was time to eat three hours ago."

I look at the clock on the computer. How did I lose track of time? *I guess that happens when you're reading about a psychotic woman abusing her children.* "I thought it was eight."

"You've been in here for twelve hours," he says. "Take a break. There's a meteor shower tonight, you need to eat, and I made you a margarita."

Margaritas and tacos. *Doesn't take much.*

•••

I ate on the back porch while we sat in rocking chairs and watched the meteor shower. There weren't very many at first, but now we're seeing one every minute, at least.

At one point, I moved from the porch to the yard. I'm on my back in the grass, staring up at the sky. Jeremy finally gives in and positions himself next to me.

"I forgot what the sky looked like," I say quietly. "I've been in Manhattan for so long now."

"That's why I left New York," Jeremy says. He points to the left, at the tail end of a meteor. We watch it until it disappears.

"When did you and Verity buy this house?"

"When the girls were three. Verity's first two books had released by then and were doing really well, so we took the plunge."

"Why Vermont? Do either of you have family here?"

"No. My father died when I was in my teens. My mother died three years ago. But I grew up in New York State, on an alpaca farm, if you can believe that."

I laugh, turning to look at him. "Seriously? Alpacas?"

He nods.

"How, exactly, does one make money raising alpacas?"

Jeremy laughs at this question. "They don't, really. Which is why I got a degree in business and went into real estate. I didn't have any interest in taking over a debt-ridden farm."

"Do you think you'll go back to work soon?"

My question gives Jeremy pause. "I'd like to. I've been waiting on the right time so it won't be a huge adjustment to Crew, but it never feels like the right time."

If we were friends, I would do something to comfort him. Maybe grab his hand and hold it. But there's too much inside me that wants to be more than his friend, which means we can't be friends at all. If an attraction is present between two people, those two people can only be one of two things. Involved or not involved. There is no in-between.

And since he's married...I keep my hand on my chest and I don't touch him at all.

"What about Verity's parents?" I ask, needing the conversation to keep flowing so that he doesn't hear how exaggerated he makes my every breath.

He lifts his hands from his chest in an I-don't-know gesture. "I barely know them. They weren't around much before they cut Verity out of their lives."

"They cut her out? Why?"

"It's hard to explain them," he says. "They're strange. Victor and Marjorie, insanely religious to their core. When they found out Verity was writing thriller and suspense novels, they acted like she was suddenly denouncing her religion to join a satanic cult. They told her if she didn't stop, they would never speak to her again."

That's unbelievable. So...*cold*. For a second, I empathize with Verity, wondering if her lack of maternal instinct was inherited. But my empathy evaporates when I remember what she did to Harper in her crib.

"How long did their estrangement last?"

"Let's see," Jeremy says. "She wrote her first book over a decade ago. So...more than years."

"They still haven't spoken to her? Do they even know about what's happened?"

Jeremy nods. "I called them after Chastin passed. Left them a voicemail. They never called back. Then, when Verity had her wreck, her father actually answered the phone. When I told him what had happened, to the girls and to Verity, he grew quiet. Then said, 'God punishes the wicked, Jeremy.' I hung up on him. Haven't heard from them since."

I pull a hand to my heart and stare up at the sky in disbelief. "Wow."

"Yeah," he whispers.

We're quiet for a stretch. We see two meteors, one to the south and one to the east. Jeremy points at them both times, but says nothing. When there's a lull in both the conversation and the meteors, Jeremy lifts up beside me, onto his elbow, and looks down at me.

"Do you think I should put Crew back into therapy?"

I tilt my head so that I'm staring at him. We're only a foot apart with him positioned like this. Maybe a foot and a half. It's so close, I can feel the heat coming from him.

"Yes."

He seems to appreciate my honesty. "Alright," he says, but he doesn't lower himself back to the grass. He continues to stare at me, as if he wants to ask me something else. "Did you go to therapy?"

"Yes. It was the best thing that ever happened to me." I look back up at the sky, not wanting to see the expression on his face after my next sentence. "After watching the footage of myself on that railing, I was worried that deep down, it meant I wanted to die. For weeks I tried to fight my sleep. I was afraid I'd hurt myself intentionally. But my therapist helped me realize that sleepwalking is unrelated to intention. And after several years of being told that, I finally believed it."

"Did your mother go to therapy with you?"

I laugh. "No. She didn't even want to talk to me about my own therapy. Something happened that night, when I broke my wrist, and it changed her. Our relationship, anyway. We always felt disconnected after that. My mother actually reminds me a lot of—" I stop speaking because I realize I was about to say *Verity*.

"Reminds you of who?"

"The main character in Verity's series."

"Is that bad?" he asks.

I laugh. "You really haven't read any of them?"

He lies back down on the grass, breaking eye contact with me. "Just the first one."

"Why'd you stop?"

"Because...it was hard for me to fathom that it all came from her imagination."

I want to tell him he's right to be concerned, because his wife's thoughts are eerily similar to her character's thoughts. But I don't want him to have that impression of her at this point. After all he's been through, he deserves to at least be able to preserve a positive memory of his marriage.

"She used to get so angry with me because I didn't read her manuscripts. She needed that validation from me, even though she got it from everywhere else. Her readers, her editor, her critics. For some reason, my validation seemed to be the only validation she wanted."

Because she was obsessed with you.

"Where do you get your validation?" he asks.

I turn my head toward him again. "I don't, really. My books aren't popular. When I do receive a positive review or get an email from a fan, I never feel like they're talking to me. Probably because I'm such a recluse and never do signings. I don't put my image out there, so even though there are readers who love what I do, I still haven't had the experience of being told to my face that what I do matters to someone." I sigh. "That would feel good, I imagine. For someone to look me in the eye and say, 'Your writing matters to me, Lowen.'"

As soon as I finish that sentence, a meteor shoots across the sky. We both follow it and watch as it streaks across the water, reflecting in the lake. I stare at the lake, framing Jeremy's head.

"When are you going to start on the new dock?" I ask him. He finally finished tearing the old one down completely today.

"I'm not building a new dock," he says, matter-of-fact. "I just got sick of looking at that one."

I would make him expand more on that, but he doesn't seem to want to.

He's watching me. Even though Jeremy and I have been making eye contact a lot tonight, it feels different in this moment. Heavier. I notice his eyes flicker toward my lips. I want him to kiss me. If he tried, I wouldn't stop him. I'm not even sure I would feel guilty.

He sighs heavily and lets his head roll back in the grass until he's looking at the stars again.

"What are you thinking?" I whisper.

"I'm thinking it's late. And I should probably lock you in your room now."

I laugh at his choice of words. Or maybe I laugh because I've had two margaritas. Whatever the reason, my laugh makes *him* laugh. And what almost became a moment he'd probably end up regretting turns into a moment full of relief.

I go to the office to grab the laptop so I can work in the bedroom after he goes to sleep. When he's turning out the lights in the kitchen, I open the desk drawer and grab a small handful of the manuscript to take to my room with me. I tuck the pages between the laptop and my chest.

There's a new lock on the outside of the bedroom door that I haven't seen. I don't want to examine it or figure out if it could somehow be unlocked from the inside, because I'm sure my subconscious would remember that, and I would somehow get past it.

Jeremy is behind me as I walk into the room and set my things on the bed.

"You have everything you need?" he asks from the doorway.

"Yep." I walk back to the door so I can lock it from the inside after I shut it.

"Alright, then. Goodnight."

"Alright," I repeat with a smile. "Goodnight."

I go to shut the door, but he puts his hand up, stopping me from closing it all the way. I pull it open again, and in the split second since I almost closed it, his expression has changed.

"Low," he says, his voice quiet. He leans his head against the doorframe and looks down at me. "I lied to you."

I try not to look too concerned, but I am. His words rush through me, and I think back to our conversation tonight, the conversations that came before it. "You lied about what?"

"Verity never read your book."

I want to take a step back, to mask my disappointment in the darkness. But I stay put, squeezing the doorknob with my left hand. "Why would you say that if it wasn't true?"

He closes his eyes for a brief moment while inhaling. When he opens them, he stands up straight through his exhale. He raises his arms and grips the top of the doorframe. "I'm the one who read your book. And it was good. *Phenomenal.* Which is why I suggested your name to her editor." He lowers his head a little, looking me firmly in the eye. "Your writing matters to me, Lowen."

He lowers his arms, grips the doorknob, and closes the door. I hear him latch the lock before his footsteps disappear upstairs.

I fall against the door, pressing my forehead against the wood.

And I smile, because for the first time in my career, someone outside of my agent has given me validation.

I cozy up in the bed with the chapter I brought with me. Jeremy made me feel so good just now, I don't even mind being a little disturbed by his wife before I fall asleep.

Chapter Nine

Chicken and dumplings.

It was the fifth meal I cooked after living in our new house for two weeks.

It's the only meal Jeremy ever threw against the dining room wall.

I'd known for several days that he was upset with me. I just didn't know why. We were still having sex almost every day, but even the sex felt different. Like he was disconnected. Fucking me because it was our routine and not because he craved me.

That's the reason I decided to cook the goddamn dumplings in the first place. I was trying to be nice by making one of his favorite meals. He was having a hard time adjusting to his new job. To make matters worse, he was upset with me for putting the girls in daycare without consulting him first.

Back in New York, we hired a nanny as soon as my books started selling. She would show up every morning when Jeremy left for work so that I could retreat to my office and write every day. Then she'd leave when Jeremy came home, and I'd come out of my office and we'd cook dinner together.

It was a great setup, I'll admit. I never had to care for them when Jeremy wasn't around because we had the nanny. But out here, in the middle of nowhere, nannies are hard to come by. I tried watching them myself the first two days, but that was beyond exhausting, and I wasn't getting any writing done. So, one morning last week, I was so fed up, I drove them into town and enrolled them into the first daycare I came across.

I knew Jeremy didn't like it, but he realized we had to do something if we both wanted to continue to work. I was more successful than he was, so if anyone was going to stay home and care for them during the day, it certainly wasn't going to be me.

But the girls being in daycare wasn't what was bothering him. He seemed to like the interaction they were getting with other children, because he couldn't shut up about it. But we had discovered a few months earlier that Chastin had a severe allergy to peanuts, so Jeremy was cautious. He didn't want anyone caring for her but us. He was afraid the daycare would be careless, even though Chastin was the kid I actually *liked*. I wasn't stupid. I made sure they knew all about her allergy.

Whatever it was that had him irritated with me, I was positive it was something a bowl of dumplings and a good fuck would help him forget.

I intentionally started dinner late that night so the girls would be in bed when we ate. They were only three, so luckily, they were tucked in by seven. It was almost eight when I set the table and called Jeremy to come and eat.

I tried to make it as romantic as possible, but it's hard to make chicken and dumplings sexy. I lit candles on the table and set up my playlist through the wireless speakers. I had on clothes, but underneath them, I was wearing lingerie. Something I didn't do often.

I tried to make small talk with him as we ate.

"I think Chastin is fully potty trained now," I said to him. "They've been working with her at daycare."

"That's good," Jeremy said, scrolling through his phone with one hand and eating with the other.

I waited a moment, hoping whatever it was on his phone would take a back seat to us. When it didn't, I adjusted myself in my seat and attempted to grab his attention again. I knew conversation about the girls was his favorite subject.

"When I picked them up today, the teacher said she's learned seven colors this week."

"Who?" he said, finally making eye contact with me.

"Chastin."

He stared at me, dropped his phone flat on the table, and took another bite.

What the fuck is his problem?

I could see the anger he was trying to stifle, and it made me nervous. Jeremy never got upset, and when he did, I almost always knew why he was. But this was different. It was coming out of left field.

I couldn't take it anymore. I sat back in my chair and dropped my napkin on the table. "Why are you mad at me?"

"I'm not mad." He said it too fast.

I laughed. "You're pathetic."

He narrowed his eyes and tilted his head. "*Excuse* me?"

I leaned forward. "Just *tell* me, Jeremy. Enough of this bullshit silent treatment. Be a man and tell me what your problem is."

His fists clenched and then unclenched. Then he stood up and slapped his bowl, sending it across the table and all over the dining room wall. I had never seen him lose his temper. I stiffened, wide-eyed, as he stomped out of the kitchen.

I heard him slam our bedroom door. I looked at the mess and knew I'd have to clean it up after we made up so he'd know how much I appreciated him. *Even if he was being a major fucking douche.*

I shoved my chair under the table and walked to the bedroom. He was pacing back and forth. When I closed the door behind me, he looked up and paused. He was trying so hard in that moment to put his words in order— everything he needed to say to me. As angry as I was at him for throwing the meal I had worked so hard making for him, I felt bad that he was upset.

"It's constant, Verity," he said. "You talk about her *constantly*. You never talk about Harper. You never tell me what Harper learned in school or how Harper's doing with potty training or all the cute things Harper said. It's Chastin, all the time, every day."

Shit. Even with how much I try to hide it, he still sees it. "That's not true," I said.

"It *is* true. And I've tried to keep my mouth shut, but they're getting older. Harper's going to notice that you treat them differently. It isn't fair to her."

I wasn't sure how to get out of that predicament. I could have gotten defensive, accused him of something I didn't like. But I knew he was right, so I needed to find a way to make him think he was wrong. Luckily, he turned away from me, so it gave me a moment to think. I looked up, like I was turning to God for advice. *Stupid, girl. God won't help you out of this one.*

I stepped forward, cautiously. "Baby. It's not that I like Chastin more. She's just...smarter than Harper. So she accomplishes things first."

He spins around, angrier than before I even opened my mouth. "Chastin isn't smarter than Harper. They're different. But Harper is very intelligent."

"I know that," I said, taking another step toward him. I kept my voice low. Sweet. Unoffended. "That's not what I meant. I meant...it's easier for me to have a reaction to what Chastin does because Chastin likes that. She's animated, like me. Harper isn't. I give her silent affirmation. I don't make a show of it. She's like you in that way."

His stare was unwavering, but I was almost certain he was buying it, so I continued.

"I don't push Harper when she's in those moods, so yes, I do talk about Chastin more. Sometimes I focus on her more. But only because I realize they're two different children with two different sets of needs. I have to be two different mothers to each of them."

I was good at spewing bullshit. It's why I became a writer.

Jeremy's anger was slowly melting away. His jaw wasn't as tense as he ran a hand through his hair, taking in what I had just said. "I worry about Harper," he said. "More than I should, I'm sure. I don't think treating them differently is the right thing to do going forward. Harper might notice the difference."

A month earlier, one of the daycare workers had expressed concern to me about Harper. It wasn't until that moment—when Jeremy was expressing his concern for her—that I remembered her mentioning it to me. She said she thinks we should have her tested for Asperger's. I had forgotten all about it until that moment during my fight with Jeremy. And thank God I remembered because it was the perfect way to back up my defense.

"I wasn't going to mention this because I didn't want you to worry," I said to him. "But one of their daycare teachers told me she thinks we should have Harper tested for Asperger's."

Jeremy's concern grew tenfold in that moment. I tried to subdue that concern as quickly as possible.

"I've called a specialist already." *At least I* will *put a call in tomorrow.* "They're going to call back when they have an opening."

Jeremy pulled out his phone, becoming sidetracked by the potential diagnosis. "They think Harper is on the autism spectrum?"

I took his phone from his hands.

"Don't. You'll worry yourself sick until the appointment. Let's speak to the specialist first because the internet isn't the place we need to seek out answers for our daughter."

He nodded and then pulled me in for a hug. "I'm sorry," he whispered against the side of my head. "It's been a shitty week. I lost a big client at work today."

"You don't have to work, Jeremy. I make enough money for you to spend more time at home with the girls if that would make it easier."

"I would go insane if I didn't work."

"Maybe so, but it's going to be really expensive putting three kids through daycare."

"We can afford..." He paused, pulling back. "Did you say...*three*?"

I nodded. I was lying, of course, but I wanted the mood of the night to disappear. I wanted him to be happy. And he was so happy after I told him I was pregnant again.

"Are you sure? I thought you didn't want more."

"I was sloppy with the pill a couple of weeks ago. It's still early. Really early. I found out this morning." I smiled. Then I smiled even bigger.

"You're happy about it?"

"Of course I am. Are you?"

He laughed a little, then he kissed me, and *all was back to normal. Thank God.*

I gripped his shirt in my fist and kissed him back with everything in me, wanting him to forget all about the fight we were having. He could tell by my kiss that I wanted more than just a kiss. He took off my shirt, then took off his own. He kissed me as he backed up to the bed. When he removed my pants, he saw the bra and panties I had put on for him.

"You're wearing lingerie?" he asked. He dropped his head into my neck. "And you made my favorite meal," he said, disappointed. I wasn't sure why he sounded disappointed until he pulled back, brushed hair from my face, and said, "I am so sorry, Verity. You were trying to make tonight special and I ruined it for you."

What he doesn't understand is that he could never ruin a night for me when it ends with him loving *me*. Focusing on *me*.

I shook my head. "You didn't ruin it."

"I did. I threw my food, I yelled at you." He brought his mouth to mine. "I'll make it up to you."

And he did. He fucked me slowly, kissing me the whole time, taking turns with each nipple as he sucked them. Had I breastfed, would he be enjoying my breasts as much?

I doubted it. Even after twins, my body was nearly perfect. Aside from the scar on my abdomen, the most important parts of me were still intact. Still fairly firm. And Jeremy's temple between my legs was still nice and tight.

When he had me close to the edge, he pulled out of me. "I want to taste you," he said, moving down my body until his tongue was spreading me apart.

Of course you want to taste me, I thought. *I kept things in tact for you down there. You're welcome.*

He stayed between my legs until I came for him. Twice. When he began to crawl back up my body, he paused at my stomach and kissed me there. Then he was inside of me again, his mouth on mine. "I love you," he whispered between kisses. "Thank you."

He was thanking me for being pregnant.

He made love to me with so much care, with so much compassion. It was almost worth faking the pregnancy just to have him love me like that again. To get our connection back.

If there was one good thing the girls brought to our life, it was that Jeremy seemed to love me the most when I was pregnant. Now that he thought I was about to give him a third child, I could already feel his love multiplying again.

There was a small part of me that was concerned about faking the pregnancy, but I knew I had options if I didn't get pregnant that week. Miscarriages were just as easy to fake as pregnancies.

16

It's been another week of reading Verity's manuscript, and I'm bored. I'm finding it repetitive. Chapter after chapter of detailed sex with Jeremy. Very little to do with her children. She wrote two paragraphs about Crew's birth, but then went on to talk about the first time they were able to fuck after Crew was born.

It got to a point where I started feeling jealous. I don't like reading about Jeremy's sex life. I skimmed a chapter this morning, but finally tossed it aside to get back to work. I finished the outline for the first book today and submitted it to Corey for feedback. He said he'd forward it to the editor at Pantem, because he still hasn't read any of Verity's books and wouldn't know if the outline is sufficient. Until I hear back from them, I don't really want to start on the second outline. If they come back wanting changes, it will have been work wasted.

I've been here almost two weeks now. Corey says they processed my advance and it should hit my account any day now. Once I get the feedback from Pantem, it'll likely be time for me to move on. I've done all I can do in Verity's office. If it weren't for not having anywhere to go until that money hits my account, I'd have already left.

I hit a wall today. I'm burnt out from working so much these past two weeks. And I could read more of Verity's autobiography, but I'm really not in the mood to read about all the ways Verity can suck her husband's dick.

I miss television. I haven't stepped foot in their living room since I arrived here almost two weeks ago. I leave the confines of Verity's office and make myself a bag of popcorn, then sit on the living room sofa and turn on the television. I deserve to be a little lazy because tomorrow is my birthday, but I'm not planning on telling Jeremy that.

I keep glancing at the top of the stairs because I have the perfect view of it from the couch, but Jeremy is nowhere. I haven't seen much of him over the last couple of days. I think we both know how close we came to kissing the other night, and how inappropriate that would have been, so we've been avoiding each other.

I turn the channel to HGTV and settle into the couch. I've watched about fifteen minutes of a house remodel when I finally hear Jeremy coming down the stairs. He pauses mid-step when he sees me in the living room. Then he descends the rest of the stairs and makes his way over, joining me on the couch. He sits in the middle, close enough to reach over and grab a few pieces of my popcorn, but far enough away that we aren't in danger of touching.

"Research?" he says, propping his feet up on the coffee table in front of him.

I laugh. "Of course. Always working."

He grabs more popcorn this time, cupping some in his hand. "Verity would binge-watch TV when she had writer's block. She said it sometimes sparked new ideas."

I don't want to talk about Verity, so I change the subject. "I finished an outline today. If it gets approved tomorrow, I'll probably leave in a couple of days."

Jeremy stops chewing and looks at me. "Yeah?"

I like that he doesn't seem happy about the thought of me leaving. "Yes. And thanks for letting me stay longer than I should have."

He holds my stare. "Longer than you should have?" He starts chewing again and faces the television. "I don't think it's been long *enough*."

I don't know what he means by that. If he thinks I didn't do enough work while I was here, or if he's saying it selfishly, like he didn't get to spend enough time with me.

Sometimes, especially right now, I feel how much he's drawn to me, but then other times it seems like he works so hard to deny whatever attraction there might be between us. And I get that. I do. But is this how he's going to spend the rest of his life? Giving up huge parts of himself to care for a woman who is just a shell of the person he married?

I understand he made vows, but at what cost? His entire life? People get married assuming they'll live long, happy lives together. What happens when one of those is cut short, but the other is expected to live out those vows for the rest of their life?

It doesn't seem fair. I know if I were married and my husband were in Jeremy's predicament, I wouldn't want my husband to feel like he could never move on. But I'm not sure I'll ever be as obsessed with a man as Verity was with Jeremy.

The show ends and another one begins. Neither of us speaks for several minutes. It's not that I have nothing to say—I have a *lot* to say. I just don't know that it's my place.

"I don't know very much about you," Jeremy says. His head is against the back of the couch and he's looking at me, casually. "Have you ever been married?"

"Nope," I say. "Came close a couple of times, but it never worked out."

"How old are you?"

Of course, he would ask me that when my age will expire in just over an hour. "You wouldn't believe me if I told you."

Jeremy laughs. "Why wouldn't I?"

"Because I'll be thirty-two. *Tomorrow*."

"Liar."

"I'm not lying. I'll show you my driver's license."

"Good, because I don't believe you."

I roll my eyes and then go to the master bedroom to grab my purse. I bring back my driver's license and hand it to him.

He stares at it, shaking his head. "What a shitty birthday," he says. "Hanging out with people you barely know. Working all day."

I shrug. "If I wasn't here, I'd just be alone in my apartment."

He stares at my driver's license a moment longer. When he runs his thumb over my picture, I get actual chills. He didn't even touch me—he touched my fucking *driver's* license—and it turned me on.

I am pathetic.

He hands it back to me and stands up.

"Where are you going?"

"To make you a cake," he says, walking out of the living room.

I smile and then follow him to the kitchen. Jeremy Crawford baking a cake is something I don't want to miss.

•••

I'm sitting on the island in the middle of the kitchen, watching him put icing on the cake. In all the days I've been here, this is only the second time I've actually had fun. We haven't talked about Verity or our tragedies or the contract for the past hour. While the cake was baking, I sat on the bar, my legs dangling off the edge of it. Jeremy leaned against the counter in front of me and we talked about movies, music, our likes and dislikes.

We've actually started getting to know each other outside of everything that ties us together. He was relaxed the night we went out to dinner with Crew, but I haven't seen him this at ease inside these walls since I arrived.

I can almost—*almost*—understand Verity's addiction to him.

"Go back to the living room," he says as he pulls the candles from a drawer.

"Why?"

"Because. I have to walk in with your cake and sing you 'Happy Birthday.' Give you the full effect."

I roll my head and jump off the bar, then go back to the couch. I mute the television because I want to hear him singing me happy birthday without interruptions. I keep hitting the information button on the remote, checking the time. He's waiting for it to turn midnight to make it official.

Right when it hits midnight, I can see the flicker of candles as he makes his way around the corner. I laugh when he starts to sing quietly so he doesn't wake up Crew.

"Happy birthday to you," he whispers. He's cut a single slice of cake and stuck a candle in the top of it. "Happy birthday to you."

I'm still laughing when he reaches the couch, slowly kneeling down on it so he doesn't spill the cake or risk the candle being blown out when he sits next to me.

"Happy birthday, dear Lowen. Happy birthday to you."

We're facing each other on the couch so I can make a wish and blow out the candle, but I'm not sure what to wish for. I've been lucky enough to land a really great job. I'm about to get more money than I've ever had in my bank account at one time. The only thing in my life that I feel like I want right now that I don't have is *him*. I look him in the eye, then blow out the candle.

"What'd you wish for?"

"If I tell you, it won't come true."

The way he smiles at me seems heavily flirtatious. "Maybe you can tell me after it comes true."

He doesn't hand me the cake. He makes a show of it, slicing into it with a fork. "Do you know what the secret ingredient is to making such a moist cake?"

He holds out the fork and I take it from him. "What is it?"

"Pudding."

I take a bite of the cake and smile. "It's really good," I say with a mouthful.

"*Pudding*," he says again.

I laugh.

He holds the plate, and I take another bite, then offer him the fork. He shakes his head. "I had a bite in the kitchen."

I don't know why, but I wish I had seen that. I also wish I knew if he tasted like chocolate.

Jeremy lifts a hand. "You have icing on your..." He points at my mouth. I brush at it, but he shakes his head. "Right here." He slides his thumb across my bottom lip.

I swallow the bite of cake.

His thumb doesn't leave my lip. It lingers there.

Fuck. I can't breathe.

I'm aching everywhere because he's so close, but I don't know what I'm allowed to do about it. I want to drop my fork, I want him to drop the plate of cake, I want him to kiss me. But I'm not the married one here. I don't want to make the first move and he *shouldn't* make the first move, but I'm desperate for him.

He doesn't drop the cake. Instead, he leans across me and places it on the end table. In the same fluid movement, he brings his hand to my head and presses his lips to mine. Even after all the anticipation I've held for this moment, it still feels completely unexpected.

I close my eyes and drop the fork on the floor, leaning back into the arm of the couch. He follows me, crawling on top of me, our lips never disconnecting. I part my lips, and he sweeps his tongue inside my mouth. The slowness of the kiss doesn't last long. As soon as we get our first tastes of each other, the kiss becomes manic. It's everything I imagined kissing him would feel like. Radiation, explosives, dynamite. Anything and everything dangerous.

We taste like chocolate as we trade kisses, back and forth, push and pull. His hand is tangled in my hair, and with every second this kiss continues, we become infused with the couch beneath us, him relaxing into me as I melt into the cushions.

His mouth leaves mine in search of other parts of me he seems eager to taste. My jaw, my neck, the tops of my breasts. It's as if he's been starving himself of me. He's kissing me and touching me with the hunger of a man who's been fasting his whole life.

His hand is sliding up my shirt and his fingers are warm, trickling over my skin like drops of hot water.

He's back at my mouth, but only momentarily. Long enough to find my tongue before he pulls back and takes off his shirt. My hands go to his chest like they belong there, pressed against the curves of his abdomen. I want to tell him this is what I wished for when I blew out my candle, but I'm afraid any conversation will lead him to think about what we're doing and how we shouldn't be doing it, so I remain quiet.

I lean my head back against the arm of the couch, wanting him to explore even more of me.

He does. He pulls off my shirt and sees that I'm not wearing a bra beneath my pajamas. He groans, and it's beautiful, and then he takes my nipple into his mouth, forcing a whimper to escape my lips.

I lift my head to watch him, but my blood runs cold when my eyes are pulled to the figure standing at the top of the stairs. She's just standing there, watching her husband as his mouth roams over my breast.

My entire body stiffens beneath Jeremy.

Verity's fists clench at her sides before she rushes back in the direction of her room.

I gasp, shoving him, pushing him. "Verity," I say, breathless. He stops kissing me and then lifts his head, but he doesn't move. "Verity," I say again, wanting him to understand that he needs to get the fuck off me.

He lifts up onto his arms, confused.

"Verity!" I say again, but with more urgency. It's all I can say. My fear has taken hold of me and I struggle to inhale, to exhale.

What the fuck?

Jeremy is on his knees now, gripping the back of the couch as he moves away. "I'm sorry."

I pull my knees up and scoot to the far end of the couch, away from him. I cover my mouth. "Oh, God." The words crash against my trembling fingers.

He tries to touch my arm reassuringly, but I flinch. "I'm sorry," he says again. "I shouldn't have kissed you."

I'm shaking my head because he doesn't understand. He thinks I'm upset and feel guilty that he's married, but I *saw* her. Standing. She was *standing*. I point to the top of the stairs. "I saw her." I whisper it, quietly, because I'm terrified to say it louder. "She was standing at the top of the stairs."

I can see the confusion cross his face as he turns to look at the stairs. He looks back at me. "She can't *walk*, Lowen."

I'm not crazy. I stand up and back away from the couch, covering my bare chest with my arm. I point at the stairs again, finding my voice this time. "Your fucking wife was standing at the top of the fucking *stairs*, Jeremy! I know what I saw!"

He sees in my eyes that I'm telling the truth. Two seconds pass before he's off the couch and running up the stairs, toward her bedroom.

He's not leaving me down here alone.

I grab my shirt, pull it on over my head, and then run after him. I refuse to be alone in this house for another second.

When I reach the top of the stairs, he's standing in her doorway, staring into her room. He hears me approaching. And then he just...leaves. He brushes past me without making eye contact and stomps down the stairs.

I take several steps until I'm close enough to peek into her room. I only glance in there for one second. It's all the time I need to see that she's in bed. Under the covers. *Asleep*.

I shake my head, feeling my knees wanting to buckle. *This can't be happening.* I somehow make it to the stairs, but I only make it halfway down them before I have to sit. I can't move. I can barely draw a breath. My heart has never beat this fast.

Jeremy is at the bottom of the stairs, looking up at me. He probably doesn't know what to think about what just happened. *I* don't know what to think. He walks back and forth in front of the stairs, looking at me every now and then, I'm sure because he's waiting for me to start laughing at my tasteless joke. *It wasn't a joke.*

"I saw her," I whisper.

He hears me. He looks at me, not with anger, but with apology. He walks up the stairs and helps me up, then keeps his arm around me as he leads me back down. He takes me to the bedroom and closes the door, then wraps himself around me. I bury my face in his neck, wanting the image of her out of my head. "I'm sorry," I tell him. "I just... Maybe I haven't been getting enough sleep... Maybe I..."

"It's my fault," Jeremy says, interrupting me. "You've been working for two weeks without a break. You're exhausted. And then I—*we*—it's paranoia. Guilt. I don't know." He pulls back, holding my face with both hands. "I think we both need about twelve hours of solid sleep."

I'm convinced by what I saw. We can blame it on exhaustion or guilt, but I saw her. I saw everything. Her fists clenched at her sides. The anger in her expression before she rushed away.

"Do you want some water?"

I shake my head. I don't want him to leave. I don't want to be alone. "Please don't leave me alone tonight," I beg.

His expression doesn't reveal what he's thinking at all. He nods, just a little, then says, "I won't. But I need to turn off the TV and lock the doors. Put the cake in the fridge." He heads for the door. "I'll be back in a few minutes."

I go to the bathroom and wash my face, hoping the cold water will help calm me. It doesn't. When I return to the bedroom, Jeremy is sliding the lock across the top of the door. "I can't stay all night," he says. "I don't want Crew to get scared if he wakes up and can't find me."

I climb into the bed and face the window. Jeremy climbs in behind me, then wraps himself around me. I can feel his heartbeat, and it's almost as fast as mine. He shares the pillow with me, finds my hand, and slides his fingers through mine.

I try to mimic his pattern of breathing so that mine will slow down. I'm breathing through my nose because my jaw is clamped too tight to take in normal breaths. Jeremy presses a kiss to the side of my head.

"Relax," he whispers. "You're okay."

I try to relax. And maybe I do, but it's only because we both lie here for so long, it's hard for muscles to retain that much tension after a while. "Jeremy?" I whisper.

He runs a thumb across my hand to let me know he hears me.

"Is there a chance... Could she be faking her injuries?"

He doesn't answer right away. Almost as if he has to give the question some thought. "No," he finally says. "I saw the scans."

"But people get better. Injuries heal."

"I know," he says. "But Verity wouldn't fake something like this. No one would. It would be impossible."

I close my eyes, because he's trying to reassure me that he knows her well enough to know that she wouldn't do something like that. But if there's one thing I know that Jeremy doesn't...it's that he doesn't know Verity at *all*.

17

I went to bed convinced I had seen Verity at the top of the stairs last night.

I woke up full of doubt.

I've spent most of my life not trusting myself in my sleep. Now I'm starting to not trust myself when I'm awake. *Did I see her? Was it a hallucination because of stress? Did I feel guilty for being with her husband?*

I lay in bed for a while this morning, not wanting to leave the room. Jeremy left my bed sometime around four this morning. I heard him lock the door, then he texted me a minute later and told me to text if I needed him again.

Sometime after lunch today, Jeremy knocked on the door to the office. When he came inside, he looked like he hadn't slept. He hasn't slept much this week at all because of me. From his point of view, I'm a hysterical mess of a woman who wakes up in his wife's bed in the middle of the night and then claims I see his wife standing at the top of the stairs after he finally kisses me.

I thought he had come to the office to ask me to leave, and honestly, I'm more than ready to go, but the money still hasn't hit my account. I'm kind of stuck here until it does.

He had come to my office to let me know he got another lock. For *Verity's* door this time.

"I thought it might help you sleep. Knowing there's no way she could leave the room if that were even possible."

If that were even possible.

"I'll only lock it at night, when we're asleep," he continues. "I told April her door comes open at night because of drafts in the house. I don't want her to think it's there for any other reason."

I thanked him, but after he'd gone, I didn't feel reassured at all. Because part of me worried that he'd put the lock there because *he* was worried. Of course I wanted him to believe me, but if he believed me, that meant it might be true.

In this case, I would rather be wrong than right.

I'm struggling with what to do with Verity's manuscript now. I want Jeremy to understand his wife in the way that I now understand her. I feel like he deserves to know what she did to his girls, especially since Crew spends so much time up there with her. And I'm still full of suspicion since he spoke of Verity talking to him. I know he's only five, so there's a chance he was confused, but if there's even a remote possibility that Verity could be faking it, Jeremy deserves to know.

But I haven't worked up the courage to give the manuscript to him yet because it *is* just a remote possibility that she's faking it. It would be more plausible to believe I was seeing things due to exhaustion and sleep deprivation than it would be to think a woman could fake a disability of that extent for months on end. *Without any apparent reason.*

There's also the fact that I haven't finished it yet. I don't know how it ends. I don't know what happened to Harper or Chastin, or if the timeline of this manuscript even covers those events.

There isn't much left to read. I'll probably only be able to digest one chapter before needing to take a break from the horror of this manuscript. I make sure the door to the office is closed, and I start the next chapter and decide to skip it, along with several others. I don't even want to read about a simple kiss, much less more sex. I don't want to ruin the kiss we shared by reading about him doing that with another woman.

When I've skipped yet another intimate scene and reach the chapter I feel may be an explanation for Chastin's death, I double-check the office door again before starting it.

Chapter Thirteen

I got pregnant with Crew within two weeks of lying to Jeremy about my pregnancy. It's as if fate were on my side. I thanked God with a prayer, even though I don't believe he had a hand in it.

Crew was a good baby (I'm assuming). By that point, I was making so much money, I was able to afford a full-time nanny at our new house. Jeremy was staying home with the kids after quitting his job and didn't think a nanny was really necessary, so I called the nanny our housekeeper, *but she was a nanny.*

She enabled Jeremy to work on the property every day. I had new windows installed in my office so I could watch him from almost every angle.

Life was good for a while. I did all the easy parts of mothering and Jeremy and the nanny did all the hard parts. And I traveled a lot. I had book tours and interviews, which I didn't really like leaving Jeremy for, but he preferred to stay home with the kids. I grew to appreciate those breaks, though. I noticed when I was gone for a week, the attention Jeremy gave me when I returned home was like the attention he used to pay me before the kids came along.

Sometimes I would lie and say I was needed in New York, but I would hole up in an Airbnb in Chelsea and watch television for a week. Then I'd go home, and Jeremy would fuck me like I was his virgin. Life was great.

Until it wasn't.

It happened in an instant. It was like the sun froze and darkened on our lives, and no matter how hard we tried, the rays couldn't reach us after that.

I was standing at the sink, washing a chicken. *A fucking raw chicken.* I could have been doing anything else...watering the lawn, writing, knitting, *anything* else. But I will forever think of that fucking disgusting raw chicken when I think about the moment we were told we lost Chastin.

The phone rang. *I was washing the chicken.*

Jeremy answered it. *I was washing the chicken.*

He raised his voice. *Still washing the fucking chicken.*

And then the sound...that guttural, painful sound. I heard him say *no* and *how* and *where is she* and *we'll be right there.* When he ended the call, I could see him in the reflection of the window. He was in the hallway, gripping the doorframe like he was going to fall to his knees if he didn't. I was still washing the chicken. Tears were streaming down my cheeks, my knees were weak. My stomach began to lurch.

I vomited on the chicken.

That's how I'll always remember one of the worst moments of my life.

On our entire drive to the hospital, I was wondering how Harper had done it. Had she smothered her like in my dream? Or had she come up with a more clever way to murder her sister?

They had been at a sleepover at their friend Maria's house. They'd been there several times before. And Maria's mother, Kitty—*what a silly name*—knew all about Chastin's allergies. Chastin never traveled without her EpiPen, but Kitty had found her unresponsive that morning. She dialed 9-1-1, and then called Jeremy as soon as the ambulance took her.

When we arrived at the hospital, Jeremy still had that faint hope that they were wrong and that Chastin was okay. Kitty met us in the hallway and kept saying, "I'm sorry. She wouldn't wake up."

That's all she told us. *She wouldn't wake up.* She didn't say, *She's dead.* Just, *She wouldn't wake up,* like Chastin was some kind of spoiled brat who wanted to sleep in.

Jeremy ran down the hall, into the patient hallway of the E.R. They escorted him out and told us we needed to wait in the family room. Everyone knows that's the room where they put the surviving members after someone has died. That's when Jeremy knew she was gone.

I'd never heard him scream like that. A grown man, on his knees, sobbing like a child. I'd have been embarrassed for him if I wasn't right there with him.

When we finally got to see her, she'd been dead less than a day, but she didn't smell like Chastin. She already smelled like death.

Jeremy asked so many questions. All the questions. *How did it happen? Did they have peanuts in the house? What time did they go to sleep? Was her EpiPen taken out of her bag at all?*

All the right questions, all the devastatingly right answers. It was over a week before her cause of death was confirmed. Anaphylaxis.

We were hyper vigilant about her peanut allergy. No matter where they went or who they were left with, Jeremy spent half an hour telling the mother their routine, explaining how to use the EpiPen. I always thought it was overkill since we'd literally only had to use it once in her entire life.

Kitty was well aware of her allergy and kept nuts out of their reach when the girls were there. What she wasn't aware of was that the girls had snuck into the pantry and grabbed a handful of snacks to take back to their room in the middle of the night. Chastin was only eight; it was late at night and dark when the girls decided they wanted a snack. Harper said they didn't realize anything they were eating contained peanuts. But when they woke up the next morning, *Chastin wouldn't wake up.*

Jeremy went through a period of denial, but he never questioned that Chastin unknowingly ate the nuts. But I did. I knew. *I knew.*

Every time I looked at Harper, I could see her guilt. I had been waiting on this to happen for years. *Years.* I knew, from when they were six months old, that Harper would find a way to kill her. And what a perfect murder she committed. Even her own father would never suspect her.

Her mother, though. *I* was a little harder to convince.

I missed Chastin, obviously, and I was saddened by her death. But there was something unpleasant in how hard Jeremy took it. He was devastated. Numb. After she'd been dead for three months, I was growing impatient. We'd only had sex twice since her death, and he hadn't even kissed me with tongue either time. It's like he was disconnected from me, using me to get off, to feel better, to get a quick rush of something other than agony. I wanted more than that. I wanted the old Jeremy back.

I tried one night. I rolled over and put my hand on his dick while he was asleep. I rubbed my hand up and down, waiting for it to grow hard. It didn't. Instead, he brushed my hand away and said, "It's okay, Verity. You don't have to."

He said it like he was doing me a favor. Like he was turning me down for *my* reassurance.

I didn't need reassurance.

I didn't.

I've had over eight years to accept it. I knew it was coming—I had dreamt about it. I gave Chastin all the love I had every minute she was alive because I knew it would happen. I knew Harper would do something like that to her. Not that it could ever be proven that Harper had any involvement. Even if I had tried to prove it to him, Jeremy would never believe me. He loves her too much. He'd never believe such an atrocious thing—that a twin could do that to her own sister.

Part of me felt responsible. Had I just tried choking her again as an infant, or leaving an open bottle of bleach near her as a toddler, or ramming the passenger side of my car into a tree while she was unbuckled with the airbag turned off, all of it could have been avoided. So many potential accidents I could have staged. *Should* have staged.

Had I stopped Harper before she acted, we would still have Chastin.

And then maybe Jeremy wouldn't be so fucking *sad* all the time.

18

Verity is in the living room. April brought her down in the elevator right before she left for the evening. An unusual change in their routine that I'm not sure I like.

April said, "She's wide awake this evening. I thought I'd let Jeremy put her to bed tonight." She left her in front of the television, her wheelchair parked near the sofa.

Verity is watching *Wheel of Fortune*.

Or...staring in that direction, anyway.

I'm standing in the doorway to the living room, looking at her. Jeremy is upstairs with Crew. It's dark outside, and the living room light isn't on, but there's enough light from the television that I can see Verity's expressionless face.

I can't imagine anyone going to such great lengths to fake an injury for this long. I'm not even sure how someone could pull it off. Would she startle at a loud noise?

Next to me, near the entryway to the living room, is a bowl full of decorative glass balls mixed in with wooden ones. I look around, then pluck one of the wooden ones out of the bowl. I toss it in her direction. When it hits the floor in front of her, she doesn't flinch.

I know she's not paralyzed, so how does she not even flinch? Even if her brain damage is too severe to understand the English language, she'd still be alarmed by noise, right? Have some kind of reaction?

Unless she's trained herself to not react.

I watch her for a little longer before I start to creep myself out with my own thoughts again.

I return to the kitchen, leaving her alone with Pat Sajak and Vanna White.

There are only two chapters left of Verity's manuscript. I'm praying I don't find a part two anywhere before I leave here because I can't take the ups and downs of it all. The anxiety I get after every chapter is worse than the anxiety I get after I sleepwalk.

I'm relieved she had nothing to do with Chastin's death, but disturbed by her thought process during all of it. She seemed so detached. Two-dimensional. She'd lost her fucking daughter, yet all she thought about was how she should have killed Harper, and she was fed up with waiting for Jeremy to get over his grief.

Disturbing is putting it mildly. Luckily, it's coming to an end soon. Most of the manuscript details things that happened years ago, but this last chapter was more recent. Less than a year ago. Months before Harper's death.

Harper's death.

It's the thing I plan to get to next. Maybe tonight. I don't know. I haven't slept well the last few days, and I'm worried after I finish the manuscript, I won't be able to sleep at *all*.

I'm making spaghetti for Jeremy and Crew tonight. I try to focus on dinner and not at all on Verity's lack of a soul. I purposely timed this meal so that April would be gone before dinner was ready. And I'm hoping Jeremy takes Verity up to bed before it's time to eat. My birthday is almost over, and I'll be damned if I eat my birthday meal seated next to Verity Crawford.

I'm stirring the pasta sauce when I realize I haven't heard the television in a few minutes. I carefully loosen my grip on the spoon, placing it on the stove next to the pan.

"Jeremy?" I say, hoping he's in the living room. Hoping he's the reason there's no sound coming from the television anymore.

"Be down in a second!" he calls from upstairs.

I close my eyes, already feeling the quickening of my pulse. *If this bitch turned off that goddamn television, I'm walking out that front door without shoes on and I'm never coming back.*

I clench my fists at my sides, growing really tired of this shit. This house. And that fucking creepy-ass, psychotic woman.

I don't tiptoe into the living room. I stomp.

The television is still on, but it's no longer making noise. Verity is still in the same position. I walk over to the table next to her wheelchair and snatch up the remote. The television is now on mute, and I am over this. I'm *over* this. *Televisions don't just mute themselves!*

"You're a fucking cunt," I mutter.

My own words shock me, but not enough to walk away. It's as if every word I read of her manuscript fans the flames inside of me. I unmute the television and drop the remote on the couch, out of her reach. I kneel down in front of her, positioning myself so that I'm directly in her line of sight. I'm shaking, but not from fear this time. I'm shaking because I am so angry at her. Angry at the type of wife she was to Jeremy. The kind of mother she was to Harper. And I'm angry that all this weird shit keeps happening and I'm the only one who is witnessing it. I'm tired of feeling crazy!

"You don't even deserve the body you're trapped in," I whisper, staring straight into her eyes. "I hope you die with a throat full of your own vomit, the same way you attempted to kill your infant daughter."

I wait. If she's in there...if she heard me...if she's faking it...my words would reach her. They would make her flinch or lash out or *something*.

She doesn't move. I try to think of something else to say that would make her react. Something she wouldn't be able to keep her composure after hearing. I stand up and lean into her, bringing my mouth to her ear. "Jeremy is going to fuck me in your bed tonight."

I wait again...for a noise...for a movement.

The only thing I notice is the smell of urine. It fills the air. My nostrils.

I look down at her pants right when Jeremy begins to descend the stairs. "Did you need me?"

I back away from her, accidentally kicking the wooden ball I tossed toward her earlier. I motion toward Verity while bending down for the ball. "She just... She needs to be changed, I think."

Jeremy grabs the handles of her wheelchair and pushes her out of the living room, toward the elevator. I bring a hand to my face, covering my mouth and nose as I exhale.

I don't know why I've never been curious about who bathes her or changes her. I assumed the nurse took care of most of that, but she obviously doesn't do it all. That Verity is incontinent and has to wear diapers and be bathed makes me feel even sorrier for him. Jeremy is now taking her upstairs to do both of those things and it makes me angry.

Angry at Verity.

Surely her current state is a result of the terrible human she's been to her children and to Jeremy. Now, for the rest of his life, Jeremy will have to suffer the consequences of Verity's karma.

It isn't right.

And even though she flinched at nothing I said, the fact that I seemed to scare her has me convinced she's in there. *Somewhere.* And now she knows I'm not afraid of her.

•••

I ate dinner at the table with Crew, who played on his iPad the whole time. I wanted to wait for Jeremy, but I knew he didn't want Crew to eat alone and it was getting past his bedtime. While Jeremy was tending to Verity, I put Crew to bed. By the time Jeremy got her showered, changed, and put to bed, the spaghetti was cold.

Jeremy finally comes downstairs as I'm washing the dishes. We haven't talked much since our kiss. I'm not sure what the vibe will be between us, or if we're going to be awkward and go our separate ways after he eats. I can hear him behind me, munching on garlic bread as I continue to wash the dishes.

"Sorry about that," he says.

"What?"

"Missing dinner."

I shrug. "You didn't miss it. Eat."

He takes a bowl out of the cabinet and fills it with spaghetti. He puts it in the microwave and then leans into the counter next to me. "Lowen."

I look at him.

"What's wrong?"

I shake my head. "Nothing, Jeremy. It's not my place."

"It is now that you said that."

I don't want to have this conversation with him. It really isn't my place. This is his life. His wife. His house. And I'm only going to be here for another two days at the most. I dry my hands on a towel just as the microwave beeps. He doesn't move to open it because he's too busy staring at me, attempting to coax more out of me with that look.

I lean against the island and sigh, dropping my head back. "I just...I feel bad for you."

"Don't."

"I can't help it."

"You can."

"No. I can't."

He opens the microwave and pulls out his bowl. He sets it on the counter to cool off and then faces me again. "This is my life, Low. And I can't do anything about it. You feeling sorry for me doesn't help."

I roll my head. "But you're wrong. You *can* do something about it. You don't have to live like this, day in and day out. There are facilities, places that can take much better care of her. She'll have more opportunity. And you and Crew won't be tied to this house every day for the rest of your lives."

Jeremy's jaw hardens. I knew I shouldn't have said anything. "I appreciate that you think I deserve better. But put yourself in Verity's shoes."

He has no idea how far I've walked in Verity's shoes over the past two weeks. "Believe me, I have been." I make a frustrated fist and tap it on the counter, trying to find a better way to word it all. "She wouldn't want this for you, Jeremy. You're a prisoner in your own home. *Crew* is a prisoner in this home. He needs to get away from this house. Take him on vacations. Go back to work and put her in a facility where she can receive full-time care."

Jeremy is shaking his head before I even get the sentence out. "I can't do that to Crew. He's lost both of his sisters. He can't go through another loss like that. At least if she's here, Crew can still spend time with her."

He didn't indicate his own desire to have her here. Only Crew's.

"Take moments, then," I tell him. "You can put her in a facility part time so it's not weighing you down. Bring her home on the weekends, when Crew is out of school."

I walk over to him and take his face in my hands. I want him to see how much I worry for him. Maybe if he sees that someone actually cares about his well being, he'll take this conversation more seriously.

"Take moments for yourself, Jeremy," I say quietly. "Selfish moments. You deserve to live a life where you have moments that have nothing to do with her and everything to do with you and what *you* want."

I feel his teeth clench beneath my palms. He pulls away from me and presses his hands into the granite, dropping his head between his shoulders. "What *I* want?" he says quietly.

"Yes. What do *you* want?"

His head falls backward and he laughs, once, like that was a stupid question. Then he says one word, like it's the easiest question he's ever answered.

"*You.*"

He pushes off the counter and marches toward me. He grips my waist with both hands and presses his forehead to mine, looking into my eyes with nothing but need. "I want *you*, Low."

My relief is met with a kiss. It's different from our first kiss. This time he's patient as his lips move lazily against mine and his hand curves around the back of my neck. He's savoring the taste of me, drawing up my desire with every motion of his tongue. He bends a little, lifting me, and then he wraps my legs around his waist.

We're leaving the kitchen, but I don't want to open my eyes until we're alone behind a locked door. Verity isn't ruining it for me this time.

Once we're in the master bedroom, he releases his grip on me and I slide down him, our lips slipping apart. He leaves me standing next to my bed as he walks toward my bedroom door.

"Take off your clothes." He says it without facing me, as he's locking my bedroom door.

It's a command. One I'm eager to follow now that the door is locked. We watch each other undress. He takes off his jeans as I'm taking off my shirt, and then his shirt comes off with my jeans. I remove my bra as his eyes move over me. He's not touching me, not kissing me, just watching me.

So many emotions flood me as I remove my panties: fear, excitement, irritation, desire, trepidation. I slide my panties down my hips, over my legs, and then kick them off. When I stand up straight, I am on full display.

He soaks me up with his eyes as he removes the last of his clothing. Something inside me shifts, because no matter how accurate Verity's physical descriptions of him were, I wasn't prepared for the full magnitude of his body.

We're both standing there, naked, our breaths exaggerated.

He takes a step closer, his eyes on my face and nowhere else. His warm hands slide up my cheeks and through my hair as he brings his mouth down on mine again. He kisses me, soft and sweet, with just a tease of his tongue.

His fingers trickle down the length of my spine and I shiver.

"I don't have a condom," he says as he cups my ass and pulls me against him.

"I'm not on the pill."

My words don't prevent him from lifting me and lowering me to the bed. His lips circle my left nipple, briefly, then brush across my mouth as he hovers over me. "I'll pull out."

"Alright."

The word makes him smile. He whispers, "Alright," against my lips as he begins to push into me. We're both so focused on connecting, we aren't even kissing. Just breathing against each other's mouths. I squeeze my eyes shut as he tries to fit his entire length inside me. It hurts for a few seconds, but when he starts to move, the pain is replaced by a pleasurable fullness that makes me moan.

Jeremy's lips meet my cheek, and then my mouth again before he pulls back. When I open my eyes, I see a man who, for once, isn't thinking about anything other than what's right in front of him. There's no distant look in his eyes. It's just him and me in this moment.

"Do you have any idea how many times I've thought about being with you?" It's a rhetorical question, I'm assuming, because his kiss that immediately follows prevents me from answering it. He cups my breast while he kisses me. After about a minute of this position, he pulls out of me and rolls me flat onto my stomach. He enters me from behind, lowering his mouth to my ear as he pulls out. "I'm going to take you in every position I've imagined us in."

His words feel as though they settle in my stomach and catch fire. "Please," is all I say.

With that, he places a palm against my stomach and pulls me onto my knees, pressing my back against his chest without slipping out of me.

His breath is warm against the back of my neck. I snake a hand up and grip his head, pulling his mouth against my skin. That position lasts about thirty seconds before his hands slip to my waist. He rotates me so that we're facing each other and then slides me back onto him.

I feel weak against his strength, his arms effortlessly moving me around the bed every few minutes. I realize, in all the times I've read about his intimacy with his wife, she always had to have some form of control over him.

I relinquish all my control to him.

I let him take me however he wants me.

And he does, for over half an hour. Every time he seems close to release, he pulls out of me and kisses me until he takes me again, kisses me, repositions me, takes me, kisses me, repositions me. It's a cycle I never want to end.

Eventually, we're in what I'm assuming is one of his favorite positions, him on his back, his head on a pillow, my thighs on either side of his head. But I'm not sure if we ended up in this position because of him or because of me. I've yet to lower myself onto his mouth because I'm staring at the teeth marks on his headboard.

I close my eyes because I don't want to see them.

His palms are sliding up my stomach, to my breasts. He cups my breasts in his hands, and then he begins to slowly part me with his tongue. I let my head fall back and I moan so loud, I have to cover my own mouth.

He seems to like the noise because he does the exact same thing with his tongue again, and the ecstasy that surges through me propels me forward until I'm gripping the headboard. I open my eyes, my mouth inches away from the headboard. Inches away from the bite marks Verity left behind from all the times he had her in this same position.

When Jeremy's fingers slide down my stomach and accompany his mouth, I have nowhere for my screams to go. With the position he has me in, I'm compelled to lean forward and stifle the sounds of my climax.

I bite down on the wood in front of me.

I can feel Verity's teeth marks beneath mine. Different. Unaligned with my own. I bite harder into the wood as I come, determined to leave deeper marks than she ever did. Determined to think only of Jeremy and me every time I look at this headboard in the future.

Verity is mostly confined to one room, but her presence looms in almost every room in this house. I no longer want to think about her when I'm in this bedroom.

After I come, I pull away from the headboard and open my eyes, seeing the fresh marks I've left behind. Just as I run my thumb over them to wipe away my saliva, Jeremy pushes me onto my back and I'm suddenly beneath him again. He doesn't even need to enter me to reach his climax. He presses himself against my stomach and I feel the warmth spilling onto my skin as his mouth finds mine.

I can tell by his frantic kiss that this is going to be a long night.

19

Our second round happened in the shower half an hour later. Our hands were all over each other, our mouths were one, and then he was inside me again, my palms flat against the shower wall as he thrust into me beneath the spray of the water.

He pulled out and came on my back before washing me clean.

We're in the bed again, but it's almost three in the morning, and I know he's going to go back to his room soon. I don't want him to. Being with him in this way is everything I imagined it would be and, somehow, I feel okay being inside this house when I'm also wrapped in his arms. He makes me feel safe from the things he doesn't even realize are dangerous.

He has me tucked against him, an arm wrapped around me as I lie against his chest. His fingers are tracing up and down my arm. We've been fighting sleep, asking each other questions. The questions have taken a more personal turn because he just asked me what my last relationship was like.

"It was shallow."

"Why?"

"I'm not sure it was even a relationship," I say. "We defined it that way, but it only revolved around sex. We couldn't figure out how to fit into each other's lives outside of the bedroom."

"How long did it last?"

"A while." I lift up and look at him. "It was with Corey. My agent."

Jeremy's fingers pause on my arm. "The agent I met?"

"Yes."

"And he's still your agent?"

"He's a great agent." I lay my head back down on his chest, and Jeremy's fingers resume their movement down my arm.

"That just made me a little jealous," he says.

I laugh because I can feel him laughing. After it's quiet for a beat, I ask him a question I've been curious about. "What was your relationship like with Verity?"

Jeremy sighs, and my head moves with his chest. Then he positions us so that I'm on the pillow and he's on his side, making eye contact with me. "I'll answer your question, but I don't want you to think bad of me."

"I won't," I promise, shaking my head.

"I loved her. She was my wife. But sometimes I wasn't sure we really knew each other. We lived together, but it's as if our worlds weren't connected." He reaches up and touches my lips, tracing over them with the tips of his fingers. "I was insanely attracted to her, which I'm sure you don't want to hear, but it's true. Our sex life was great. But the rest of it... I don't know. I felt like there was something missing in the beginning, but I stayed and I married her and we started our family because I always believed that deeper connection was within reach. I thought I'd wake up one day and look her in the eyes and then it would click, like that mythical puzzle piece had finally snapped into place."

It's not lost on me that he mentioned loving her in the past tense. "Did you eventually find that connection?"

"No, not like I had hoped. But I've felt something close to it—a fleeting intensity that proved a deeper connection can exist."

"When was that?"

"Several weeks ago," he says quietly. "In a random coffee shop bathroom with a woman who wasn't my wife."

He kisses me as soon as that sentence escapes him, like he doesn't want me to respond. Maybe he feels guilty for saying it. For momentarily feeling a connection with me after trying to feel that connection with his wife for so many years.

Even if he doesn't want me to react to that admission, I feel something grow inside me, like his words sink into me and expand in my chest. He pulls me against him and I close my eyes, tucking my head against his chest. We don't speak again before we fall asleep.

I wake up about two hours later to his voice in my ear.

"Shit." He sits up and most of the covers go with him. "*Shit.*"

I rub my eyes as I roll onto my back. "What is it?"

"I didn't mean to fall asleep." He reaches to the floor and then begins pulling on his clothes. "I can't be in here when Crew wakes up." He kisses me, twice, and then walks toward the door. He unlocks it, then pulls on it.

The door doesn't budge.

He jiggles the handle as I sit up in bed, pulling the covers over my exposed breasts.

"Shit," he says again. "The door is stuck."

Something drops inside me, and I'm abruptly ripped from the pleasure of last night. I'm back in the moment, in yet another scenario where I feel desolate inside this eerie house. I shake my head, but Jeremy is facing the door so he can't see me. "It isn't stuck," I say quietly. "It's locked. From the outside."

Jeremy turns his head and looks at me, his face giving way to concern. Then he tries pulling the door with both hands. When he realizes I'm right and that the door is latched on the outside, he starts beating on it. I remain where I am, scared of what he might find when he finally gets that door open.

He tries everything to open it, but then he resorts to calling out Crew's name. "Crew!" Jeremy yells, beating on the bedroom door.

What if she took him?

I'm not sure she would have. She doesn't even like her kids. But she likes Jeremy. *Loves* Jeremy. If she knew he was in this room with me last night, she'd probably take Crew out of spite.

Jeremy's mind hasn't gone there yet. In his head, Crew is playing a prank on us. Or the lock somehow accidentally latched itself when he closed the door last night. Those are the only plausible explanations to him. Right now, he merely sounds annoyed. Not at all concerned.

Jeremy glances toward the alarm clock on the nightstand and then beats on the door again. "Crew, open the door!" He presses his forehead against it. "April will be here soon," he says quietly. "She can't find us in here together."

That's where his head is?

I'm thinking his wife kidnapped his son in the middle of the night, and he's worried he's going to be caught fucking the houseguest.

"Jeremy."

"What?" he says, beating against the door again.

"I know you think it isn't plausible. But...did you lock Verity's door last night?"

Jeremy's fist pauses against the door. "I can't remember," he says quietly.

"If by some bizarre chance it was Verity who locked us in here...Crew probably isn't here anymore."

When he looks at me, his eyes are full of fear. Then, in one swift movement, he stalks across the bedroom and unlocks the window. He lifts it, but there are two panes of glass. The second one isn't giving way as easily as the first. Without hesitation, he reaches to the bed and pulls a pillow case off of a pillow. He wraps his hand in the case, punches through the glass, kicks it, and then crawls out the window.

Several seconds later, I hear him unlock my bedroom door as he passes it and heads for the stairs. He's already in Crew's bedroom before I make it out of the master. I hear him run across the hall to Verity's room. When he makes it back to the top of the stairs, my heart is in my throat.

He shakes his head. He bends over, clasping his knees, out of breath. "They're asleep."

He squats, as if his knees were about to give way, and he runs his hands through his hair. "They're *asleep*," he says again, with relief.

I'm relieved. But I'm not.

My paranoia is starting to reach Jeremy.

I'm not doing him any favors by bringing up my concerns. April walks through the front door moments later. She looks at me, then at Jeremy squatting at the top of the stairs. He glances up and sees April staring at him.

He stands and walks down the stairs, not looking at me or April as he heads to the door, pulls it open, and walks outside.

April looks from me to the front door.

I shrug. "Rough night with Crew."

I don't know if she buys it, but she walks up the stairs like she doesn't give a shit if I'm telling the truth or not.

I go to the office and close the door. I pull the rest of the manuscript out and begin to read. I have to finish this today. I need to know how it ends, if it even *has* an ending. Because I'm at the point now where I feel like I need to show this manuscript to Jeremy. He needs to know that he was right when he felt they never really connected. Because he didn't really know her.

Things aren't right in this house, and until he mistrusts that woman upstairs as much as I do, I have a feeling something else is going to happen. The other shoe is going to drop.

After all, this is a house full of Chronics. The next tragedy is already long overdue.

Chapter Fourteen

I t's easy to remember everything about the morning Harper died because it only happened a few days ago. I remember how she smelled. *Like grease. She hadn't washed her hair in two days.* What she was wearing. *Purple leggings, a black shirt, and a knitted sweater.* What she was doing. *Sitting at the table with Crew, coloring.* The last thing Jeremy said to her that day. *I love you, Harper.*

Chastin had been gone six months that day. *To* the day. Which meant I had spent one hundred eighty-two and a half days building resentment for the child responsible.

Jeremy had slept upstairs the night before. Crew cries for him almost every night, so for the last two months, he's been sleeping in the guest bedroom upstairs. I tried to tell him it's not good for Crew. He's spoiling him. But Jeremy doesn't listen to me anymore. His primary focus are his two remaining children.

It's strange how we have one less child for him to focus on, yet that somehow turned into requiring *more* of his focus.

We've had sex four times since Chastin died. He can't seem to get it up anymore when I try. Not even when I suck his dick. The worst part is that it doesn't even seem to bother him. He could take Viagra, but he refuses. He says he just needs more time to adjust to life without Chastin.

Time.

You know who *didn't* need time? Harper.

She didn't even go through an adjustment period after Chastin's death. She never cried. Not even a single tear. It's weird. It isn't normal. Even *I* cried.

I guess it makes sense that Harper wouldn't cry. Guilt can do that to a person.

Maybe guilt is why I'm writing it all down.

Because Jeremy needs to know the truth. Someday, somehow, he'll find this. And then he'll realize how much I fucking loved him.

Back to the day Harper got what was coming to her.

I was standing in the kitchen, watching her color. She was showing Crew how to color on top of another color to make a third color. They were laughing. Crew's laugh was understandable, but Harper's? Inexcusable. I was tired of holding in my anger.

"Are you even upset that Chastin is dead?"

Harper lifted her eyes to meet my gaze. She was pretending to be afraid of me. "Yes."

"You haven't even cried. Not once. Your twin sister died and you act like you don't even *care*."

I could see the tears welling up in her eyes. Funny how the kid Jeremy believes can't express emotion can bring on the tears when she's being called out.

"I *do* care," Harper said. "I miss her."

I laughed at her. My laughter brought on the *actual* tears. She scooted her chair back and ran up to her bedroom.

I looked at Crew and flicked a hand in Harper's direction. "*Now* she cries."

Figures.

Jeremy must have passed her upstairs, because I could hear him knocking on her door. "Harper? Sweetie, what's wrong?"

I mimicked him, using a squeaky child-like voice. "*Sweetie, what's wrong?*"

Crew giggled. At least I'm funny to the four-year-old.

A minute later, Jeremy walked into the kitchen. "What's wrong with Harper?"

"She's mad," I lied. "I wouldn't let her go play by the lake."

Jeremy kissed me on the side of my head. It felt genuine and it made me smile. "It's a nice day out," he said. "You should take them to the shore."

He was behind me, so he didn't see me roll my eyes. I should have thought of a better lie to excuse Harper's tears, because now he wanted me to take them outside and play with them.

"I wanna go to the water," Crew said.

Jeremy grabbed his wallet and his keys. "Go tell Harper to get her shoes on. Your mom will take you. I'll be back before lunch."

I turned around and faced him. "Where are you going?"

"Groceries," he said. "I told you this morning."

He did say that.

Crew ran upstairs, and I sighed. "I'd rather do the shopping. You stay and play with them."

Jeremy walked up to me, wrapping an arm around me. He pressed his forehead to mine, and I felt that gesture go straight to my heart. "You haven't written in six months. You don't go outside. You don't play with them." He pulls me in for a hug. "I'm getting worried about you, babe. Just take them outside for half an hour. Get some Vitamin D."

"Do you think I'm depressed?" I said, pulling back. That was laughable. *He* was the depressed one.

Jeremy set his keys on the counter so he could hold my face with both of his hands. "I think we're both depressed. And we will be for a while. We need to look out for each other."

I smiled at him. I liked that he thought we were in this together. Maybe we were. He kissed me then, and for the first time in a long time, he kissed me with tongue and very little grief. It felt like old times. I pulled him to me and lifted onto my toes, deepening the kiss. I felt him harden against me, without coercion this time.

"I want you to sleep in our room tonight," I whispered.

He smiled against my lips. "Okay. But there won't be much sleeping."

His tone of voice, his heated eyes, that grin. *There you are, Jeremy Crawford. I've missed you.*

After Jeremy left, I took his damn children to play by the water. I also took the last book I'd written in my series. Jeremy was right, it had been six months since I'd written anything. I needed to get back in the groove. I already missed a deadline, but Pantem was lenient, thanks to the tragic "accidental" loss of Chastin.

They'd probably be even more lenient on my deadline if they knew what had really happened to her.

Crew walked out onto the dock toward the canoe. I tensed, because the dock is old and Jeremy didn't like them being on it. But Crew didn't weigh much, so I relaxed a little. I doubted he could fall through.

He sat down at the edge of the dock and stuck his feet in the canoe. I was surprised it hadn't floated away yet. It was hanging by a threadbare rope.

Crew doesn't know it, and maybe he'll find out one day, but he was conceived in that canoe. The week I lied and told Jeremy I was pregnant was the most prolific week of sex we'd had to date. But I'm pretty sure it was the canoe that did the trick. It's why I wanted to name him Crew. I wanted a nautical-themed name.

I missed those days.

There were a lot of things I missed, actually. Mostly I missed our lives before we had children. The twins, anyway.

Sitting on the shore that day, watching Crew, I wondered what it would be like to only have him. It would be another adjustment if Harper were to pass, but I figured we'd get through it. I wasn't much help after Chastin died because for a while, I was grieving too. But if Harper were to pass, I could be more help to Jeremy during his recovery.

This time, there would be very little grief on my part since all my grief was reserved for Chastin.

Maybe most of Jeremy's grief was reserved for Chastin, too.

It was a possibility.

I used to assume that the individual deaths of a person's children would be equally difficult for them. Losing a second or even third child would hurt just as much as the first experience.

But that was before Jeremy and I lost Chastin. Her death made us swell with grief. It filled every crevice inside of us, every limb.

If the canoe were to capsize with the children in it—if Harper were to drown—Jeremy might not have room for more grief. Maybe he was at full capacity.

When you've already lost one child, you might as well have lost them all.

With no room for more grief and Harper no longer around, the three of us could become the perfect family.

"Harper."

She was several feet from me, playing in the sand. I stood up and wiped the back of my jeans. "Come on, sweetie. Let's go for a ride in the canoe with your brother."

Harper jumped up, unaware as she stepped foot onto the dock that she'd never know what the earth felt like beneath her feet again.

"I get front," she said. I followed her to the edge of the dock. I helped Crew climb in first, then Harper. Then I sat down and carefully lowered myself into the boat. I used the paddle to push away from the dock.

I was in the back of the boat, and Crew was in the middle. I paddled us out to the middle of the lake as they leaned over the edge, running their fingers in the water.

The lake was calm as I looked around. We lived in a cove with 2,000 feet of shoreline, so we didn't get much of the lake traffic out here. It was a quiet day.

Harper sat up straight in the canoe and wiped her hands on her leggings. She turned around, her back to Crew and me.

I leaned forward, close to Crew's ear. I covered his mouth with my hand. "Crew. Sweetie. Hold your breath."

I gripped the edge of the canoe and leaned all my weight to the right.

I heard a small yelp. I wasn't sure if it came from Crew or Harper, but after the yelp and the initial splash, I heard nothing. Just pressure. The silence pressed against my ears as I kicked my arms and legs until I broke through the surface.

I could hear splashing. Harper's scream. Crew's scream. I swam toward Crew and wrapped my arms around him. I looked toward the house, hoping I could make it back to shore with him. We were farther out than I'd realized.

I started swimming. Harper was screaming.

Splashing.

I continued to swim.

She continued to scream.

Nothing.

I heard another splash.

More nothing.

I kept swimming and refused to look back until I could feel the mud seep between my toes. I gripped at the surface of the lake like it was a life vest. Crew was gasping and coughing, bobbing up and down, clinging to me. It was harder than I thought it would be to keep him afloat.

Jeremy would thank me for this. For saving Crew.

He'd be devastated, of course, but thankful, too.

I wondered if we'd sleep in the same bed that night. He would be exhausted, but he would want to sleep in the same bed as me, hold me, make sure I was okay.

"Harper!" Crew yelled as soon as he cleared his lungs of water.

I covered Crew's mouth and dragged him to the shore, plopping him down on the sand. His eyes were wide with fear. "Mommy!" he cried, pointing behind me. "Harper can't swim!"

Sand was all over me, stuck to my hands, my arms, my thighs. My lungs felt like fire. Crew tried to crawl back toward the water, but I pulled his hand and made him sit down. The ripples from the commotion of the water were still lapping at my toes. I looked out at the lake, but there was nothing. No screaming. No splashing.

Crew was growing more and more hysterical.

"I tried to save her," I whispered. "Mommy tried to save her."

"Go get her!" he screamed, pointing out at the lake.

I wondered then how it would look if he told anyone I didn't go back out into the water. Most mothers wouldn't leave the water until they'd found their child. I needed to get back in the water.

"Crew. We need to save Harper. Do you remember how to use Mommy's phone to call Daddy?"

He nodded, wiping tears from his cheeks.

"Go. Go to the house and call Daddy. Tell him Mommy is trying to save Harper and he needs to call the police."

"Okay!" he said, running up to the house.

He was such a good brother.

I was cold and out of breath, but I trudged back out into the lake. "Harper?" I said her name quietly, afraid if I called too loudly, she'd get a second wind and pop up out of the water.

I took my time. I didn't want to go too far and risk touching her, bumping into her. What if there was still life in her and she clung to my shirt? Tried to pull me under?

I was aware I needed to be out here when Jeremy showed up. I needed to be crying. Cold. On the verge of hypothermia. Bonus points if I was taken away in an ambulance.

The canoe was upside down, closer inland than when it flipped. Jeremy and I had flipped the canoe a couple of times before, so I was aware there were air pockets when it was positioned like it was. What if Harper had swam to it? What if she had clung to it and was hiding under it? Waiting to tell her daddy what I had done?

I worked my way to the canoe. I moved carefully, not wanting to touch her. When I reached the capsized boat, I held my breath and went under the water. I popped up inside the canoe.

Oh, thank God, I thought.

She wasn't there.

Thank God.

I heard Crew calling my name from far away. I ducked under the water and popped up outside the canoe.

I screamed Harper's name, full of panic, like an actual devastated mother would.

"Harper!"

"Daddy is coming!" Crew yelled from the shore.

I started screaming Harper's name even louder. The police would be here soon, before Jeremy.

"Harper!"

I went under several times so that I'd be out of breath. I did that, over and over, until I could barely stay afloat. I screamed her name and didn't stop until a police officer was pulling me out of the water.

I continued to scream her name, throwing in the occasional, "My daughter!" and "My baby girl!"

One person was in the water looking for her. Then two. Then three. Then I felt someone fly past me, onto the dock. He ran to the end and jumped in head first. When he popped up, I saw that it was Jeremy.

I can't describe the look on his face as he yelled for her. It was a look of determination mixed with horror mixed with psychosis.

I was crying real tears at that point. I was hysterical. I wanted to smile at how appropriately hysterical I was, but I didn't because part of me knew I had messed up. I could see it in Jeremy's face. This one would be even harder for him to recover from than Chastin.

I didn't anticipate that.

She'd been under water for over half an hour when he finally found her. She was tangled in a fishing net. I couldn't tell if it was green or yellow from where I sat on the beach, but I remembered Jeremy losing a yellow fishing net last year. What are the odds that I tipped the canoe in the exact spot it was tangled beneath the surface? Had the fishing net not been there, she probably would have made it to shore.

After she was untangled, the men helped Jeremy lift her onto the dock. Jeremy tried to perform CPR until the paramedic made it to the edge of the dock. And even then, he wouldn't stop.

He wouldn't stop until he had no choice. The dock began to cave in, and Jeremy rolled right off the edge of it, catching Harper in his arms. Three other men remained on the dock, reaching for her body.

I wondered if that moment would haunt him. Having to catch his dead daughter's body as she fell on top of him in the water.

Jeremy wouldn't let go of her. He found his footing in the water and carried her, all the way to the shore. When he reached the sand, he collapsed, still holding her. He pressed his face into her sopping wet hair, and I heard him whispering to her.

"I love you, Harper. I love you, Harper. I love you, Harper."

He said it over and over as he held her. His sadness made me ache for him. I crawled to him, to her, and I wrapped my arms around them both. "I tried to save her," I whispered. "I tried to save her."

He wouldn't let go of Harper. The paramedics had to pry her from his arms. He left me there, with Crew, while he climbed into the back of the ambulance.

Jeremy didn't ask me what had happened. He didn't tell me he was leaving. He didn't look at me at all.

His reaction wasn't quite what I had planned, but I realized he was in shock. He'd adjust. He just needed time.

20

'm gripping the toilet as I vomit. I was sick before I even finished the chapter. I'm shaking, as if I had been there. Like I witnessed firsthand what that woman did to her daughter. *To Jeremy.*

I press my forehead against my arm, struggling with what to do.

Do I tell someone? Do I tell Jeremy? Do I call the police?

What would the police even be able to do with her?

They'd lock her up somewhere. A mental institution. Jeremy would be free of her.

I brush my teeth, staring at my reflection. After I rinse my mouth out, I stand up straight and wipe my mouth. As my hand moves across my face, I can see the scar in the mirror. I never thought this scar would become insignificant to me, but it's starting to feel that way. What I went through with my mother is nothing compared to this.

What happened between us was a disconnect. A broken bond.

This was *murder*.

I grab my bag and search for my Xanax. The pill is clenched in my fist as I walk to the kitchen. I pull a shot glass out of the cabinet and pour Crown Royal into it, all the way to the top. I pick up the shot glass, just as April rounds the corner. She pauses, staring at me.

I stare right back as I pop the pill into my mouth and down the shot.

I go back to my room and close my door, locking it. I pull the blinds down over the hole in the window to block out the sun.

I close my eyes and pull the covers over my head as I wonder what the hell I should do.

•••

I wake up sometime later, feeling a warmth travel down my body. Something touches my lips. My eyes flick open.

Jeremy.

I sigh against his mouth as he lowers himself on top of me. I welcome the comfort of his lips. Little does he know that every ounce of sadness his kiss is eliminating is sadness I feel for *him*. For a situation he knows nothing about.

I adjust the covers, pulling them out from between us so there's no barrier. He's still kissing me as he rolls onto his side, pulling me against him.

"It's two o'clock in the afternoon," he whispers. "You feeling okay?"

"Yes," I lie. "I'm just tired."

"Me too." He feathers his fingers down my arm, then grabs my hand.

"How did you get in here?" I ask, knowing the door was locked from the inside.

He smiles. "The window. April took Verity to the doctor, and Crew won't be home from school for another hour."

The rest of the tension built up inside me somehow seeps out with that news. Verity isn't in this house, and I'm at instant peace.

Jeremy lays his head on my chest, facing my feet as his fingers explore my panty line. "I checked the lock. It appears, if you slam a door hard enough, it could latch into place."

I don't respond to that because I'm not sure I believe it. I'm sure there's a chance, but I think the chance that it was Verity is greater.

Jeremy lifts my T-shirt—another one that belongs to him. He kisses a spot between my breasts. "I like it when you wear my shirts."

I run my fingers through his hair and smile. "I like it when they smell like you."

He laughs. "What do I smell like?"

"Petrichor."

He's dragging his lips down my stomach. "I don't even know what that means." His voice is a mumble against my skin.

"It's a word that describes the smell of fresh rain after warm weather."

He moves until his mouth is close to mine. "I had no idea there was a word for that."

"There's a word for everything."

He kisses me briefly, then pulls back. His eyebrows draw together as he contemplates. "Is there a word for what I'm doing?"

"Probably. What are you referring to?"

He traces my jaw with a finger. "This," he says quietly. "Falling for a woman when I shouldn't."

My heart sinks, despite his admission. I hate that he feels guilty for how he's feeling. I understand it, though. No matter the condition of his marriage or his wife, he's sleeping in their bed with another woman. There's not much justification for that.

"Do you feel guilty?" I ask him.

"Yes." He regards me silently for a moment. "But not guilty enough to stop." He lays his head on the pillow next to me.

"But it will stop," I say. "I need to go back to Manhattan. And you're married."

His eyes seem to be protecting thoughts he doesn't want to speak out loud. We're both quiet as we stare at each other for a while. He eventually leans in to kiss me before saying, "I thought about what you said in the kitchen last night."

I don't speak in fear of what he's about to say. Was he open to everything I had to say? Does he agree that the quality of his life is just as important as Verity's?

"I called a nursing facility who will take her during the week, starting Monday. She'll come home three weekends a month." He waits for my reaction.

"I think that's the best thing for all three of you."

As if I see it happen in real time, the grief begins to evaporate. From him, from this house. The wind is blowing through the window, the house is quiet, Jeremy looks at peace. It's in this moment I decide what to do about the manuscript.

I'm not going to do anything.

Proving that Verity murdered Harper wouldn't make Jeremy feel better. It would make him feel worse. It would open up so many wounds. It would rip the fresh wounds open even wider.

I'm not convinced that Verity is safe to be around, but there are ways to uncover that with time. I think Jeremy just needs better security. A monitor in Verity's room, connected to a motion sensor on the weekends she's here. If she really is faking her injuries, he'll find out. And if he does find out, he'll never allow her around Crew again.

And now that she's going to a facility, she'll be monitored even more closely.

Right now, things feel okay. Safe.

"Stay another week," Jeremy says.

I was planning on leaving in the morning, but now that I know Verity will be gone soon, I'm excited about the idea of being here with him all week, without April, without Verity.

"Okay."

He raises an eyebrow. "You mean *alright*."

I smile. "Alright."

He presses his mouth to my stomach, kisses me, and then climbs back on top of me.

He doesn't remove the shirt I'm wearing as he slides into me. He makes love to me for so long, my body grows lithe against his movements. When I feel the muscles of his arms begin to tense beneath my fingertips, I don't want it to end. I don't want him to leave my body.

I wrap my legs tightly around him and bring his mouth to mine. He groans, sinking into me even deeper. He's kissing me when he comes, his lips rigid, his breaths shallow, making no attempt to pull out. He collapses on top of me, still inside me.

We're quiet, because we both know what we just did. We don't discuss it, though.

After Jeremy catches his breath, he slips out of me and lowers his hand, sliding his fingers between my legs. He watches me as he touches me, waiting for me to reach my climax. When I do, I'm not worried about how loud I am because we're the only ones here, and it's bliss.

When it's over and I relax against the bed, he kisses me one last time.

"I need to sneak out now before everyone gets home."

I smile at him, watching as he dresses. He presses a kiss to my forehead before walking across the room to climb back out the window.

I don't know why he didn't use the door, but it makes me laugh.

I pull a pillow over my face and smile. What has come over me? Maybe this house is fucking with my head, because half the time I'm ready to get the hell out of here and half the time I never want to leave.

That manuscript is definitely fucking with my head. I feel like I'm falling in love with the man, and I've only known him for a few weeks. But I'm not only falling in love with him in real life. I've fallen in love with him because of Verity's words. Everything she revealed about him has given me insight into the kind of person he is, and he deserves better than what she gave him. I want to give him what she never did.

He deserves to be with someone who will put her love for his children before anything else.

I pull the pillow off my face and I place it under my hips, lifting them so that everything he just left inside me doesn't seep out.

21

I dreamt about Crew when I fell back asleep. He was older, about sixteen. Nothing significant happened in my dream, or at least, if it did, I can't remember it. I only remember the feeling I had when I looked into his eyes. Like he was evil. It was as if everything Verity had put him through and everything he'd seen was embedded into his soul, and he had carried that with him through childhood.

It's been several hours since then, and I can't help but wonder if keeping silent about the manuscript is in Crew's best interest. He saw his sister drown. He saw his mother do very little to help her. And while he is very young, there's a possibility that memory will stay with him. That he'll always know she told him to hold his breath before she tipped the canoe over on purpose.

I'm in the kitchen with him, just Crew and myself. April left about an hour ago, and Jeremy is upstairs, putting Verity to bed. I'm seated at the kitchen table, eating Ritz crackers and peanut butter, staring at Crew as he plays on his iPad.

"What are you playing?" I ask him.

"Toy Blast."

At least it's not Fallout or Grand Theft Auto. There's hope for him yet.

Crew glances up at me, seeing me take a bite of my cracker. He sets down his iPad and crawls onto the table. "I want one," he says.

It makes me laugh, watching him crawl across the table to reach the peanut butter. I hand him the butter knife. He spreads a huge glob onto a cracker and takes a bite, sitting back on his knees. His eyes fill with excitement. "It's good."

Crew licks the peanut butter off the knife and I scrunch up my nose. "Gross. You aren't supposed to lick the knife."

He giggles, like it's funny.

I lean back in my seat, admiring him. For all he's been through, he's a good kid. He doesn't whine, he's quiet, he still somehow finds humor in the small things. I don't think he's an asshole, anymore. Not like the first day I met him.

I smile at him. At his innocence. And again, I begin to wonder if he has any recollection of that day. I wonder if Crew's memories would determine which therapeutic program is best for him. Since his own father doesn't know the extent of what he's been put through by Verity, I feel like that's on me. I'm the one with the manuscript. I'm the one with the responsibility to tell Jeremy if I think his son has been damaged more than he thinks.

"Crew," I say, reaching down to the jar of peanut butter, spinning it with my fingers. "Can I ask you a question?"

He gives me one exaggerated nod. "Yup."

I smile, wanting him to feel comfortable with my line of questioning. "Did you used to have a canoe?"

He pauses in the middle of licking the butter knife again. Then he says, "Yes."

I scan his face for clues that I should stop, but he's not giving me any. "Did you ever play in it? Out on the water?"

"Yes."

He licks the knife again, and I feel a little relief that he doesn't seem too disturbed by my conversation. Maybe he doesn't remember anything. He's only five; his perception of reality as it happens is different from an adult's. "Do you remember being in the canoe? With your mother? And Harper?"

Crew doesn't nod or say yes. He stares at me, and I can't tell if he's scared to answer the question or if he just doesn't remember. He glances down at the table, breaking eye contact with me. He sticks the knife into the jar again and puts it in his mouth, closing his lips over it.

"Crew," I say, scooting closer to him, placing a gentle hand on his knee. "Why did the boat tip over?"

Crew's eyes flick back to mine and he pulls the knife out of his mouth for a moment, long enough to say, "Mommy said I shouldn't talk to you if you ask me questions about her."

I feel the color drain from my face as he casually licks the knife again. I grip the edge of the table, my knuckles white. "She. . . Your mother talks to you?"

Crew stares at me for a few seconds without giving me an answer, and then he shakes his head with a look in his eye that makes me feel like he's about to backtrack. He realizes he shouldn't have said that.

"Crew, does your mommy pretend she can't talk?"

Crew's teeth clench down while the butter knife is still in his mouth. I see the knife slip up between his teeth, into his gums.

Blood begins to slide down his front teeth, onto his lips. I shove my chair back hard enough that it hits the floor as I grab the handle of the butter knife and pull it out of Crew's mouth.

"Jeremy!"

I cover Crew's mouth with my hand, looking around for a towel that might be within reach. There's nothing. Crew isn't crying, but his eyes are full of fear.

"Jeremy!" I'm screaming now, partly because I need him to help me with Crew and partly because what just happened terrified me.

Jeremy is here now, in front of Crew, tilting his head back, looking inside his mouth. "What happened?"

"He..." I can't even say it. I'm gasping for air. "He bit the knife."

"He needs stitches." Jeremy scoops him up. "Grab my keys. They're in the living room."

I rush to the living room and swipe Jeremy's keys from the table. I follow them to the garage, to Jeremy's Jeep. Crew has tears in his eyes as if the pain is setting in. Jeremy opens the back door and puts Crew in his booster seat. I open the front door to climb into the Jeep.

"Lowen," Jeremy says. I turn around just as he closes Crew's door. "I can't leave Verity here alone. I need you to stay."

My heart plummets deep into the pit of my stomach. Jeremy is helping me down from the Jeep before I can object. "I'll call you after they see him." He grabs his keys from my hand, and I'm frozen in one spot as I watch him back out of the garage. He turns his Jeep around and peels out of the driveway.

I look down at my hands, covered in Crew's blood.

I don't want to be here anymore, I don't, I don't, I hate this job.

A few seconds pass before I realize it doesn't matter what I want. I'm here, and so is Verity, and I need to make sure her door is locked. I rush back into the house, up the stairs to her room. Her door is wide open, probably because Jeremy rushed downstairs in a hurry.

She's in her bed. The covers are halfway off her body, and one of her legs is dangling, as if Jeremy heard me screaming before he could get her all the way in the bed.

Not my problem.

I slam the door shut and lock it, then think about what I can do next to ensure my own safety. I rush downstairs when I remember seeing the baby monitor in the basement. The last place I want to be is in the basement, but I power through my fear, using the light on my cell phone, and walk down the stairs. When I was down here with Jeremy, I didn't give the basement much of an inspection. But I know some of the boxes that were stacked up were closed.

As I shine my light around the room, I notice almost all of the boxes have been moved and opened, as if someone were rummaging through them. The thought that it might have been Verity makes my mission more urgent. I don't want to be down here longer than I need to be. I head for the area where I saw the baby monitor sticking out of a box. It was right on top when I noticed it the first time—in one of the only unopened boxes.

It's been moved.

Right when I'm about to give up my search out of fear of being down here, I see the box on the floor a few feet away. I grab the monitor and the receiver and head back for the stairs, my heart heavy in my feet as I try and ascend the steps. Relief spreads through me when the door opens and I escape.

I untangle the cords, then plug the dusty monitor into an outlet next to Verity's computer. I rush back upstairs, but before I reach the top, I stop. I turn around. I go to the kitchen and grab a knife.

When I've reached Verity's room again, I clutch the knife in my hand and unlock her bedroom door. She hasn't moved. Her leg is still dangling off the bed. I keep my back to the wall as I move to her dresser and set the other half of the monitor on the dresser. I point it at her bed and plug it in.

I walk back to the door and hesitate before exiting her room. I step forward, still clutching the knife, then lift her leg as fast as I can and drop it on the bed. I throw the covers over her, lift the bed rail, and then slam her door shut when I'm back out in the hallway.

I lock it.

Fuck this shit.

I'm panting by the time I make it to the kitchen sink. I wash the blood off my hands, which has dried to my skin. I spend a few minutes cleaning it off the table and floor.

Then I go back to the office and sit down in front of the monitor.

I make sure my cell phone camera is on video mode in case she moves. If she moves...I want Jeremy to see it.

I wait.

For an entire hour, I wait. I watch my phone for Jeremy's call. I watch the monitor for Verity's lies. I'm too scared to leave the office and do anything other than wait. The tips of my fingers grow sore from the constant tapping against the desk.

When another half an hour goes by, I realize I've resorted to doubting myself again. *She would have moved by now.* Especially since she hasn't even opened her eyes. She didn't see me set up the monitor because her eyes were closed, so she wouldn't even know it was there.

Unless she opened them as I was running down the stairs. If that's the case, she saw the monitor and knows I'm watching her.

I shake my head. *This is driving me insane.*

There's one chapter left of her manuscript. I need to put this all to rest if I'm going to stay in this house for another week. I can't continue with the back and forth of thinking I'm in danger and thinking I'm crazy. I grab the last several pages and keep my chair pointed at the video monitor. I'll read as I keep an eye on her movements.

Chapter Fifteen

It's only been a few days since Harper died, but I feel my world has shifted more in those few days than in all my years on this earth.

The police took my report. Twice. It's understandable that they'd want to ensure there weren't any holes in my story. It's their job. Their questions were simple enough. Easy to answer.

"Can you explain to us what happened?"

"Harper leaned over the edge of the canoe. It tipped over. We all went under, but Harper never came up. I tried to find her, but I was running out of breath and needed to get Crew to safety."

"Why were your children not in life vests?"

"We thought we were in shallow water. We were so close to the dock at first, but then...we weren't."

"Where was your husband?"

"He was at the grocery store. He told me to take the kids to the water before he left."

I answered all their questions amidst bouts of sobs. Occasionally I would double over, as if her death were physically affecting me. I think my performance was so good, it made them uncomfortable to ask me more questions.

I wish I could say the same for Jeremy.

He's been worse than the detectives.

He hasn't let Crew out of his sight since Harper passed. The three of us have been sleeping downstairs together in the master—Crew in the middle, Jeremy and me separated by yet another child. But tonight was different. Tonight I told Jeremy I wanted him to hold me, so he put Crew on the other side of him and Jeremy lay in the middle. I clung to him for half an hour, hoping we could fall asleep that way, but he wouldn't stop with the fucking questions.

"Why did you take them in the canoe?"

"They wanted to go," I said.

"Why weren't they in life jackets?"

"I thought we were close to the shore."

"What was the last thing she said?"

"I can't remember."

"Was she still above water when you made it to the shore with Crew?"

"No. I don't think so."

"Did you know the canoe was about to tip over?"

"No. It all happened so fast."

The questions stopped for a while, but I knew he was still awake. Finally, after several minutes of silence, he said, "It just doesn't make sense."

"What doesn't make sense?"

He pulled back, putting space between my face and his chest. He wanted me to look at him, so I lifted my head.

He touched my cheek, gently, with the backs of his fingers. "Why did you tell Crew to hold his breath, Verity?"

That's the moment I knew it was over.

That's the moment *he* knew it was over.

For a man who thought he knew his wife... That was the first time he'd ever really understood the look in my eyes. And I knew, no matter how hard I tried to convince him...he would never believe me over Crew. He wasn't that kind of man. He put his kids first before his own wife, and that's the one thing I dislike the most about him.

I tried, though. I tried to convince him. It's hard to be convincing when tears are streaming down your cheeks and your voice is shaking when you say, "I said that as we were tipping. Not before."

He watched me for a moment. And then he released me. Pulled away from me for what I knew would be the very last time. He rolled over and wrapped his arms around Crew, like he was his own personal body of armor.

His protector.

From *me*.

I tried to lie still with no reaction so that he'd think I fell asleep, but all I did was cry quietly. When my tears began to increase, I walked to my office and I closed the door before Jeremy could hear me sobbing.

When I got to my office, I opened my manuscript and began to type. It feels as though there's nothing left to say. No future to write about. No past to redeem.

Am I at the end of my story?

I don't know what happens next. Unlike my prediction of Chastin's murder, I don't know how my life will end.

Will it be at the hands of Jeremy? Or will it be by my *own* hand?

Or maybe it won't end at all. Maybe Jeremy will wake up tomorrow and see me sleeping next to him. Maybe he'll remember all the good times, all the blow jobs, all the swallowing. And he'll realize how much more time we'll have to do those things now that we only have one child.

Or...maybe he'll wake up convinced that Harper's death was not an accident. Maybe he'll report me to the police. Maybe he'll want to see me suffer for what I did to her.

If that's the case...*so be it*.

I'll just drive my car into a tree.

The End

22

I don't even have time to absorb that ending before I hear Jeremy's Jeep pulling into the garage. I stack the pages together into a pile and then glance at the monitor. Verity still hasn't moved.

He suspected her?

I squeeze my neck, trying to ease all the tension that last chapter infused into my muscles. How could he still take care of her? Bathe her and change her for the rest of his life? Feel like he owes her the promise of his vows?

If he truly thought she killed Harper, how could he stand to be in the same house as her?

I hear the garage door open, so I walk to the office door and step out into the hallway. Jeremy is holding Crew in his arms at the foot of the stairs.

"Six stitches," he whispers. "And a lot of pain meds. He's out cold for the night." He walks Crew upstairs to put him to bed. I don't hear him check on Verity before he begins to make his way back down again.

"Want some coffee?" I ask him.

"Please."

He follows me into the kitchen, where he hugs me from behind, sighing into my hair as I start a pot of coffee. I lean my head against his, full of so many questions. But I say nothing because I don't even know where to start.

I spin around while the coffee brews and wrap my arms around him. We hold each other in the kitchen for several minutes. Until he releases his hold on me and says, "I need to shower. I have dried blood all over me."

I notice it then. The drops on his arms, the smears on his shirt. It's starting to be our thing, being covered in blood. I'm glad I'm not superstitious.

"I'll be in the office."

We kiss, and then he runs upstairs. I wait for the coffee to finish brewing so I can make myself a cup. I'm still not sure how to approach him with all my questions, but after reading that last chapter, I have so many. I think it might be a long night.

I hear his shower start when I finish pouring myself a cup of coffee. I carry it back to the office with me and then spill it all over the floor. The cup shatters. The hot liquid splashes my legs and begins to seep under my toes, but I can't move.

I am frozen in place as I stare at the monitor.

Verity is on the floor. On her hands and knees.

I lunge for my phone at the same time I scream Jeremy's name.

"Jeremy!"

Verity's head tilts to the side, as if she heard my scream from upstairs. Before I can open my camera app with unsteady fingers, she crawls back into her bed. Gets back into position. Stills herself.

"Jeremy!" I yell again, dropping my phone. I run to the kitchen and grab a knife. I run up the stairs, straight to Verity's room. I unlock her door and swing it open.

"Get up!" I yell.

She doesn't move. Doesn't even flinch.

I rip the covers off her. "Get *up*, Verity. I *saw* you." I'm full of rage as I lower the side of her hospital bed. "You aren't getting away with this."

I want Jeremy to see her for who she really is before she has an opportunity to hurt him. To hurt Crew. I grab her by the ankles and pull on her legs. I have her halfway out of the bed when I feel someone rip me from her. I'm swung around, carried to the door. He plants my feet on the floor of the hallway.

"What the *hell* are you doing, Lowen?" Jeremy's face and his voice are so full of anger.

I step forward, pressing my hands against his chest. He pulls the knife away from me and grips my shoulders. "Stop."

"She's faking it. I saw her, I swear, she's faking it."

He steps back into her room and slams the door in my face. I open the door, and he's lifting Verity's legs back onto the bed. When he sees me entering the room again, he tosses the covers over Verity and shoves me out into the hallway. He turns and locks her door, then grabs me by the wrist and pulls me behind him.

"Jeremy, no." I'm grabbing at his wrist that's locked tightly around mine. "Don't leave Crew up here with her."

My voice is pleading, but he can't hear the worry. He can only see what he thinks he knows, what he walked into. When we reach the stairs, I back up, shaking my head, refusing to descend them. *He needs to take Crew downstairs.* He grabs me by the waist and lifts me over his shoulder and carries me down the stairs, straight to my room. He sets me down onto the bed, gently, even in the midst of his anger.

He walks to my closet. Grabs my suitcase. My things. "I want you to leave."

I lift up onto my knees and move to the foot of the bed, where he's shoving all my things into the suitcase. "You have to believe me."

He doesn't.

"Goddammit, Jeremy!" I point toward the upstairs. "She's *crazy*! She's been lying to you since the day you met her!"

I've never seen so much distrust and hatred pouring out of a human. The way he's looking at me has me so terrified, I scoot away from him.

"She's not faking it, Lowen." He tosses his hand in the air, toward the direction of the stairs. "That woman is helpless. Practically brain-dead. You've been seeing things since you got here." He shoves more clothes into my suitcase, shaking his head. "It's impossible," he mutters.

"It isn't. And you know it isn't. She killed Harper and you *know* it. You suspected it." I climb off the bed and rush to the door. "I can prove it."

He follows after me as I run to Verity's office. I grab the manuscript, every page of it, and I turn around just as he reaches me and I shove it against his chest. "Read it."

He catches the pages. Looks down at them. Looks back up at me. "Where did you find this?"

"It's hers. It's all there. From the day you met her up until her car wreck. *Read* it. At least read the last two chapters, I don't care. Just, please, read it." I'm exhausted, and I have nothing else in me but pleas. So I beg him. Quietly. "Please, Jeremy. For your girls."

He's still looking at me like he doesn't trust a single word coming out of my mouth. He doesn't have to. If he would just read those pages—see what his wife was truly thinking in the moments she was with him—he'll know I'm not the one he needs to worry about.

I can feel the fear welling up in me. The fear of losing him. He thinks I'm crazy—that I was trying to hurt his wife. He wants me to leave his home. He wants me to walk out of here and he never wants to see me again.

My eyes sting as the tears begin to fall down my cheeks.

"Please," I whisper. "*Please*. You deserve to know the truth."

23

I expect it to take him a while to read the entire thing. I'm sitting on my bed, waiting. The house is quieter than it's ever been. Unsettling, like the calm before a storm.

I stare at my suitcase, wondering if he's still going to want me to leave after this. The entire time I've been here, I've been holding on to that manuscript, keeping it a secret from him. He may never forgive me for it.

I know he'll never forgive Verity.

My eyes flick up to the ceiling when I hear a crash. It wasn't loud, but it sounded like it came from the room Jeremy is in. He hasn't been up there for very long, but it's enough time to at least skim the manuscript and know that Verity was not at all the woman he thought she was.

I hear a cry. It's low and quiet, but I hear him.

I fall onto my side and hug the pillow as I squeeze my eyes shut. It kills me to know how much he's hurting right now as he reads page after page of a truth so harsh, it never should have been written.

Footsteps are above me now, moving around upstairs. He hasn't been up there nearly long enough to read the entire thing, but I can understand that. If I were him, I would have skipped to the end to see what really happened to Harper.

I hear a door open. I run across the hall to the office and look at the monitor.

Jeremy is standing in Verity's doorway, looking at her. I can see both of them from the monitor. "Verity."

She doesn't answer him, obviously. She doesn't want him to know she's a threat. Or maybe she's been faking it because she's afraid he'll turn her into the police. Whatever her reason, I have a feeling Jeremy isn't going to walk away from the room until he gets his answer.

"Verity," he says, stepping closer to her. "If you don't answer me, I'm calling the police."

She still doesn't answer him. He walks over to her, reaches down, and pulls one of her eyelids open. He stares at her for a moment, then walks toward the door. *He doesn't believe me.*

But then he pauses, like he's questioning himself. Questioning what he read. He turns around and walks over to her. "When I walk out of this room, I'm taking your manuscript straight to the police. They'll put you away and you'll never see me or Crew again if you don't open your eyes and tell me what's going on in this house."

Several seconds pass. I'm holding my breath, waiting for her to move. Hoping she moves so that Jeremy will know I'm telling the truth.

A whimper escapes my throat when she opens her eyes. I slap my hand over my own mouth before it turns into a scream. I'm afraid I'll wake Crew, and this is not something he needs to walk into.

Jeremy's whole body tenses, and then he grabs his head in both hands as he backs away from her bed. He meets the wall. "What the *fuck*, Verity?"

Verity begins to shake her head adamantly. "I had to, Jeremy," she says, sitting up on the bed. She's getting into a defensive pose, as if she's terrified of what he might do.

Jeremy is still in disbelief, his face full of anger and betrayal and confusion. "This entire time...you've been...." He's trying to keep his voice down, but he looks like he's about to explode into a rage. He turns and releases his anger with a fist against the door. It makes Verity flinch.

She holds up her hands. "Please, don't hurt me. I'll explain everything."

"Don't *hurt* you?" Jeremy spins around, taking a step forward. "You *killed* her, Verity."

I can hear the anger in his voice, and it's just over the monitor. But Verity has a front row seat to it. She tries to jump off the bed to escape him, but he doesn't allow it. He grabs her by the leg and yanks her back onto the bed. When she starts to scream, he covers her mouth.

They struggle. She's trying to kick him. He's trying to hold her down.

Then his other hand forms a circle around her throat. *No, Jeremy.*

I run straight up to Verity's room and stop short when I reach the doorway. Jeremy is on top of her. Her arms are trapped beneath his knees, her legs are kicking at the bed, her feet are digging into the mattress as she wheezes.

She's trying to fight back, but he overpowers her in every way.

"Jeremy!" I rush to him and try to pull him off of her. All I can think of is Crew and Jeremy's future and how his anger is not worth a life. *His* life. "Jeremy!"

He isn't listening. He refuses to let go of her. I try to get in his face, to calm him, to talk sense into him. "You have to stop. You're crushing her windpipe. They'll know you killed her."

Tears are streaming down his cheeks. "She killed our daughter, Low." His voice is full of devastation.

I grab his face, try to pull him to me. "Think about Crew," I say, my voice low. "Your son will not have a father if you do this."

I see the slow change in him as my words sink in. He eventually pulls his hands from her throat. I double over, gasping for as much breath as Verity is right now. She's sputtering, trying to inhale. She tries to speak. Or scream. Jeremy covers her mouth and looks at me. There's a plea in his eyes, but it's not a plea for me to call for help. It's a plea for me to help him figure out a better way to end her.

I don't even argue with him. There is not a single cell in her body that deserves to live after all she's done. I step back and try to think.

If he chokes her, they'll know. His handprints will be on her throat. If he smothers her, particles from the pillow will be in her lungs. *But we have to do something*. If he doesn't, she'll get away with it somehow because she's manipulative. She'll end up hurting him or Crew. She'll kill him just like she killed her daughter. Just like she tried to kill Harper as an infant.

Just like she tried to kill Harper as an infant.

"You have to make it look like an accident," I say, my voice quiet, yet loud enough to be heard over the noises she's making beneath the palm of his hand. "Make her vomit. Cover her nose and mouth until she stops breathing. It'll look like she aspirated in her sleep."

Jeremy's eyes are wide as he listens to me, but there's understanding there. He pulls his hands from her mouth and then shoves his fingers down her throat. I turn my head. I can't watch.

I hear the gagging, and then the choking, and it feels like it goes on forever. *Forever.*

I sink to the floor, my whole body wracked with tremors. I press my palms against my ears and attempt to ignore the sounds of Verity's last breaths. Of her last movements. After a while, the sound of three people's lungs turns into two.

It's only Jeremy and me breathing right now.

"Oh, God, oh, God, oh, God..." I can't stop whispering it over and over as the enormity of what we've just done begins to register.

Jeremy is quiet, other than the cautious breaths he's releasing. I don't want to look at her, but I need to know it's over.

When I turn my body to face her, she's staring at me. Only this time, I know she isn't in there, hiding behind that vacant stare.

Jeremy is on his knees by the bed. He checks her pulse, then his head collapses between his shoulders. He sits, his back to the bed as he catches his breath. He brings both hands to his face, cradling his head. I don't know if he's about to cry, but I would understand it if he did. He's been hit with the reality that his daughter's death wasn't an accident. That his wife—the woman he devoted so many years of his life to—was not at all the person he believed her to be. That she was manipulating him the entire time.

Every good memory he's ever had with his wife died right along with her tonight. Her confessions ripped him apart, and I can see it in the way he's doubled over now, attempting to process the last hour of his life. The last hour of *Verity's* life.

I slap my hand over my mouth and I start to cry. I can't believe I just helped him kill her. *We just killed her*.

I can't stop looking at her.

Jeremy stands and then lifts me into his arms. My eyes are closed as he carries me out of the room and down the stairs. When he lays me on the bed, I want him to crawl in with me. Wrap his arms around me. But he doesn't. He starts pacing the room, shaking his head, muttering under his breath.

We're both in shock, I think. I want to reassure him, but I'm too scared to speak or move or accept that this is real.

"Fuck," he says. And then, louder. "*Fuck!*"

And there it is. Every memory, every belief, everything he thought he knew about Verity is sinking in.

He looks at me and then strides over to the bed. His trembling hand pushes back my hair. "She died in her sleep," he says, his words both quiet and rigid. "Okay?"

I nod.

"In the morning..." His voice is mixed with so much breath as he tries to stay calm. "In the morning, I'll call the police and tell them I found her when I went to wake her up. It'll look like she aspirated in her sleep."

I haven't stopped nodding. He's looking at me with concern, with empathy, with apology. "I'm sorry," he says. "I'm so sorry." He leans down and kisses me on the top of my head. "I'll be right back, Low. I need to go straighten up the room. I need to hide the manuscript."

He kneels down so that he's eye to eye with me, as if he wants to make sure I'm getting it. That I understand him.

"We went to bed like normal. Both of us, around midnight. I administered her meds, and then, when I woke up at seven to get Crew ready for school, I found her unresponsive."

"Okay."

"Verity died in her sleep," he repeats. "And we're never going to discuss this again after tonight. After this moment...right now."

"Alright," I whisper.

He blows out a slow breath. "Alright."

After he leaves the room, I can hear him moving things around, walking back and forth, first to his room, then Crew's room, then Verity's room, then the bathroom.

He walks to the office and then the kitchen.

Now he's back in bed with me. Holding me. He holds me tighter now than he ever has before. We don't sleep. We only fear what the morning will bring.

24

Seven months later

Verity died in her sleep seven months ago.

Crew took it hard. So did Jeremy, publicly. I left the morning she died and went back to Manhattan. Jeremy had a lot to deal with that week, and I'm sure it would have been even more suspicious had I stayed in his home following the death of his wife.

My outline was approved, as well as the two subsequent outlines. I turned in the first draft of the first novel two weeks ago. I've requested an extension on the deadline for the next two novels. It's going to be hard working on them with a newborn.

She hasn't arrived yet. She's not due for another two and a half months. But I'm confident, with Jeremy's help, I'll be able to catch up on any work I fall behind on. He's great with Crew, and he was great with the girls, so I know he'll be great with our baby girl when she arrives.

We were shocked at first, although not surprised. Things like this happen when you aren't careful. I worried how Jeremy would take it, becoming a father again after losing two children so close together. But I realized after seeing his excitement that Verity was wrong. Losing one child, or even two, doesn't mean you've lost them all. Jeremy's grief over the deaths of his daughters is separate from his joy over the impending birth of a new one.

Even after all he's been through, he's still the best man that has ever entered my life. He's patient, attentive and a much better lover than Verity could have possibly described him to be. After her death, when I had to go back to Manhattan, Jeremy called me every day. I stayed away for two weeks—until everything began to settle. When he asked me to come back, I was there that same night. I've been with him every day since then. We both knew we were rushing things, but it was hard being apart. I think my presence brought him comfort, so we didn't worry about the timing or if our relationship was too much, too soon. In fact, we didn't even discuss it. The definition of our relationship was unspoken. It was organic. We were in love and that's all that mattered.

He decided to sell the house shortly after we found out I was pregnant. He didn't want to remain in the same town where he and Verity had lived. And honestly, I didn't want to remain in that house with all those terrible memories. We started fresh three months ago in North Carolina. With the advance and Verity's life insurance, we were able to pay cash for a home right on the beach in Southport. Every evening, the three of us sit on the deck of our new home and watch the waves crash against the shore.

We're a family now. We aren't made up of all the members of the family Crew was born into, but I know

Jeremy is appreciative that Crew has me in his life. And he'll be a big brother soon.

Crew seems to be adjusting well. We did put him in therapy, and Jeremy sometimes worries it'll do more harm than good, but I reassure him of all the good therapy did for me as a child. I have faith that Crew will easily forget the bad memories if we give him enough good ones to cover them up with.

Today is the first time we've stepped foot in their old house in months. It's eerie, but necessary. I'm getting too close to my due date to travel again, so we're using this opportunity to clear out the house. Jeremy has received two offers on it already, and we don't want to have to drive back up here during my last month of pregnancy to empty it out.

The office was the hardest room to clear out. There was so much stuff that probably could have been salvaged, but Jeremy and I spent half the day putting everything through the shredder. I think we both just want that part of our lives to be over. Gone. Forgotten.

"How are you feeling?" Jeremy asks. He walks into the office and places a hand on my stomach.

"I'm good," I say, smiling up at him. "You almost finished?"

"Yep. A few more boxes on the porch and we'll be done." He kisses me, just as Crew runs into the house.

"Stop running!" Jeremy calls out over his shoulder. I push myself out of the desk chair and follow Jeremy with it as I roll it toward the door. He grabs one of about ten boxes left on the porch and begins to carry it to the car. Crew slips around me to run outside, but pauses, then comes back into the house.

"I almost forgot," he says, rushing toward the stairs. "I have to get my stuff out of mom's floor."

I watch as he runs upstairs, toward Verity's old bedroom. It was empty last time I checked. But a moment later, Crew comes walking downstairs with papers in his hand.

"What are those?" I ask him.

"Pictures I drew for my mom." He shoves them in my hands. "I forgot she used to keep them in the floor."

Crew runs outside again. I look down at the pictures in my hands. The old familiar feeling I carried around with me while staying in this house has returned. *Fear.* Everything starts flashing through my head. The knife that was on the floor in Verity's room. The night I saw her on the monitor, on her hands and knees, like she was digging at the floor. Crew's passing words just now.

I forgot she used to keep them in the floor.

I rush up the stairs. And even though I know she's dead and isn't in there, I'm still terrified as I walk down the hallway to her room. My eyes fall to the floor, to a piece of wood Crew failed to put back in place after he took out his pictures. I kneel down and pick up the loose piece of flooring.

There's a hole in the floor.

It's dark, so I reach my hand inside and feel around. I pull out something small. *A picture of the girls.* I pull out something cold. *The knife.* I reach in again and feel around until I find an envelope. I open it and pull out a letter, then drop the empty envelope to the floor next to me.

The first page is blank. I blow out a steady breath and lift it, revealing the second page.

It's a handwritten letter to Jeremy. Fearfully, I begin to read.

Dear Jeremy,

I hope it's you who finds this letter. If it isn't you, I hope it will get to you somehow because I have a lot to say.

I want to start off with an apology. I'm sure by the time you read this, I'll have left in the middle of the night with Crew. The thought of leaving you alone in the home where we shared so many memories together makes me ache for you. We had such a good life with our children. With each other. But we're Chronics. We should have known our heartache wouldn't end with Harper's death.

After years of being the perfect wife to you, I never expected this career that I love and devote most of my time to would ultimately be what ended us.

Our lives were perfect until we somehow flipped into an alternate dimension the day Chastin died. As much as I try to forget where it all started to go wrong, I was cursed with this mind that never forgets a single thing.

We were in Manhattan having dinner with my editor Amanda. You were wearing that thin grey sweater I loved—the one your mother bought you for Christmas. My first novel had just released and I signed the new two-book deal with Pantem, which is why we were at that dinner. I was discussing my next novel with Amanda. I don't know if you tuned this part of the conversation out, but I'm guessing you did because writer talk always bored you.

I was expressing my concerns to Amanda because I wasn't sure which angle to take with the new book. Should I write something completely different? Or should I stick to the same formula of writing from the villain's point of view that made my first novel so successful?

She suggested I stick to the same formula, but she also wanted me to take even more risks with the second book. I told her it was difficult for me to make a voice in my novel sound authentic when it wasn't at all how I think in my everyday life. I was worried I wouldn't be able to improve my craft with the next book.

That's when she told me to try an exercise she learned in grad school called antagonistic journaling.

This would have been a great time for you to be paying attention at that dinner, but you were on your phone, probably reading an eBook that wasn't mine. You caught me staring and you looked up at me, but I just smiled at you. I wasn't mad. I was happy you were there with me and being patient while I received advice from my new editor. You squeezed my leg under the table, and I directed my attention back to Amanda, but my focus was on your hand as it trailed circles around my knee. I couldn't wait to get back to our place that night because it was our first night away from the girls together, but I was also very interested in the advice Amanda was giving me.

She said antagonistic journaling was the best way to improve my craft. She said I needed to get into the mind of an evil character by writing journal entries from my own life. . . things that really happened. . . but to make my inner dialogue in the journal entry be the opposite from what I was actually thinking at the time. She told me to start by writing about the day you and I met. She said I should write down what I was wearing, where we met and what our conversation was that night, but to make my inner dialogue more sinister than it actually was.

It sounded simple. Harmless.

I'll give you an example from a paragraph I just wrote above.

I look over at Jeremy, hoping he's paying attention. He isn't. He's staring down at his fucking phone again. This dinner is a huge deal for me. I realize this isn't Jeremy's scene—these fancy dinners and meetings in Manhattan—but it's not like I force him to do this all the time. Instead, he's reading someone else's eBook, being completely disrespectful to this entire conversation.

He reads all the time, yet he doesn't feel comfortable reading MY books? It's an insult in the highest form.

I'm so embarrassed by his audacity, but I know I need to mask my embarrassment. If Amanda notices the irritation on my face, she might notice Jeremy's disrespect.

Jeremy looks up at me, so I force a smile. I can save my anger for later. I give my attention back to Amanda, hoping she doesn't notice Jeremy's behavior.

A few seconds later, Jeremy squeezes my leg, right above my knee, and I stiffen beneath his touch. Most of the time, I crave it. But in this moment the only thing I crave is a husband who supports my career.

And that's how easy it is for a writer to pretend to be someone they aren't.

As soon as we got back to our place, I went straight to my laptop and wrote about the first night we met. I pretended my red dress was stolen in my alternate version. I pretended I was there to hopefully fuck rich men, which was absolutely not true. You should know me better than that, Jeremy.

I wasn't very good at making myself much of a villain the first time I tried it, so I made it a habit of writing down our milestone moments.

I wrote about the night you proposed to me, the night I found out I was pregnant, the day I gave birth to the girls. Every time I wrote about a new milestone, I got better and better at being inside the mind of a villain. It was exhilarating.

And it helped.

It helped immensely, which is why I was able to create such realistic, terrifying characters in my novels. It's why they sold, because I was good at it.

By the time I had finished my third novel, I felt I had mastered the craft of writing from a point of view that wasn't at all mine. The exercises had helped me so much, I decided to combine all of my journal entries into an autobiography that could be used to teach other authors how to master their craft. I needed to tie the chapters together with an overall storyline so that the autobiography was more cohesive, so I pushed the envelope with every scene to make it more jarring. More disturbing.

I don't regret writing it because my only intention was to eventually help other writers, but I do regret writing about Harper's death just days after it happened. My mind was in such a dark space though, and sometimes, as a writer, the only way to clear your mind is to let the darkness spill out onto a keyboard. It was my therapy, no matter how hard that may be for you to understand.

Besides, I never thought you would read it. Beyond that first manuscript, you never read anything I wrote.

So why...why did you choose to read that one?

It was never meant for anyone to read and believe. It was an exercise. That's it. A way to tap into the dark grief that was eating at me and eliminating it with every stroke of the keyboard. Putting all the blame onto this fictional villain I had created in that autobiography was one of the ways I coped.

I know this letter is hard for you to read, but it can't be any harder than the manuscript was to read the night you found it. And if we're ever going to come to a place of forgiveness, you need to keep reading so you'll know the absolute truth about that night. Not the version you discovered days after Harper died.

When I took Harper and Crew out on the lake that day, I was trying to be good for them. That morning, you mentioned how I didn't play with them anymore, and you were right. It was so hard because I missed Chastin so much, but I also had these two beautiful children who still needed me. And Harper really did want to go to the water that day. It's why she ran upstairs crying, because I had told her no. I never scolded her for her lack of emotions like I stated in the manuscript. I was using artistic freedom to further the plot. It's an insult that you believe I would speak to one of our children that way. It's an insult that you believe any of that manuscript—or that I was capable of harming them.

Harper's death was an accident. Her death was an accident, Jeremy. They wanted to go in the canoe, and it was so beautiful that day. And yes, I should have put life vests on them, I realize that. But how many times had we gone in that boat without them? The water wasn't that deep. I had no idea the fishing net was beneath the surface. If it weren't for that fucking fishing net, I would have found her and helped her to shore and we all would have laughed about the day the boat tipped over.

I can't even tell you how sorry I am for not doing everything, anything differently that day. If I could go back, I would, and you know I would.

When you got there and pulled her out of the water and held her, I wanted to rip my heart out and feed it to you because I knew you no longer had one of your own. I didn't want to live for another second after seeing your anguish. My God, Jeremy. To lose both of them. Both of them.

I watched your suspicion come to a head a few nights after Harper passed. We were in bed when you started asking me all those questions. I couldn't even believe you would think I would do something like that on purpose. And even if it was a fleeting thought, I saw the love you had for me leave your body and flitter away like it was never even there. Our entire past...all the great moments we shared together. It just left.

Because, yes, I did tell Crew to hold his breath. I told him to hold his breath as the canoe was tipping over. I was trying to help him. I thought Harper would be fine because we've played in that lake many times before, so my focus was on Crew after we fell into the water. I grabbed him and he was panicking, so I tried to make it back to the dock as fast as I could before he caused us both to drown. Not even thirty seconds had passed before I realized Harper wasn't right behind us.

To this day, I blame myself. I was her mother. Her protector. And I assumed she'd be fine, so I focused on Crew for thirty seconds too long. I immediately tried to swim back and find her, but the canoe had shifted farther out because of the commotion of the water. I couldn't even find where she'd gone under, and Crew was still fighting me—panicking. I knew if I didn't get him to the shore in that exact moment, all three of us would drown.

I searched for her with everything in me, Jeremy. You have to believe me. Every part of me drowned in that lake with her.

I didn't blame you for suspecting me. I probably would have allowed my mind to explore every possible scenario if the roles had been reversed and she drowned under your supervision. It's natural, to assume the worst in people, even if that assumption is only for a split second.

I thought you'd wake up the next day after our conversation in the bed and you would realize how ridiculous your indirect accusation had been. I didn't even try to change your mind that night because I was too full of grief to care. To argue. It had only been days since she passed, and I honestly just wanted to die. I wanted to walk out into the lake that night and join her, because her death was my fault. It was an accident, yes. But if I'd made her wear a vest, if I'd been able to grab her and Crew together, she'd still be alive.

I couldn't sleep, so I went to my office and opened my laptop for the first time in over six months.

Imagine it for a moment. A mother, grieving the loss of both of her daughters, writing a fictional work-up that accused one of them of murdering the other.

It was beyond disturbing. I realize that, which is why I cried the entire time I typed. But I thought, maybe, if I released my guilt and my grief onto this fictional villain I had created, it would somehow help me in a twisted way.

I wrote all about Chastin's death. I wrote all about Harper's. I even went back to the beginning of the manuscript and added foreshadowing so the entire thing would match our new grim reality. And in a way, it did help ease a small fraction of my guilt and pain, being able to blame this fictional version of myself rather than accept the blame in real life.

I can't explain the mind of a writer to you, Jeremy. Especially the mind of a writer who has been through more devastation than most writers combined. We're able to separate our reality from fiction in such a way that it feels as if we live in both worlds, but never both worlds at once. My real world had grown so dark that I didn't want to live in it that night. It's why I escaped from it and spent the night writing about a world darker than the one I was living in. Because every time I worked on that autobiography, I found relief in closing the laptop. I found relief in walking out of my office and being able to close the door on the evil I created.

That's all it was. I needed for the imaginary version of my world to be darker than my real world. Otherwise, I would have wanted to leave them both.

After spending the entire night and some of the morning working on the manuscript, I finally reached the last page. I felt the manuscript was done at that point because, really, what more could I have added? It felt as though our world was over. The end.

I printed it out and stuffed it away in a box, thinking one day in the future I'd get back to it. Maybe add an epilogue. Maybe I would burn it. Whatever the plan was, I was not expecting you to somehow read it. I was not expecting you to believe it.

After being up all night writing, I slept most of the day. When I finally woke up that night, I couldn't find you. Crew was already asleep, but you weren't up there with him. I was standing in the hallway wondering where you had disappeared to when I heard a noise in my office.

The noise was you. I'm not sure what kind of sound you had made, but it was worse than either of the days we found out the girls had died. I walked toward my office to console you, but I stopped short before opening the door because your cries had turned into rage. Something crashed against the wall. I jumped back—wondering what was happening.

That's when I remembered the laptop. The autobiography was the last file I had opened.

I swung open the door to explain what I knew you had just read. I'll never forget the look on your face as you stood there and looked at me from across the room. It was complete and utter...misery.

Not like the sadness of someone who just found out one of their children died. It was a consuming sadness, like every happy memory we had ever had as a family was erased with every new word of that manuscript you had read. Gone. There was nothing left inside you but hatred and destruction.

I shook my head, tried to speak. I wanted to say, "No. It's not true, Jeremy. It's okay, it's not true." But all I could get out was a fearful and pathetic, "No."

The next thing I knew, you were dragging me by my throat to the bedroom. I was no match for your strength as you held my arms down with your knees and squeezed my throat even tighter.

If you'd given me five seconds. Just five seconds to explain, I could have saved us. I tried so hard to say, "Just let me explain," but I couldn't breathe.

I'm not sure what the sequence of events was after that. I know I passed out. Maybe you panicked because you realized you had almost killed me. If I had died on that bed, you would have been arrested for my murder. Crew wouldn't have a father.

I woke up in the passenger seat of my Range Rover and you were behind the wheel. There was tape on my mouth, and my hands and feet were bound together. Again, I just wanted to explain that what you read wasn't true—but I couldn't talk. I looked down and realized I didn't have on a seatbelt. And in that moment, I knew what you were doing.

It was one simple sentence in my manuscript, about how I should turn off the passenger airbag and drive my car into a tree while Harper was unbuckled so her death would look like an accident.

You were going to kill me and make my death look like an accident. I had unknowingly written my own death in the last two sentences of my manuscript. "So Be It. Maybe I'll just drive my car into a tree."

I realized in that moment, if you were ever suspected of my death, all you had to do was provide the manuscript. Had I died, it would have been the perfect suicide letter.

Of course, we both know how that part of the story ended. I'm assuming you removed the tape from my hands and feet, placed me into the driver's side of the vehicle, and walked back home where you waited for the police to come notify you that I had died.

Your plan didn't quite work out, though. I'm not sure I'm relieved that it failed. It would almost be easier if I had died in that wreck because pretending to be injured has been difficult. I'm sure you're wondering why I've been deceiving you for so long.

I have very little memory of that first month after Harper's death. I'm assuming I was in a medically induced coma because of the swelling on my brain. But I remember the day I came out of it very clearly. I was alone in the room, thank God, which gave me time to process what needed to happen next.

How would I explain to you that every negative word you read was a lie? You wouldn't believe me if I tried to deny that manuscript, because I wrote it. Those words were mine, no matter how untrue they were. Because who would believe it was a lie? Certainly not someone who didn't understand the writing process. And if you were aware that I had recovered, you would turn me in to the police, if you hadn't already. I'm sure an investigation would have followed Harper's death had I not had that wreck. And with my own husband against me, I have no doubt that I would be convicted of her murder because it would be my own words used against me.

For three days I pretended to still be in a coma when anyone would enter my room. Doctors, nurses, you, Crew. But I was careless one day and you caught me with my eyes open as you walked into the hospital room. You stared at me. I stared back. I saw your fists clench, as if you were pissed that I had woken up. As if you wanted to walk over and wrap your fingers around my throat again.

You took a few steps toward me, but I decided not to follow you with my eyes because your rage terrified me. If I pretended not to be aware of my surroundings in that moment, there was a chance you wouldn't try to end my life again. A chance you wouldn't go to the police and tell them I had recovered.

So I pretended for weeks because I felt it was my only means of survival. I was going to fake the extent of my brain injuries until I could figure out how to fix the situation I was in.

Don't think it wasn't hard. It was humiliating at times. I wanted to give up. Kill myself. Kill you. I was so angry at where our lives had ended up, and after all those years of marriage you could even, for one second, believe any of that manuscript to be true. I mean seriously, Jeremy. Do men really believe women are that obsessed with sex? It was fiction! Of course I loved making love to you, but most of the time it was to please you because that's what couples do for each other. It wasn't because I couldn't live without it.

You were a good husband to me and whether you believe it to be true, I was a good wife to you. You're still a good husband to me. You believe in your heart that I murdered our daughter, yet you still ensure I'm taken care of. Maybe it's because you think I'm no longer in here—that all the evil parts of me died in that wreck and I'm merely someone you feel sorry for now. I think that's why you brought me home because with all Crew has been through, your heart is too good to keep him away from me. You knew after losing both of his sisters, the complete loss of his mother would do even more damage to him.

Despite what my manuscript stated, your love for our children is the thing I've always cherished most about you.

There have been moments throughout these past few months when I've wanted to tell you I'm here. That it's me. That I'm okay. But it would be a waste of breath. We can't get past two murder attempts, Jeremy. And I know if you find out I'm faking this before I'm able to leave, your third attempt at killing me will be successful.

I'm not going through all this effort in hopes that I'll eventually change your mind and prove to you how wrong you were. You will never fully trust me again.

Everything I'm doing is for Crew. All I can think about is my little boy. Everything I've done from the day I woke up in that hospital has been for Crew. As much as I don't want to take Crew away from you, I have no choice. He's my child and he needs to be with me. He's the only one who knows I'm still in here—that I still have thoughts and a voice and a plan. It feels safe, being myself with him, because he's only five. I know if he told you I speak to him, you would pass it off as an active imagination, or even trauma from all he's been through.

He's the reason I searched so hard for that manuscript. I know, if you ever find us after I leave here, you'll try to use it against me. You'll want him to believe it as you believed it.

The first night after you brought me home, I snuck to the office to delete the manuscript from the laptop, but you had already deleted it. I tried to find the one I had printed, but I couldn't remember where it was. There were blank spots in my memory after the wreck, and that was one of them. But I knew I needed to get rid of both of them so you couldn't use it against me.

I searched everywhere, any chance I got for that manuscript, as quietly as I could. My office, the basement, the attic. I even searched around the bedroom a few times while you were asleep on your bed. I just knew I couldn't leave with Crew until I had destroyed the proof you would use against me.

I also had to wait until I could get my hands on money but I wasn't quite sure how to do that since I couldn't very well drive to the bank.

When I overheard your conversation with Pantem Press about their brilliant idea of continuing the series with a new author, I knew that was my way out.

When you hired an overnight nurse and left for your meeting with them in Manhattan, I snuck into my office and opened a new checking account online.

Within days of that meeting, the new co-author was moving into the house to start on the series. Which means it will only be a matter of time before the money for the remaining three books will finally be in the account and I'll be able to transfer the funds to my new account and get Crew out of here.

All I have to do is bide my time, but the new co-author has been making it difficult. She somehow got her hands on the printed manuscript I've been searching for. I'm sure you thought by deleting the file, you were ridding the house of it. But you didn't. Now it's two against one. I don't even care about destroying the manuscript at this point. I only care about getting out of here.

I admit, it's my fault she's growing suspicious. I know it freaks her out when she catches me looking at her, but you can't blame me. This woman has entered your life, is taking over my career, is falling in love with you. And from what I can tell, you're falling in love with her, too.

I heard you fucking her in our bedroom a couple of hours ago. As much as I'm hurting, I'm equally as angry. However, you're so occupied with her right now I feel it's the safest time to write this letter. I locked the door to the master bedroom so I'll be able to hear you trying to get out. It'll provide me with enough time to hide this letter and get back in place before you can make it upstairs.

It's been tough, Jeremy. Not gonna lie. All of it. Knowing you believed my words more than you believed my actions over the course of our marriage. Knowing I've had to resort to this level of deceit to save myself from being convicted of one of the most atrocious things a mother could do. Knowing you're falling in love with another woman while I spend day after day pretending to be unaware of what our lives have turned into.

But I keep pushing through because I'm confident that I'll get out of here as soon as that money comes, which is why I'm leaving you this note.

Maybe you'll find it, maybe you won't.

I hope you do. I really hope you do.

Because even after you tried to choke me to death and crash my car into a tree, I can't find it in myself to hate you. You have always been fierce in your protection of our children, which is exactly how parents should be. Even if that means eliminating the parent who has become a threat to them. You truly believe in your heart that I am a threat to Crew, and even though it kills me to know you believe that, it also gives me life knowing how much you love him.

When Crew and I finally get out of here, I'll call you someday and I'll tell you where to find this letter. After you read it, I hope you'll find it in you to forgive me. I hope you'll find it in you to forgive yourself.

I don't blame you for what you've done to me. You were a wonderful husband until you couldn't be. And you were the best father in the world. Hands down.

I love you. Even still.

Verity

25

I drop the letter to the floor.

I grip my stomach as a pain seers through it.

She didn't do it?

I don't want to believe anything I just read. I want to believe Verity is cruel and deserves what we did to her, but I'm not sure she did.

Oh, God. What if it's true? This woman lost her daughters and then her husband tried to kill her and then... we *did* kill her.

I sit back, staring at the letter as if it's a weapon that harnesses the power to destroy the life I've recently built with Jeremy.

So many thoughts are running through my mind, I press against my temples because my head is pounding. *Jeremy already knew about the manuscript?*

Had he really already read it before I gave it to him? Did he *lie* to me?

No. He never denied knowing it existed. In fact, now that I think back on that moment, his exact words were, "Where did you find this?"

It's too much to take in. I can't process everything she said and everything that's happened. I stare at the letter for so long, I forget where I am and that Jeremy and Crew are downstairs and that any minute, he'll come looking for me.

I crawl forward and grab the pages. I shove the knife and picture back into the floor, then cover the hole with the wood. I take the pages to the bathroom and I lock the door behind me. I kneel in front of the toilet and I start ripping each page into tiny shreds. I flush some of the paper and eat as many pieces of the letter I can find with Jeremy's name. I want to make sure no one ever reads a word of this.

Jeremy would never forgive himself. *Never.* If he found out the manuscript wasn't real and that Verity never harmed Harper, he wouldn't be able to survive that kind of truth. The truth that he murdered his innocent wife. That *we* murdered his innocent wife.

If it even *is* the truth.

"Lowen?"

I flush the rest of the pieces of paper in the toilet. I flush again for good measure, just as Jeremy knocks on the door.

"You okay?" he asks.

I turn on the water and try to calm my voice. "Yes." I wash my hands, then take a sip of water to ease the dryness in my mouth. I look in the mirror and recognize the terror in my eyes. I close them, attempting to push it back. All of it. Every terrible thing I've witnessed in my thirty-two years.

The night I stood on the railing.

The day I saw the man being crushed beneath the tire.

The manuscript.

The night I saw Verity standing at the top of the stairs.

The night she died in her sleep.

I push it all back. I swallow it like I swallowed her letter.

I blow out a breath and then open the door and smile at Jeremy. He reaches up and runs a hand down the side of my head. "You okay?"

I swallow my fear, my guilt, my sadness. I cover it all up with a convincing nod. "I'm alright."

Jeremy smiles. "Alright," he says quietly, threading his fingers through mine. "Let's get out of here and never come back."

He holds my hand throughout the house and doesn't let go until he opens my door and helps me into his Jeep. As we're driving away, I watch the house grow smaller in the rearview mirror until, finally, it disappears.

Jeremy reaches across the seat and rubs my stomach. "Ten more weeks."

There's an excitement in his eyes. One I know I was able to put there, even after all he's been through. I brought light into his darkness, and I will continue to be that light so he'll never be lost in the shadows of his past.

He will never know what I know. I'll make certain of that. I will take this secret to my grave with me so Jeremy doesn't have to.

I have no idea what to believe, so why put him through more anguish? Verity could have written that letter as a way to try and cover her tracks. It could have been another ploy at manipulating the situation and everyone involved.

And even if Jeremy really was the reason for her wreck, I can't blame him. He believed Verity maliciously murdered his child. I can't even blame him for ultimately following through with her murder when he found out she had been deceiving him about her injuries. Any parent in his position would have done the same. *Should* have done the same. We both believed in our hearts that she was a threat to Crew. To *us*.

No matter which way I look at it, it's clear that Verity was a master at manipulating the truth. The only question that remains is: Which truth was she manipulating?

The End

Acknowledgements

Thank you for taking a chance on this book. It's a departure from the emotional love stories I usually write, so I very much appreciate you coming on this journey with me. I have a lot of people to thank. Bear with me.

1) My mother. Always. With every book I write, it gets harder to find that same level of excitement I had while writing my first book. Without fail, my mother always brings that back to me. She makes me believe I have a brilliant mind, when really it's mediocre. She makes me think the book I'm writing is the best book I've ever written, even though she says it with every book I write. Sometimes I'll call her in the middle of the night and say, "Please, just read this one chapter!" And she will. Or she at least pretends to. Either way, it keeps me moving forward and is the sole reason any of my novels ever reach completion. Thank you, Mom. Your belief in me makes me want to believe in myself.

2) My favorite group on Facebook, Colleen Hoover's CoHorts. We're close to eighty thousand members now, yet it still feels like such a close-knit community. When someone is having a bad day, you encourage them. When

someone can't afford a book, you help them. When someone has something to celebrate, you celebrate with them. There is nothing but absolute love and support in this group, and I will defend that 'til the end. We have no room for negativity or (metaphorical) dicks. But we do have plenty of room for new readers if you want to come check us out. I LOVE YOU, COHORTS!

3) Lauren Levine. I will forever be grateful to you for being part of the team that brought Confess to life. And while witnessing one of my books become an actual TV show was a phenomenal experience, it has been nothing compared to your friendship. Your support is unmatched. Someday I will return the favor.

4) Tarryn Fisher. I don't even know where to start. I'm very lucky to have supportive people in my life, but I'm not sure anyone wants to see me succeed like you do. You celebrate the success of others like no one I know. You are the Tarryn to my Colleen. Because you literally are.

5) Lin Reynolds. You're my favorite sister.

6) Murphy Fennell. You're also my favorite sister.

7) To my granny, Vannoy Gentles. You are too sweet to read a book like this. Which is exactly why I'll be giving you the first physical copy. ;)

8) To those of you who are in my life because of the book world but would continue to be in my life without it. Chelle Lagoski Northcutt, Kristin Phillips Delcambre, Pamela Carrion, Laurie Darter, Kay Miles, Marion Archer, Jenn Benando, Karen Lawson, Vilma Gonzalez, Susan Gilbert Rossman, Tasara Vega, Anjanette Guerrero, Maria Blalock, Talon Smith, Melinda Knight and about two

hundred more of you, THANK YOU for always being willing to let me run paragraphs, chapters, and entire novels by you. And for all you do to support my career. I love each and every one of you.

9) E.L. James. Your successful career does not impress me nearly as much as your soul. You're amazing in so many ways, but my favorite thing about you is the love and appreciation you have for your readers. You set a great example to authors everywhere.

10) Kim Holden. I just wanted to thank you for being you. Keep being that. #DoEpic

11) Caroline Kepnes. One time, years ago, I wrote half of a book in second person, only to be told by my publisher that one of their other authors was soon releasing a book in second person and I might want to rethink it. I didn't know you. I muttered profanity in your direction, as I had to rewrite half of my book. When my publicist mailed me your book to read early, I cursed even more as I read it because it was so great. And then, somehow, we became friends after I sent you a message and threatened to murder you. I believe my friendship with you has a weirder beginning than any other friendship I have. Which makes it perfect. I am so grateful you are in my life. Even though I'm a little afraid of your mind. Congratulations on your new phenomenal television series.

12) To the entire Book Bonanza and Bookworm Box teams, you all have made my life more manageable than I could have ever imagined. The work and dedication you put into Book Bonanza and The Bookworm Box is unmatched. Thank you, thank you, thank you.

13) Johanna Castillo. We had almost seven great years together. I'm heartbroken you are no longer my editor, but ecstatic for your new adventures. One thing that will never change is our friendship. I miss you and can't wait to see where your new journey takes you!

14) Jane Dystel. In the beginning of my career, I was a fish lost at sea without a single clue about this business. It's been seven years now, and I am STILL a fish lost at sea without a single clue about this business. But with you at my side, I never have to worry. Thank you for taking all the stressful pieces of this business I don't want to deal with and attacking them like no one else could. I am beyond grateful for you.

15) Lauren Abramo. You are a machine. I hope you take a full week off for the holidays and turn off your phone. I've never known anyone more dedicated and organized than you. Your patience with my lack of organization knows no bounds. Thank you for all you do!

16) Elissa Down. Thank you for bringing Owen and Auburn to life in Confess. You're a phenomenal director and an equally phenomenal human. Working with you was such a wonderful experience, I hope we get to do it again.

17) Brooke Howard. I just love you. Everything about you. Thank you for putting up with me. 18) Joy and Holly Nichols. Y'all are two of my favorite people. I'm so happy y'all are in my life now.

19) Stephanie Cohen. I pretty much owe everything to you. All of it. You are amazing in so many ways and I am so lucky our paths crossed. I can't imagine my life without you in it. I can't imagine I would even have this career

if it weren't for you. You are the epitome of what humans should strive to be, and I mean that. I know it isn't easy running my life because I make it way more difficult than it should be. But because of you, I don't have to change who I am. Thanks for that.

20) Erica Ramirez and Brenda Perez. My favorite sister duo and two of the sweetest people I have the pleasure of knowing. I appreciate you both so very much and am so lucky to have you both in my life.

21) Book Club. I know I'm the worst book club member, but thank y'all so much for that one night every month when we just get to hang out, talk books, and eat cake. It's my favorite night of the month.

22) Melinda Knight. I'm so grateful for you and your whole family. All you guys have done for our charity is appreciated. I'm so happy that Calc and Emma have each other. Now move to Hopkins County, already.

23) Tiffanie DeBartolo. Thank you for your books and thank you for your excellent taste in music. You are my goto when I need good art in my life.

24) Kim Jones. Thank you for…well…maybe I'll remember by the time I write the acknowledgments for my next book.

25) Social Butterfly, Murphy Rae, Marion Making Manuscripts, Karen Lawson, Elaine York. Thank y'all for the edits, the marketing, the cover design, the formatting, and the work each of you put into this book.

26) Shannon O'Neill. Thank you for all you've done for The Bookworm Box and the book community in general. You are a shining star in this industry.

27) KA Tucker. I still want to collaborate on a book with you, so I'm thanking you in advance for agreeing to it. I've been told what you put into this world will manifest, so this is me, manifesting our collaboration.

28) Tillie Cole. I know we don't know each other all that well, but I just wanted to thank you for your insta stories. Watching you talk is like therapy for me. You should probably bill me for all the therapy sessions I've saved money on now that I have your stories.

29) Jenn Sterling. I need new post cards for my computer, Jenn. Get on it. I miss your face. I'm so happy to see you happy.

30) Abbi Glines. Thank you for all you've done for me this year. I know it isn't easy being away from that precious family of yours, but I am and always will be grateful for your friendship and the time you give. You're a rockstar.

31) Ariele Fredman Stewart. Thank you for letting me steal a name from you. You shouldn't have such great taste in names and terrible taste in friends. I love you.

32) Kathryn Perez. How you've handled the past year of your life has been nothing short of inspiring. Thank you for being you, for being there for me, and for being so positive in a world that sometimes makes that difficult.

33) BB Easton. Will you say hello to Ken for me?

34) Dina Silver. Your cat is dumb.

35) Kendall Ryan. Thank you for taking time out of your busy schedule to give me advice and encouragement. I appreciate it more than you know!

36) Levi, Cale, and Beckham. I love you all so much. You make me proud every day. Please don't read this book.

37) Heath Hoover. You aren't allowed to read this book, either. I love you and I would like to stay married to you.

38) Thank you to bloggers. The hard work you put into your careers simply because you love books is inspiring. I'm sorry the ARCs for this particular book were such a hot mess. That happens when you don't finish the book until four days before release. I will do better next time, I promise. Thank you for ALL you do.

39) TIKTOK! Specifically BookTok. Thank. You. So. Damn. Much.

40) Thank you to Grand Central Publishing for believing in this book and wanting to see it reach a wider audience. I can't wait to work with you on future projects.

41) To every one of you reading these acknowledgments. Whether you're here because you hate this book or here because you love it, the important thing is that you are reading. Thank you for that. Now that you've finished this one, go devour another one.